THE FUNNY MAN

A NOVEL

JOHN WARNER

SOHO

For Kathy, always

———

Published by Soho Press, Inc.
853 Broadway
New York, NY 10003

Library of Congress Cataloging-in-Publication Data

Warner, John, 1970–
The funny man / John Warner.
p. cm.
ISBN 978-1-56947-973-5
eISBN 978-56947-974-2
1. Comedians—Fiction. I. Title.
PS3623.A86328F86 2011
813'.6—dc22
2011018280

Printed in the United States of America

10 9 8 7 6 5 4 3 2 1

PART I
The Rise (The Fall)

1

THE COURTROOM IS not a space conducive to comedy. For one thing the ceiling is too high; too much space for jokes to float up and fade. And then there's the layout, the way the various people—judge, defendant, prosecutor, jury—are isolated in their zones. Laughter is like a virus, more easily spread when people are in proximity to each other, and the only person anywhere near me is Barry, my lawyer.

Not that I'm in the mood to try out any new material, even if Barry hadn't hinted that levity is a bad idea when you're charged with manslaughter by saying, "The only one who gets to be funny in here is the judge and if the judge is funny I'm allowed to laugh, but you aren't. *You* are going to be as serious as ass cancer."

The viewing area is empty, the judge's decision to prevent a "spectacle." I didn't object, and neither did Barry, which is odd because he seems to enjoy an audience almost as much as I used to. Because I'm famous, there's been high demand to see the trial. Depending on the news outlet this is either the trial of the year or the decade. I am a top story every night. There are at least ten

Web sites dedicated entirely to the trial's goings on, reporting the tiniest of minutia. There are daily tweets on what the jury orders out for lunch. A large crowd hoping for a glimpse of something interesting gathers in a roped-in designated free speech area out in front of the courthouse every day. On the cable news crawl you will find my name scrolling by at five minute increments. Apparently, I spark the synapses of the national consciousness.

Crowds used to be my thing, but lately, I sometimes like to imagine myself as the main character in one of those postapocalyptic movies where there is only one person with one loyal dog companion left on Earth and that vision feels pretty damn good, relative to the present circumstances anyway.

No, two people. I would like there to be two people left on Earth (with or without the dog), me being one of them.

Barry and I must now enter and leave the courthouse from below ground in a car with dark windows because otherwise the paparazzi would never allow us down the courthouse steps. They would slowly melt me to a puddle under the heat and glare of their camera lights.

As is, when the car leaves the underground garage, they stand in front of the vehicle, blocking its way until they get more than enough pictures. They seem willing to risk their lives for these pictures (of the car, not even of me since the windows are blackened), one hand braced on the car's hood while they fire away with their cameras, defying the car to run them over.

I killed a man, that's not in doubt. We're not arguing about that. I said as much to the first cops on the scene when they approached with their guns and their flashlights drawn, the guns aimed at my torso, the flashlights focused on my hands, because it was in my hands that I still held the gun and they asked, "Did you shoot this guy?" and I said, "Yeah." And one of the cops said, "Hey, I know you," and the other cop said, "Me too."

In the mug shot that you've probably seen I look blottoed, crazy, my hair electrified, my eyes sunken deep into my skull, but it's important to remember that it was raining and I was wearing a hood and there's a certain amount of shock associated with being arrested, even when you've done nothing wrong.

Plus, I was in love.

The trial is to determine if I *had* to shoot the man, if it was self-defense, if it was justified. It is illegal to shoot someone because you can, or even should, or even if they deserve it. The only way it is legal to shoot someone is if you have a reasonable belief that your life is in danger at the moment you shot the person.

The answer to the question of why I shot the man is a complicated story. However, let me lay out these undisputed facts: The gun belonged to the other man, and the other man was a well-known thief, an armed robber as had been proven in a court of law twice before. And no, I did not have to shoot him. He was disarmed, the threat neutralized. I shot him six times as an act of kindness, of mercy. No one knows this story, not even Barry, because he wouldn't believe it. It seems impossible to make the context clear. I deserve punishment for lots of things, but shooting that man is not one of them.

That night, I was walking around the city, minding my own business, feeling good, feeling really good for the first time in a long time, feeling really really good for the first time since the divorce and then the new thing bombing, my failures. Two of my failures, anyway. I was feeling good because I had gone to the ends of the Earth (another complicated story) and there I'd met *her* and in her I had been cleansed; all things suddenly seemed possible. I had spent the evening watching her the only way I could, on television, a match from Monte Carlo, tape delayed as filler. I could've been the only one watching for all I knew, but it didn't matter. It was as though each serve, every groundstroke, was a message transmitted directly to me. As she destroyed the teenager from Croatia, it was as though she was saying, *I miss you. I'll see you soon.*

It was raining, but following her match I couldn't be contained by the walls of my apartment, so I gave in to the urge to grab my coat and walk, just walk wherever, rolling everything around in my head, her smile, the sensation of our first kiss, savoring this change in fortune. We were temporarily apart due to circumstances, but I was confident that those circumstances would change. Not confident, certain. Those were moments of certainty for me. I kept the hood on my jacket pulled up, protection against the rain. I must've looked a little dumb, walking in the rain, laughing, almost giggling to myself when I thought of her.

I turned a corner and smirked because just at that moment I was thinking about how my life had turned a corner and there I was, *literally turning a corner*, and there was something funny in that, not ironic funny, coincidence funny, but there was the man with the gun saying, "Give me your wallet. No funny business."

BARRY SITS, STARING placidly at the empty bench, his hands folded on top of a blank legal pad. An expensive pen rests to one side. There are no other papers or materials either on or beneath or beside the table. I used to have my own notepad and pen, but Barry took them away from me earlier in the trial because the courtroom sketch artist noticed that I had the tendency to draw obscene doodles and this little tidbit wound up anonymously sourced in the news, which was not good, which was described on several of the websites as a "setback."

The judge is often called away for urgent business in her chambers, which means the rest of us—me, Barry, the prosecutor, the jury, the sketch artist—are left behind, waiting. If the waiting is expected to go on too long, the jury gets to go elsewhere, but I am usually expected to stay. Sometimes I imagine the judge makes us wait because she can, which isn't fair. The headlines say it themselves: FUNNY MAN ON TRIAL FOR HIS LIFE, the kind of thing that deserves a judge's full attention. Well, not exactly my life, since manslaughter is not punishable by death, but enough imprisonment to last the rest of my days is close enough to "life," in my book.

During these periods of judicial absence, Barry is serene, contemplative without being glassy or glazed, a well-dressed Buddha. Occasionally, he leans toward me as though to speak, his eyes canted up and to the right at the jury, but nine times out of ten he says nothing, or at best, a "how ya doing?"

The prosecutor, on the other hand, is busy riffling through accordion files, flagging things with Post-its, scribbling notes onto his own pad. His tie is almost always askew and there is a stack of poster-sized exhibits resting behind him, some gruesome pictures of the "victim" at the scene and later on the coroner's table. A team of three assistants sits at an auxiliary table pouring through their own files, occasionally bringing a sheet of paper to the prosecutor's attention for him to look at briefly before either shaking his head and sending them away, or grabbing it and stuffing it into one of his own files. They are like bees working in the hive.

During the prosecution's case, which has just ended, this dichotomy between the prosecution's busy hive and Barry's Buddha disposition began to bother me. The prosecutor would display one of the oversized pictures showing the "victim" on a metal table under the glare of the coroner's lights, the small pur-plish blotch between his eyes where the only bullet that mattered entered, and march back to his table to grab a piece of paper to wave at the witness and ask things like, "Isn't it true that . . . ?" And the answer from the witness always sounded very bad, very damaging to my case, a "major setback," if you will. All the while Barry maintained his look, calm yet alert, centered, speaking only occasionally to object to the way a question was phrased, after which the prosecutor would simply reword to the same effect and there came the damaging information anyway. It was as though a hand was raised to block a blow to the head, only to invite one to the gut. I'll admit, it was maddening, borderline infuriating even, and finally at the end of one of the days of the trial as Barry and I rode in the back of the car with the darkened windows, being buffeted by the paparazzi trying to shoot us through the front windshield, I exploded. There was a time where I would've gladly subjected myself to the judge and jury's harshest punishment, but I was ready to live and it seemed like Barry was helping them kill me. The car rocked gently as it eased through the mass of reporters, the driver tooting his horn with every inch.

"We're getting killed! You're killing me!" I said, my hands trembling in my lap, one eye on Barry, one on the stubbly back of the driver's head. "Even I'm going to think I'm guilty by the time this is over! Why don't you do anything? Look at all the stuff they have! The reports, the pictures, the diagrams, the re-creation animation!" I felt my face flush and I pounded my hand against the armrest as I shouted.

Barry maintained the infuriatingly calm look and placed one hand gently on my leg as the other reached for the switch that raised the divider between us and the driver. As the barrier swooshed into place, he started to speak.

"I am doing great, better than great, actually. You, on the other hand, are going to cock things up with your fidgeting and wincing every time they ask something and even a slightly unfavorable answer comes out. Half the time you look like someone's got electrodes on your nads. It's not pretty and it's not helpful."

"Not helpful! You're doing nothing! No-thing! Did you see those pictures he has? Gah! This guy is slaughtering you and you do nothing! I just want you to do something!"

I shook my fists like a frustrated baby. It was a worse moment among bad ones. Barry sighed and grabbed my arms and pulled them down and gripped me by the hands. The look on Barry's face remained unchanged, unbothered, placid, but the grip was extremely strong. I could feel my knuckles shift underneath my skin.

"You are under a misapprehension," Barry said, maintaining his grip. "You, like our prosecutor friend, believe that a trial is an exercise in logic, that Sherlock Holmes is on the scene, deducting and inducting until we arrive at a common understanding of who is guilty and why. You believe that a trial is like solving a puzzle of what happened that night in that alley, and why, each piece locking into place until the picture is clear for all to see. Yes?"

I nodded. These things had seemed self-evident to me, the page that all of us—judge, prosecution, jury—were on. This was the given, the thing to be understood and accepted and while—because of the plausibility issues—I could never tell the full story, I had been hoping that Barry would come up with a reasonable facsimile that would prove convincing to the jury. Barry loosened his grip a little and began rubbing the top of his thumb over the back of one of my hands. It felt good, actually.

"This strategy would suggest that we need to be contesting each and every inch of forensic evidence, and from there move on to destroying the credibility of their witnesses, the ones who said they heard a scuffle starting and then a scuffle ending and then maybe some pleading from an unidentified voice that is probably not the defendant, since the defendant's voice is rather recognizable, and only then a gunshot. Check that, multiple gunshots, suggesting that you may just have executed this poor wretch of a man forced to steal from people with enough money for a hundred lifetimes to feed a drug habit that has already twice landed him in jail.

"If this trial is an exercise in logic," he continued, "we should want to muddy the picture of that puzzle so the jury can't tell if they're looking at a picture of Mount Rushmore, or a basket full of golden retriever puppies, or an autumn scene in New England, right?"

I nodded again, relaxing slowly. My hands puddled inside of Barry's grip. His skin was downy soft. We held onto each other like husband and wife at the wedding altar. Barry continued.

"You believe that trials are won and lost on the basis of who presents the most compelling arguments in the most cohesive and logical fashion, but as history and experience have shown, this is nonsense, a fundamental misunderstanding of human nature and decision making. Here's an analogy. I assume you've voted before. Do we happen to elect the person who is most qualified, who is best prepared for the challenges of the office? Do we sort through the criteria for being a good president, weigh the pros and cons, and then select the right person for the right time? No, we do not, because human beings are irrational creatures. We are subject to swings of emotion. We are governed by illogic. You, above all, should recognize this by now, considering your life."

I opened my mouth to protest, but no sound came out.

"A trial is not a logic puzzle. A trial is not Tetris. A trial is a story. A trial has characters and conflict and action and symbolism and theme and a climax, and all those other things. Now, I bet you can picture the climax we're hoping for. I know I can. In fact, I visualize it daily. It is part of my morning ablutions, all of us turned toward the jury, quiet enough in the courtroom to hear a pin drop, breaths held in anticipation as the foreperson unfolds the slip of paper and reads from it, despite already knowing what's printed there, and says, 'Not guilty, Your Honor.' Would you agree that this is the climactic moment we're hoping for?"

I nodded. I hadn't dared visualize it before, but as he spoke it appeared before me and I had the urge to run toward it.

"Good. So we're on the same page there. Now, to bring about this climax, something very important has to happen and that is that regardless of whether or not you committed the act in the way the prosecution alleges, when we get to that moment, we need that jury to *want* you to be innocent. Let me say that again in a slightly different way. It doesn't matter if you are or are not innocent on the facts of the case. It is not *what* happened that matters, it is *why* it happened. They must be rooting for you to be innocent. In rooting for you to be innocent they will realize that they have the power to make it so and after we hear that verdict you'll be shaking my hand and hugging me and pounding me on the back as tears roll down your cheeks. But . . ."

"But?"

"Yes, there is a *but*. I didn't want to have to share this with you, but at this point, we have no real choice. As part of our trial preparation we have been focus grouping you."

"Focus grouping?"

"Yes, we gathered the unemployed, the elderly, the unemployed, the unclever, the unemployed, in short, the sorts of people who were likely to—and indeed did—wind up in a jury of your peers, and we asked them about you, what they know, what they think, and it was not pretty."

"No?"

"No. The words most commonly associated with you among our target potential jury demographic were *untalented, successful,* and *bad husband and father.*"

Barry said the words matter-of-factly, a declaration as straightforward as name, rank, and serial number.

"Successful is good, though, right?"

"Not when coupled with *untalented*, no. The perception is that your success is unearned, either a fluke or a function of a decaying society, an early sign of the end-times-type thing. If the world were a better place we never would have heard of you. You are a symptom of a collective societal weakness for the gimmicky and trivial. The overwhelming feeling among these people is that you should just go away. To these people, you're not likable enough to pity, not interesting enough to hate. Either of these could be compelling reasons for a jury to find you not guilty. Right now, you are simply what is happening and they're eager to move on to whatever is next while still recognizing the need for closure with regards to your particular tale. They feel that you are holding them hostage. They wish for resolution, but don't particularly care what it is. 'Just get it over with,' they say. 'Whatever,' they say. Needless to say, this narrative is toxic to our chances. They want you gone because they can't bring themselves to look away.

Barry released my hands and sat back in the seat and turned his eyes forward. The driver had wormed free of the paparazzi and we were speeding down an avenue, the lights going green for us as though by Barry's command, the soft shocks of the town car absorbing all bumps. I stared at Barry, still gape-mouthed, my mind swirling, disordered like a snow globe shaken and dropped, and finally asked, "So which am I going to be? Hero or villain?"

"That's what we're going to find out."

2

O N THE SMALL, nightclub stage, the funny man says funny
things to the small audience arranged around the small tables
before him. As the laughter fades between these funny things,
the funny man hears ice shift in cocktail glasses and throats being
quietly cleared. Toward the end, someone lets loose a big, wet
cough that sounds tubercular and a drunk man orders his next
round loud enough to drown out a punchline. All in all, though,
a damn good night.

This is maybe the five or six hundredth time the funny man
has tried his hand at this and "damn good" is a significant
improvement over his initial attempts. The number of people
he has performed for has varied from none to slightly more
than none, to seven (including three bachelor party revelers
who were unconscious, greening upchuck crusted to their
shirtfronts), all the way up to 125 when he was scheduled on a
night when there was a rumor that a "comedy legend" would
be doing a rare club appearance to work on new material. The
legend never appeared because it was the funny man who started

the rumor, maybe the cleverest thing he had done in his life up to that point.

Six years the funny man has been coming to this club, from the moment he was old enough for his parents to trust him to drive alone into the city, fueled by an indestructible belief that he was indeed funny and that someday people would pay to hear him say and do funny things. The funny man doesn't know where this belief, or the seemingly inexhaustible fuel that accompanied his desire to have others agree with this self-assessment, came from. This belief remained unshaken despite the number of times someone, unsolicited, had shouted up to him on the stage, "Fuck you, you're not fucking funny." (Forty-nine.) The funny man had been told to "eat shit," to "die," to "eat shit and die," and to "eat shit and die horribly," which actually made *him* laugh. Shielded by the stage lights blocking the funny man's view, patrons had yelled at the funny man to fuck himself, to fuck his mother and to fuck himself with his mother's dick, and yet at every opportunity he climbed on to the stage, hopeful each time that it would go, if not "damn good," at least "pretty good." If you want to call that a sickness, that's your business.

The club is the only venue that matters, the place where all of the famous funny men (and women, though there aren't that many women) have been spawned. They come to the club as embryos and the stage is where they gestate and careers are either birthed or aborted. The club is small and ugly and certainly not the kind of place that should be seen in daylight under any circumstances, but it is and always has been *the* place. The hopeful funny people come to bomb until the day they no longer bomb and then they are said to have "passed," at which time you are allowed to perform on a Friday or Saturday night and you earn twenty dollars for the privilege.

But this night, for the funny man, no bombing, only applause, or mostly applause among the usual indifference. One of the things the funny man has come to realize during his times on stage is that the people in the club who are not shitfaced into oblivion want to laugh. They are almost desperate to laugh, having paid their fifteen-dollar cover charge and drunken their required minimum of drinks. They are like cans of soda shaken up, ready to explode and all it takes is to open them. It is the funny man's job to unearth the funny things they already hold in their brains, they just don't know it yet. And yet, so many of the prospective funny people bomb, or tank, or flop, because the wannabe funny people are equally desperate to get them to laugh and the mutual desperation meets like two magnets tuned to the same poles, pushing each other farther and farther apart until there is only silence, or even worse, a comic who turns on the audience, seeking laughs in that guy's mole, or her oversized breasts, blaming them for his (it is always a he) own shortcomings, the most significant of which is that he just isn't funny.

Upon finishing, the funny man thanks the audience for having him and tells them that they're really too, too kind. As is custom, he introduces the next performer and steps from the stage lights into darkness and wipes the sweat from his brow and this moment always reminds the funny man of the moment after orgasm where just instants before you were thinking that this is the best thing ever and then all of the sudden it's all, "what's the big deal?" and then two minutes later you feel kind of dirty about the whole thing.

Near the bar, a man loudly claps two fat hands together, whistles with his fingers at his lips, and then claps again, repeating the sequence long after the rest of the room is silent. The man is round and dumpy like those toys that can't be knocked down. He gestures the funny man backstage. The funny man follows. The man's neck is thick and wrinkled like a Shar-pei.

The clapping man claps the funny man on the back. Regular people are not allowed backstage, so the funny man knows this man is irregular. He is part of the industry. "That was killer," the man says. "You killed. That slayed me. Funny, funny shit. I'm dying here." The clapping man leans on a chair and breathes heavily as he hands the funny man a card. "You've cracked the code. You just need a 'thing' now. That's the clincher. A thing. The arrow through the head, the inflated surgical glove, water-melons and sledgehammers, crazy hair, screeching, turtlenecks, obesity, something. Call me when you get one," he says. "I'll take you places."

The funny man looks down at the card as he massages the back of his own neck. The other hopeful funny men lounging around the broken-down couches sucking on beers and smoking themselves into early graves look at him with deep and intractable loathing. *Talent Agent* the card says, with a number below. "Where?" he asks, looking up, but the man has already left. On the way home he rolls this word around his head: *Talent.* "I have talent," he thinks. "Talent talent talent."

AT HOME, IN the apartment, the funny man spoons gray mush into the child's mouth. The child laughs and claps his hands. "More?" the funny man asks the child. He can't imagine wanting more of the stuff. It looks unbelievably disgusting. A new bit begins to form in his head, something about feeding babies high-end pureed food if we want to get them to eat, but as the child stretches his mouth as wide as it will go, the funny man must concentrate on aiming the spoon and the bit is lost.

"He can't get enough," the funny man says to his wife.

"Tell me about it," she replies, lifting a heavy breast with the back of her hand. The funny man laughs and she smiles back at him. The wife finishes tying the apron portion of her waitress uniform around her waist. She tucks a pen and order slip into the appropriate slots. She looks old-fashioned and hot to the funny man. A real throwback, this wife of his.

The funny man and his wife first met in the library at their college when the funny man's future wife scanned his books for checkout and she smiled at him. The child was conceived in the very same library only a few weeks after they first met and mere days from their graduation, which meant the wife was fat with the growing child at the hasty fall wedding, but despite this, despite both of their mothers weeping copiously and constantly throughout the ceremony, and the whispers and her belly pressing against each and every guest as they were greeted in the receiving line, at that moment in the kitchen, neither the funny man nor his wife regretted squeezing themselves into the narrow shelves and giving in to what called them. The funny man knows he is no prize, can imagine his wife's father saying, "He wants to be a what?" "When?" and "You've got to be kidding," when they were told of his life's dream, the wedding, and the gestating baby all in one conversation.

As she's on her way out, the funny man shows his wife the clapping man's card.

"What do you think?" he says.

"I think that Mrs. Kowalski is wondering where our rent is." She kisses the funny man long and well on his mouth. The funny man's hand lingers on her backside as she walks away and leaves for work and he thinks about how when she arrives home he will unwrap her apron, spinning her like a top back into his arms, and that maybe it's time to do the next stupid thing, like make another baby.

In the living area, the funny man places toy blocks back into the toy chest and imagines the voice-over for his television biography that one day will air on one of the high-numbered cable channels: *Like many of the great funny men, the outward mask of laughter hid a complex and private nature.* He feels neither complex, nor private, so that is something he will have to work on. He knows he is a simple man with a simple wish. He has had this wish for as long as he remembers and he has not been shy about announcing it to anyone who cared (or didn't). There is a home movie of the funny man at Christmastime, age five or six, and he has been given a microphone that amplifies through a radio turned to the proper FM frequency. In the movie he marches around the house, inter-mittently shouting into the microphone. It is clearly the best toy ever. The camera shakes a little because his father is laughing at the antics. The child funny man looks up into the camera and his father asks him what he wants to be when he grows up, and the child funny man holds the microphone to his mouth, and even though he doesn't even really know what it means and is simply saying it because it is the answer his parents gave when he asked them whose job it is to make people laugh, he says, loudly and clearly, "a comedian."

The funny man next thinks of the off-Broadway play that he will one day write and perhaps produce as well after he is already a famous funny man. The play will have a "laugh out loud" opening, but the second half will contain an unexpected act of violence that will cause the critics to call the play "important" and "intriguing" and "unexpected." There may be brief nudity as well. The funny man may even star in it with an actress most known for her sitcom work who is trying to stretch creatively. The play will cause people to expand their estimation of the funny man. No longer will he just be the funny man, but the funny man who wrote an off-Broadway play that filled every single one of its folding chairs.

The funny man rolls the child onto its back and tickles its belly. The funny man notices that the skin at the child's joints is wrinkled like the back of the talent agent's neck.

"Laugh," he says to the child, and the child does. Kicks the air too.

The funny man's wife supports this habit of going to the club at night and trying to induce drunk strangers to laugh by waiting tables because her degree in Spanish does not translate into a higher paying job and the funny man pledged to take care of the child, "as if he were my own," which got quite a good laugh from the funny man's wife since they both knew full well where the child came from. The funny man remembers the moment like it was just a year and a half ago, which it was. Money is tight and the best meals are ones his wife carts home cold from her work, but the funny man, despite his visions of future grandeur, cannot imagine wanting anything more than this apartment in this, the best city in the world, this woman, this child, which is of course why he can put so much focus into making all these impossibly large dreams happening.

On the future televised biography of the funny man's life, they will interview a host of lesser funny men to talk about the career of the funny man. The funny man vows that he will never appear in one of these televised biographies about someone else, because only people less famous than the subject at hand agree to be interviewed for them. It is like volunteering for the junior varsity.

The funny man imagines one of these lesser funny men being filmed in his Coral Gables living room while sitting in an ugly, floral-print easy chair. "Who shot the curtains, right?" this lesser funny man will say to the camera operator as the lighting is adjusted. "But what are you going to do? It's the wife's taste and you've got to keep her happy." The camera operator will smile wanly and ask this lesser funny man if he's ready.

"Does the pope shit in his hat?"

On camera, the lesser funny man will gesture with his hands, and talking about the funny man say something like, "You've got to understand that the best humor comes from a dark place, and if you spend a lot of time in that place, your head's going to wind up being a little *farchadat*."

The funny man has heard this often, mostly backstage at the club where there is a kind of competition for who is the most fucked-up, who is darkest, who is most despairing, who has the worst tales of early abuse that have marked them for the self-flagellation that is professional comedy. Early on, the funny man tried playing these reindeer games, but he was making stuff up, stories borrowed from characters in the soap operas he would watch instead of going to class and deep down he knows that his mind is not even partly cloudy, let alone black and stormy. This is one of his biggest concerns, actually, that he is not screwed up enough to have anything interesting to say.

The best thing about the child is that recently his little personality has begun to emerge. Early on, the funny man found the boy distressingly inert, a warm, sleeping, crying, pissing, shitting lump that was a pleasant couch companion when watching the game, as long as he was sleeping and not shitting or crying. The funny man started calling the boy BP, short for *baked potato*, because he was often swaddled in a silver blanket that looked like foil. The funny man's wife frowned at this in a way that said she thought it was adorable. It got ninety seconds in his act. But now, the child can no longer be contained by the swaddling. He loves to thrash his arms and legs, and above all, to wave them in front of his own face before trying to see how many he can stuff inside his mouth, which the funny man finds absolutely hilarious. A chip off the old block.

Inspired, the funny man continues to tickle the child with one hand while trying to shove his other hand entirely inside his own mouth. The child's eyes shut he laughs so hard. The funny man feels his knuckles scrape past his teeth. There is a clicking noise in the back of the funny man's head that tells him either something important has happened or he has unhinged his jaw. He fights the urge to gag. Still laughing, the child thoroughly wets its diaper. The funny man removes his hand from all the way inside his mouth and smacks his lips together into a funny face that the child enjoys tremendously as he is carried to the changing table, dripping all the way.

After changing the baby, the funny man calls the number on the clapping man's card, and as it turns out, the clapping man had told the truth, though about something different than the funny man hoped. "He's dead," the voice on the line says. "He was dying and now he's dead."

"He told me I should call. He was going to take me places," the funny man says.

"He mentioned you," the voice replies. "He was my partner, said he'd seen a real funny man. I asked him if you had a 'thing.' He said, 'not yet, but he will.'"

"I do. I have a thing now," the funny man says. "I'm sure of it."

"You should come by then. We're mourning right now, but we'll have to wrap that up soon. Tomorrow."

"I'm sorry to hear . . ." the funny man says.

"Yeah, well, we all knew it was going to happen at some point or another. We're all stamped with an expiration date," the man on the other line says before hanging up.

3

THE FIRST TIME I saw the judge I was surprised she was a woman, and not a bad-looking one at that, mid-forties, shoulder-length brunette, trim, good grooming. When she entered the courtroom, we all shot to attention and as she mounted the steps to the bench, I saw a pair of stylish high heels beneath the hem of her robe and just above the heels a rather nice flash of leg. Sitting just outside my own consciousness, as I am now capable of, thanks to my therapist, I marveled at my inclination to notice the well-turned shape of a woman's leg even as I'm on trial for my life. This is a reversion to a different, darker time I thought was in the past, but was apparently resummoned when I pulled the trigger six times and killed that man.

In the midst of the worst times I self-diagnosed a sex addiction to my therapist. This was after the divorce when I was doing three sessions a week and complaining that the freedom to sleep with anyone I wanted to felt somehow confining, and how fucked-up was that? The therapist nodded thoughtfully as I described my symptoms, the "ache" I would feel when I found something attractive about a woman, an ache I was dead certain could only be satisfied by having sex with her, but then I would turn and see someone else, this one with a tiny scar on her upper lip, a slice of pale flesh that was suddenly irresistible, and the ache would turn into an anxiety and then a panic, a desperation. I would invent stories for each of them, scenarios that would bring us together, like porn, but with actual romance involved. My throat and chest would tighten and I would crumple and strangers would be asking me first if I needed help, before saying, "Hey, are you that guy?"

"It's like there's too much choice," I said to my therapist. "It's like buying toothpaste. Have you tried buying toothpaste recently? It's like a whole aisle, just toothpaste. It used to be a shelf, but now it's a whole aisle. Soon we're going to need an entire store called Just Toothpaste." I got up off of the therapist's couch and spread my arms to indicate a large store sign and pulsed my fingers to indicate flashing lights. "Just Toothpaste. Do I get tartar control? Whitening? Breath freshening? Something with sparkles in it? What about the flavor? Spearmint? Baking soda? Citrus? Fresh mint? What the fuck is fresh mint, anyway? Is there a stale mint flavor? The Just Toothpaste stores are going to have those guys like at the fancy restaurants who know everything about wine. Whaddya call them?"

"Sommeliers," the therapist said.

"Yeah, we'll need toothpaste sommeliers, toothpaste consultants just to figure out the right goddamn toothpaste. I'm telling you, doc, the choice is killing me."

"Is this in your act?" the therapist asked.

"No," I said, "should it be?"

"It's very funny."

"But you're not laughing."

"I don't laugh because I understand what's behind the joking, which isn't a laughing matter, but that doesn't mean it isn't funny."

He is and always has been a buzz kill. If I was going to kill anyone, it should've been him.

"Anyway, you're not a sex addict," he said.

"Then what am I?"

"A man."

WHEN THE JUDGE enters this time, I take care to focus on her face, which is undeniably pretty. Normally, middle age is not attractive to me, but this woman has kept it together and the age lines around her eyes and mouth are charming. Barry has warned me about this kind of thing, this appearing to be what people think I am. He said that there are two key things to know about juries: Number one, they notice everything, and number two, they've got nothing to do but talk to each other, particularly when a jury is sequestered, as they are in this trial. According to the focus groups, I'm supposed to be demonstrating respect for the process, an understanding of what's at stake, and a fundamental trust in the American system of jurisprudence, and staring at the judge's legs or grinning at the thought of her serious, but charming face are likely not in sync with those values. Under no circumstances should a man in my circumstances be grinning.

"Pinch your sack if you have to," Barry counseled.

With a brief wave of her hand the judge indicates that everyone should be seated as she settles in her high-backed chair behind the bench high above us. The judge's clerk approaches from the side to privately confer on something with the judge as the court reporter, just to the right of the witness chair, cracks his knuckles in anticipation of going back on the record. For the last week or so I've had this urge to tell the judge how impressed I am with her, how good she is at what she does. She appears overwhelmingly comfortable with each and every action, like the way she unhurriedly takes her chair, even though she must know the entire room is waiting for and looking at her, that she is the focal point. Or how she accepts a file from her clerk with a graceful flick of one wrist, while the other hand moves the stylish reading glasses hanging from a chain around her neck into place on the bridge of her nose. She has a nod she gives the court reporter that signals it's time to go back on the record that I couldn't even see until I took care to look extremely closely, but somehow it always snaps the court reporter from his dazed inactivity into a straight-backed virtuoso of the steno machine.

But what is most impressive is how she handles the lawyers. Even Barry is a lapdog in the presence of the judge. During testimony, she rarely looks directly at the witness or the questioning attorney and yet she is apparently always attentive, as demonstrated by the speed of her rulings when one of the lawyers offers an objection, followed by a slight smile to herself that seems to say, "I knew you were going to say that." When she looks at me—which is not often, mind you—I see total dispassion, which strikes me as completely right while also being probably difficult to pull off. After all, I am untalented, successful, a bad husband and father. Three-quarters of those surveyed think so. The other 25 percent likely think something worse. She must feel something about me. Everyone else does. I'd just like to tell her how much I appreciate the fine job she's doing, that in her work I recognize a true professional, that I get it.

There is at least one period during each day where it seems possible that I could say these things to her. It comes when it is just me and Barry and the prosecutor with the judge in her chambers when something needs discussing out of earshot of the jury. It is mostly Barry and the prosecutor who do the talking with the judge listening, but I still have to be there, and at the end of each conference when whatever it is that had to be decided is decided, from behind her desk the judge will look up at me over her reading glasses, he small mouth on her charming face moving and say, "Is that agreeable to you?" and I will say, "Yes, Your Honor," just as Barry has instructed me, but what I want to say, or more accurately what I want to ask, is how she got so comfortable in her own skin, how she is capable of such authenticity, because I would really like to know what that feels like again.

As I think about it, I've actually been very impressed by everyone involved with the trial, the judge, the bustling prosecutor, the court reporter, the sketch artist, even the jury. And Barry, of course. He has not disappointed. They've all played their roles marvelously. I just hope I've done my part. I may be untalented, but I try to be a pro.

At these thoughts I feel a smile playing at the corners of my mouth and I am not sure if this is my appreciation for all these jobs well done or simple nervousness that any moment this whole thing could be over. Barry has explained to me that after the prosecution completes its case it is usual for the defense to request a directed verdict of not guilty for lack of prima facie evidence. If no reasonable person could believe me to be guilty, then I will go free without having to mount any defense whatsoever. I had never heard of this before until Barry told me about this particular judicial wrinkle the day after the blowup in the town car, a salve for the wounds inflicted thus far.

"Why didn't you tell me this earlier?" I asked.

"I didn't want to get your hopes up."

"Then why are you telling me now?"

"It seems like the right thing to do at this time, considering."

"Considering?"

"Considering your apparent emotional distress."

"And could we get that, the directed verdict?" I asked. There was a surprising amount of hope in my voice. There have been periods during this time where I honestly felt like I didn't care which way this whole thing went.

"Possibly."

"Possibly or probably?" My conversations with Barry sometimes remind me of an Abbott and Costello routine. Truthfully, I've never cared for Abbott and Costello, never found them funny, though I'd never admitted it publicly since these thoughts were blasphemous for any "real" comic. Seeing those two stupid assholes do "Who's on First?" makes me want to leap through the television and knock their heads together. *Draw a diagram, fuckwads.*

"It's unusual to win on a directed verdict on a jury trial, but not unheard of."

"How not unheard of?"

Barry sighed. Usually Barry does not like to show irritation because irritation is weakness, but there it was, him briefly pinching his thumb and index finger at the bridge of his nose. I felt immediately sorry that I was such a pain in the ass. I wish I could blame it on me not being myself, but I fear it's the opposite.

"It's rare," he said.

"How rare?"

"Rare."

"Halley's Comet rare? Cubs winning the World Series rare? Rare rare? Or medium rare?"

"That's very funny," Barry replied. "The answer is rare. It could happen, but it's not likely."

But is *it going to happen*? Barry said that the ruling should come quickly, that the judge will know the motion is coming and as such will have an answer ready. Regardless of how it turns out, I know that this judge will make the right decision. She is very wise, this judge. She is very wise and very good at placing her reading glasses on her nose and she also understands the importance of attractive shoes on a woman. Sweat pools behind my knees. If I'd known this was going to happen, I would've taken an extra pill this morning. I feel rooted to the chair. If the case is dismissed I may not be able to leap with joy because the chair holds me down so strongly. If the case is dismissed, as we planned prior to the shooting, Bonnie and I will be able to be together, maybe. It was going to be difficult before and now, even with an acquittal, I will be further damaged goods, but love conquers all. (Except when it doesn't.)

I look over and see that, for once, the prosecutor is still, waiting to see if any more activity is actually going to be necessary. The jury is not present because hearing the judge's answer will prejudice their future opinions. Finally, the judge looks up at Barry and says, "I understand you have a motion for me."

4

A T THE OFFICES, the clapping man's partner sits behind a desk
with arms folded, face silent and stony as the funny man
demonstrates his "thing." Despite the assurances of his deceased
partner, he appears skeptical when it comes to the funny man's
charms. His look says, "I've seen your kind before."

The funny man rolls his head around his shoulders and blows
out his cheeks and shakes out his arms before pausing and saying,
"Jimmy Cagney with his hand all the way inside his mouth." He
has decided to dispense with any patter. The "thing" is the "thing"
and he doesn't want anything clouding this fact.

The funny man turns his back, puts a trench coat on, turns up
the collar and shoves his hand all the way inside his mouth. The
funny man turns back around and says, "You dirty rat," only it
sounds like, "*Whooar arghl whab*," because his hand is shoved all the
way inside his mouth. The clapping man's partner does nothing.
Face stony, arms still folded.

The funny man removes his hand, says, "John Wayne with his
hand all the way inside his mouth," then quickly turns his back

again, takes off the trench coat, puts on a cowboy hat and toy six-gun shooters around his waist and shoves his hand all the way back inside his mouth. He returns to face the clapping man's partner.

"*Whalks whake wah gok inunh grhuble,*" (*Looks like we got injun trouble*) the funny man says with his hand all the way inside his mouth while swaggering at the hips and using the barrel of one of the six-guns to tilt his cowboy hat slightly upward.

The funny man again removes his hand and says, "Richard Nixon with his hand all the way inside his mouth," turns back around, takes the cowboy hat and six-shooters off, puts on a suit coat and presses play on a small cassette player. The sound of helicopter blades cutting the air fills the room. The funny man faces the clapping man's partner again, ducks his head into his shoulders, furrows his brow, and makes the peace sign with the hand that is not shoved inside his mouth.

"*Foy hant tont uh crulkh,*" (*I am not a crook*), he says. The clapping man's partner's face breaks. He chuckles. His folded arms bounce on his chest. The funny man remains standing in his Nixon costume.

"*Whool ownt ave ixon oo ick rowned nymoor,*" (*You won't have Nixon to kick around anymore*).

The clapping man's partner laughs out loud. "Ha!" he says. "Ha!"

The funny man does John F. Kennedy ("*Fsk ot aht oour untree an oo or oo, fsk aht oo an oo or ouyor untree*"), John Lennon ("*Ive eece a hance*"), and Norma Desmond ("*Eyein eddie or eye ohsut,*") and with each one, the clapping man's partner laughs a little louder.

Finally, the funny man takes his hand from his mouth and holds a single finger up, asking for silence.

Something big is coming.

The funny man turns his back and puts on a frilly shirt and pirate hat. The funny man faces the clapping man's partner briefly, says, "Captain Hook with his hand all the way in his mouth." The funny man pauses and slyly arches his brow beneath the pirate hat before turning away again. He places a (fake) metal hook on one hand and a small blood packet between cheek and gum and turns to face the clapping man's partner. The funny man jams the hook into his mouth and screams, "Motherfucker!" Fake blood sprays over the desk at the clapping man's partner, who in turn opens one of the desk drawers and withdraws a sheet of paper and a small stack of money.

"This is two thousand dollars," he says. He wipes a mirthful tear from his eye. "And this is your contract. For television, we'll kill the foul language, but the kids'll love it. They want everyone working blue these days."

The funny man nods, signs the sheet of paper, and takes the money. The two shake hands.

"I am now your agent," the agent says.

THE FUNNY MAN sits in the kitchen, bouncing the child on his knee when the wife comes home. When he's bounced, the flesh on the child's cheeks jiggles in a funny way that the funny man enjoys, so they do this often. When he proposed to his wife, not long after she revealed her pregnancy and only minutes after she had deposited her breakfast in the toilet, the funny man had gotten on one knee and presented the small diamond, purchased on a 100 percent installment plan and said, "It may not be easy, but I promise it will always be fun." He has held up the bargain thus far and he has something very exciting and he thinks fun planned for her.

"Honey, could you get me some cornflakes?" the funny man says. He smiles and nods toward the cupboard. He turns the child to face toward his wife so there's an audience of two. She looks at the funny man like he might actually be the extremely stupid person he is acting like.

"Could you get yourself royally fucked?" she says.

"But I'd really like some cornflakes. Maybe you would too," he says. He wiggles his eyebrows at her Groucho-style. This is going better than the funny man could have hoped. The setup and reversal are really well constructed. He has learned quite a bit performing for those drunks in those clubs.

The wife storms to the cupboard, grabs the cereal and two bowls, slams them down to the table and pours. Five one-hundred dollar bills fall out. She holds her hand over her mouth like she's received a great surprise. He knows it is not about the money, that the money itself doesn't matter (though it is a great help). It is about the fulfilling of the compact they made with their partnership. He has come through for them.

"You might also want to check the diaper pail," the funny man says. "I think it needs emptying." The wife runs to the bedroom and sprints back, fanning five hundred more dollars in her hand. She starts to smile.

"I think something fell behind the toilet," the funny man says. The wife leaves and returns again, holding the jewelry box open. The small, diamond earrings sparkle from inside. Her hands shake so hard she cannot place them successfully in her ears. The funny man takes them from her and carefully removes the hoops that occupy the spot where the diamonds belong.

"Did you rob a bank?" she says.

"I did not. But I would if you wanted me to." The funny man leans in closely as he pulls the final earring free. He kisses her on the lobe and can feel her shudder.

"It's like some kind of movie," she says.

"Hang up your apron, Rosie, your hash-slinging days are over," the funny man says.

"You know my name's not Rosie."

The funny man carefully places the diamonds in his wife's ears and watches them sparkle. "Whatever," he says.

5

"WHAT ARE WE going to do now?" I say to Barry. We are in one of the private courthouse consultation rooms. I sit slumped in a chair at a small conference table, the knot of my tie pulled down so it hangs around my head like a noose. I stare at the carpet, a dark burgundy, with large, even darker stains. I imagine this is a spot where many a man's stomach has upended onto the floor. I for sure feel like that could be me any moment. I have been lower in my life, but this is pretty damn low.

Barry stands in front of me, arms folded, and gives a big smile.

"Why, we put on our defense, of course!" he says, clapping his hands and rubbing them together. "A vigorous, spirited defense!"

"As in the best defense is a good offense?"

"No," Barry says, frowning. I am clearly getting on his nerves. My act is growing stale, even with him. "That's one of the dumbest things someone can say. The best defense isn't a good offense. Why do people say that? The best defense is a good defense. Offense is offense and defense is defense. Saying the best defense is a good offense is like saying the best polar bear is an ostrich. They aren't the same thing at all. One is a flightless fowl and the other is a massive, carnivorous mammal."

"Like Tom Arnold," I say.

Barry ignores me and plows forward. "Now, our defense is multipronged, the first prong being that it's going to be a very lengthy, very thorough defense."

This sounds wretched. Thirty minutes ago I dared to imagine my freedom, the possibilities for a reborn man, my second rebirth, and now my own lawyer is telling me that even if we win the trial, victory is in the distant future. Barry continues.

"One thing our defense will do is make them forget the offense ever existed. We will erase their memories of those coroner's pictures and the victim's mother sobbing so hard she couldn't manage to answer any questions, and those ear-witness accounts claiming that you yelled 'die motherfucker,' (this is not true, by the way) either right before or right after pulling the trigger, and of the six bullets that were recovered from the victim's body. Certainly the prosecutor will try to remind the jury of these things in his closing, but they will be so distant they will sound more like rumor than fact, as in, 'I think I heard that, but it can't be right, can it?'"

Barry warms to the task, more animated than I've ever seen him. The cool courtroom customer has been replaced by something different, something giddy. He must've been rooting against his own motion for dismissal.

"The second prong is putting you, your life, your times, the very moment you killed that man in context. Right now, what does our jury know and think about you? Untalented, successful, bad husband and father." Barry ticks the items off on his fingers, one by one.

"Also you shot someone. Six times. In alleged self-defense. They look at your life and think, 'I would never do that.' They say, 'I have more self-respect than to build an entire career around a silly gimmick.' They think, 'I couldn't possibly do to my child what he did to his.' They cannot imagine pulling the trigger and ending another human life, all of which, I don't need to remind you, are things you've done. In order to put your actions in context, we are going to make your defense a veritable *This Is Your Life*.

"We are going to tell your story in the present tense to give it a sense of urgency, to put them in your shoes. We are going to give them all of the context. With context, not only will we cause the jury to understand why you have done things, why you snuffed out a life, why you were a bad husband and father, why and how you have reaped huge monetary rewards doing something trivial, we will have them believing that under the same circumstances they would have done *the exact same things*. Maybe even that you should be celebrated for having done these things. Perhaps, just possibly, if we really nail this thing, if we tie this bitch up in a bow, that you should be *emulated in doing these things*." Barry knocks his knuckles against the table, emphasizing the final part of the sentence. "We want to make them recognize that we are all the sum total of our traumas and our triumphs. It doesn't matter if they like you. They just have to understand you, why you are what you are—and not to get too 'Kumbaya' on you—that you and they are the same. You are they, we are us, us is them. Do you see the what I'm saying?"

I do, but I don't want to.

"Once we tell your story, the jury may not like you, but they will understand you. You may not have their sympathy, but you will have their empathy. They will walk several miles in your shoes and then we will put them in that alley that rainy evening, face-to-face with that man with the gun, which then somehow winds up in your hands, and we will ask them, 'given what you know, given what you've experienced, what would you have done?' and their answer will be, 'the exact same thing.' 'I would have shot that man, disarmed, on his knees, allegedly begging for his life, six times, allegedly.' In the abstract, people think they would *never* do that. We want to make them feel like they'd *definitely* do that.

"If I recall correctly," he said, continuing, "Mr. Prosecutor said early on that he 'wants to make an example of you,' so that's what we're going to do. It's just not going to be the example he's looking for."

I am deflated, one of those Mylar balloon animals sunken from ceiling to floor. I cannot see the path from here to there. It is an impossible task. If I had this life to do over again I'd be hard-pressed to think of anything I would do the same way. Untalented, bad husband and father, successful. These things are undeniably true and yet also not. I have done horrible things, but I also have done wonderful things. I have loved with all that a person is capable of. I have tried my best; there are countless poor choices littering the path behind me, but is this so different from anyone else? The thought of getting total strangers to feel what Barry proposes is out of the question at this point. I am not deserving of empathy or sympathy. I have been branded. Everyone *knows* me. The focus group said so.

The phrase *mercy of the court* pops into my head and I have a vision of getting up, leaving the room, walking down the corridor to the judge's chambers, knocking softly, entering and saying, "I throw myself at the mercy of the court," and I will crawl on my hands and knees to the judge until I am at her feet, her beautiful feet with the stylish pumps . . .

"It'll never work," I say. "I'm a monster, aren't I?"

Barry perches a single buttock on the table and looks both ways even though we both know we are alone and no one can hear us before he leans toward me, so close that our noses almost touch. I can smell his lunch, egg salad. "Let me tell you a secret," he says.

"What?"

"We're all monsters."

6

THERE ARE QUALMS, for sure. Backstage at the club the funny
man has heard all the "jokes":

> *Knock-knock.*
> *Who's there?*
> *Impressionist.*
> *Go fuck a llama, impressionists are hacks.*

Or:

> *Why did the prop comic cross the road?*
> *I don't know, why did the prop comic cross the road?*
> *Because he was hoping to get killed in traffic because he knew*
> *he was a hack and couldn't live with himself. Fuck a llama*
> *that has your grandmother's face, so it's like you're fucking your*
> *grandmother, but she's also a llama.*

The funny man had shared these opinions, had joined in the bitter laughter dismissing those who had risen out of the backstage holding area to greater heights with impressions or trunks full of junk or ventriloquism. (Don't even mention ventriloquism. Show up at the club with a dummy in a case and get ready for an ass beating followed by an invitation to fuck a semitruck full of grandma-faced llamas.) One of the most respected of the backstage hopeful funny men, the one everyone swears is a genius that the audience simply doesn't "get," once said it in a way the funny man would never forget. "You know where I carry my jokes?" he said. "Here," he said, pointing to his head. "Here," he said, pointing to his heart, "and here," he said, cupping his balls. The funny man laughed as hard as anyone. It was funny because it was true. This was the code and the funny man believed in it.

But no one ever laughs at this guy. At least no one who isn't one of the other hopeful funny men who often line up in the back to watch the unappreciated genius's sets, so impressed by his ability to tell hilarious jokes that ricochet around the room above the audience's heads. The guy's clothes that never get replaced or refreshed, his sour smell, his deteriorating teeth, the dandruff that flickers in the stage lights as it falls from his head after running his hand through his hair following yet another silence, all add up to one word for all the hopeful funny men: Integrity.

Everyone does impressions, but no one wants to be known as an impressionist. Impressionists have nothing funny of their own to say. Impressionists often get good laughs and rarely bomb, but impressionists are lame, lame, lame. Prop comics, though, are the worst. While there were plenty of *successful* prop comics, there had never been a *great* prop comic. Pryor did not use props, Carlin did not need props, Bruce occasionally pretended to be leafing through a newspaper, but he was no prop comic. Gallagher used props. Gallagher's brother, who performed as Gallagher Too, used props, Gallagher's props. Carrot Top. Ugh.

Steve Martin used props, but for some reason no one called him a prop comic. Why wasn't Martin a prop comic? It is because Martin was a genius, a postmodern surrealist comic, a creator then breaker of molds? Martin's props winked at the audience. They all agreed, props are stupid, but nonetheless, take a look at this rubber chicken. Martin was the prop. The funny man tries to take solace in the Martin example. Even if it was not possible to be a great prop comic, it was possible to be a great comic who used props. Martin's arrow through the head is in the Smithsonian.

The funny man buoys himself with these thoughts as he prepares for his first post-thing discovery performance at the club. His new talent agent has insisted on it as a test. "My instincts are unfailing," the agent said, "but still, you never know, you know?" The other hopeful funny men look at him as he drags his small trunk into the room to wait his turn.

"You having a garage sale?" one of them cracks.

"What's in the box?" another says, but before he can strike, the funny man delivers the punch line: "Your act: I'm giving it a proper burial." The joke is good enough to shut down the inquiries, everyone recognizing that it's unlikely to be topped. And anyway, they are distracted when they realize one of them has fallen asleep, which provides an opportunity for one of them to drop trou and drape his testicles and penis across the unfortunate slumberer's face in what is known as a "Roman helmet."

As usual, backstage is saturated with smoke and littered with empty beer bottles with spent cigarettes jammed down the necks. The funny man is one of the few who doesn't smoke (bad for the child), but the funny man is thirsty and nervous and would like a beer. However, he is afraid to leave his trunk unattended because he is certain that they will fuck with it because that is what he would do to them under the same circumstances. The atmosphere backstage is very all for one, one for all, us versus the audience, at least until you're suspected of having the kind of success that will allow you to escape backstage, after which you are a goddamn sellout who should fuck a llama with your grandmother's face, in a room with your parents, who are doing each other, so you're fucking your llama grandmother while watching your parents have sex.

They all saw the funny man talking to the talent agent after his last time and now he shows up with a mysterious trunk. Very, very suspicious. He looks at them now, snapping cell phone photos of their sleeping comrade, now wearing the genitalia on his face, and realizes that for them, this may be as good as it gets, these stories about backstage at the club, hanging out with so-and-so, who everyone knows, and this is what they call a brush with fame.

But the funny man senses he is about to be more than brushed, he is being slathered in fame, dipped in fame, cannonballing into the fame pool, which may be dangerous because he cannot swim.

Or this may be hindsight talking. It's hard to know for sure.

The funny man was third in line by the time he'd arrived. His agent has arranged for a better slot than usual, before the patrons are drunk and wrung-out and tired. The funny man considers asking someone to help him haul the trunk onto the stage, but knows he is unlikely to get any takers. Fortunately, he has been practicing carrying it without looking awkward or at least tripping onto his face, though that could be funny now that he thinks of it.

To the side of the stage a neon star illuminates, signaling that it's time for the current performer to wrap things up. He now has between thirty and sixty seconds to finish or he is unlikely to be invited back ever again. The schedule at the club is not to be fucked with unless a famous alumnus of the club—someone who has achieved a sitcom or movie career—decides to show up unannounced to work some kinks out of their new material, in which case the schedule is torched. The neon star is also the signal for the next performer to move into position, ready to be announced by the finishing person. At the club, backstage is not actually backstage, but is behind the audience, past a curtain and down the stairs, so the funny man carefully eases the case to the ground at the top of the stairs so as not to draw attention to himself too soon.

The man on the stage hoods his eyes with his hand and squints through the stage lights peering to the back and says, "Ladies and gentlemen, we have a truly talented professional coming next and it looks to me like he's got something special planned that I'm sure you'll enjoy. Ladies and gentlemen, please welcome . . ."

WHEN THE NEON star comes on, the funny man has just enough time for the finale. It has been going extremely well. A guy in the front row did an actual spit take when the funny man first turned around with his fist in his mouth and the funny man ad-libbed jumping off stage to mop up the mess with the sleeve of his Jimmy Cagney trench coat. By the end, just about the whole audience was convulsing with laughter and he knew that the Captain Hook twist was going to surprise and delight them. They'd never seen this before, and yet they acted like they've been waiting all their lives for it.

After his thank-yous and good nights, the funny man quickly tosses the final props into his trunk and kicks the lid closed with his foot while introducing the next performer, a good friend of his, a guy he used to drink with until he was stupid as they debated who was and who was not the greatest and laid odds on which of their current colleagues would make it out of the club. They'd bonded, these two. They were bros. Fellow warriors, foxhole mates. The funny man gives his good friend his best introduction, slathering the praise. At his name the funny man's good friend charges the stage, making it up before the funny man can even stoop to lift his trunk. He grips the funny man's hand with his right hand and clamps the left on the funny man's shoulder and menaces into his ear, "Thanks for draining the room with that weak shit. Look at these assholes, there's nothing left." His good friend lets go of the funny man's hand and shoulder and as the funny man picks up his trunk he glances at the audience and sees his good friend is right. The crowd looks wrung-out, exhausted, postcoital even. He has done that to them. Him.

The funny man doesn't even bother going backstage. He carries his trunk out the front door into the night air and normally he takes the subway, but tonight, he sticks his arm out for a cab. He isn't coming back because he doesn't need to.

⌒

OUTSIDE THE HOUSE, two production assistants roll up in the big, white rented van, and double-checking the address, note that there is no oak tree in the funny man's yard as location scouting had promised. Location scouting is almost always fucking up. It's like, why bother scouting if it's wrong? However, there is a nice, shady oak tree, with one swooping, low-hanging branch that makes its residence in the neighboring yard.

"Always something," production assistant two says to production assistant one.

"Waivers?" production assistant one asks production assistant two.

"Got 'em right here."

At the neighbor's door, PA one adjusts the slightly crooked mailbox as PA two rings the bell. The funny man's neighbor answers.

"Yes?" Seeing the two handsome young men, she pats at her frazzled hair and cinches her housecoat a touch tighter at her throat.

"Ma'am," PA two says, smiling big. "How would you like that nice, shady oak tree of yours to be nationally famous." PA one extends the waiver form with one hand, a pen with the other.

The neighbor wonders if she might still be dreaming as she signs the paper in front of her.

THE FUNNY MAN looks at his hair in the mirror. A cowlick towards the rear refuses taming. He snips it, badly, with his wife's cuticle scissors. The funny man would like to say that the recent months have been like a dream except that a dream is easier to remember and understand than what has been happening to the funny man. Following signing the contract with his agent, a series of very strange and wonderful events have carried him to this morning when his picture is to be taken for the nationally distributed magazine with a circulation of five million.

This is how his agent said it to him: "Five million circulation," emphasis on the *million*, but the funny man was most interested in the *circulation* word. His picture, accompanied by a three-hundred-word article, would soon be circulating through five million people. *Circulating* is a good word, going round and coming back again. He will be among them, part of them, circulating. If nothing else good happens for the funny man, with the picture he will achieve a level of permanence that he could only have imagined a short time ago. From his new bathroom in his new house he hears the guttural rumble of cargo trucks. They've come for him. In the end, it wasn't so tough to leave the city they both loved so dearly, the crucible in which his act was forged. The new house has three bathrooms and really, the city is a stone's throw away, provided you can throw a stone like Superman.

⌐

THE DAY AFTER his successful appearance at the club, the funny man's new agent called him and said he'd booked him for a gig that weekend, an opening slot for another comedian, but a good show, good money.

"How much money?" the funny man asked. His agent told him the figure.

"How much?" His agent told him the figure again.

"Say it again," the funny man said and his agent did so. The gig was out of town, his first gig that he would travel to on a plane instead of the subway. When he told his wife how much he was earning for approximately twenty minutes of work, she looked at the ceiling and moved her lips, doing the math in her head. "That's ten percent of what I earned all of last year," she said.

When the funny man received his boarding pass from the ticket agent he thought there must be a typo. 2A. He'd never seen a row number that small. He had spent his life up to that point confined to 24F, 37D. He had a choice of personal videos at his seat and the food was tolerable. He did not anticipate any food poisoning. At his destination, when he descended the escalator to the baggage claim area, he saw a man in a black suit wearing a driver's cap holding a dry erase board with the funny man's name on it.

At the hotel they did not ask for a credit card imprint, which was good because he didn't have one untethered to his bank account, which would not have contained nearly enough to pay for even a couple of hours in this particular hotel. His room was bigger than their apartment and a basket of consumer goods worth hundreds of dollars waited for him on the dining room table, thanking him for something he hadn't done yet. His hotel room had a dining room table. His apartment did not.

With shaky hands he dialed the phone home and when his wife answered he told her all about the trip thus far. "It's like another world," he said.

"I could get used to this," he said.

A YOUNG BOY wobbles down the street on his bike, tossing morning papers onto lawns. (It really was that kind of neighborhood.) The production assistants bounce the tractor tire out of the back of the van and roll it to the neighbor's oak tree. They throw loops of hemp over the low-hanging branch and lash the hemp to the tire so it dangles several feet off the ground. PA one climbs on.

"Push me," says PA one to PA two.

PA two grabs the tire and walks backward. "Underdog," he says, running forward as fast as he can, pushing PA one skyward.

The tree limb groans under the weight.

"Wheeeee," PA one says.

Soon, the production trucks roll up and disgorge barricades for the street, banks of lights, folding chairs, a live llama, and finally a long table of pastries and crullers.

The neighbor peeks through her curtains at the whole scene and wonders if it's safe to go outside.

THE SHOW WAS the first time he would ever do the thing for such a large audience, the first time he'd do *anything* for such a large audience and the funny man was hella nervous. Trying to bond with the headliner, the funny man asked for any useful tips. The headliner was known as a "comic's comic," a bit cerebral, a practitioner of perfectly crafted jokes larded with arcana sometimes so subtle the audience laughed several seconds behind the beat. The headliner had hosted his own series of shows (cable, not network), all of which were critically praised but mostly ignored by viewers, but still, this guy was in television and even a handful of movies here and there in parts tailored to his persona. It was widely said by other comics that the headliner should be more famous than he was, but the other comics did not really believe this because most of them didn't get the jokes either. The headliner looked up and down at the funny man. "Don't fuck up," he said.

The funny man laughed. The headliner didn't.

The crowd was almost totally silent through the funny man's opening material. He'd never been on a stage elevated so far above the audience and it was disorienting, and between bits his brain searched for each segue. Full-on amateur hour. "I'm fucking up," he thought. "I'm really fucking up." He imagined that it might be possible to jump from the stage and plunge to his death, it was so high. He would at least break a leg, which might engender some sympathy. At least they wouldn't be silent anymore, he thought. At least he was able to cram all those consumer goods from the gift basket in his suitcase. His wife would enjoy the Swiss chocolates.

But then he turned to the steamer trunk filled with the hook and his costumes for the thing, and dragging it to the front of the stage, it made a hideous squeak that got a few laughs. Working with the moment, the funny man pretended to struggle to get the trunk open, making a show of his inability to raise the lid. He kicked and cursed at the trunk, the sounds of the laughter swelling in his ears, until fully inspired, he invited someone from the front row to come up and help, a frat-boy-looking guy who looked unsure as he mounted the steps to the stage, but gave the full-on dude double-fist thrust salute into the air as the spotlight hit him. Frat-boy-looking guy strolled over to the trunk and braced himself for the effort of raising the lid that the funny man had found so impossible to move, and flinging it open, fell flat on his ass to massive applause.

When frat-boy-looking guy got home he told his parents that the show was "the coolest thing ever."

⁓

THE MAKEUP ARTIST circles the funny man and mutters something about pores. After giving up on the funny man, he turns to the funny man's wife, and shouts "perfection!" causing the funny man's wife to blush, which adds just the right amount of additional rouge to her cheeks. Oldest trick in the book.

⁓

THE FUNNY MAN could not contain his grin as he left the stage after performing the thing. It was clear that they'd never seen anything like that before and would be going home to tell their friends and neighbors about it. The headliner stood in the wings, arms crossed and frowning. "Nice job, fuckwad. A pox on you and your shitty act."

The funny man laughed. The headliner didn't.

Back at the hotel, talking on the phone, his agent said not to worry about it. "You're never opening for anyone ever again."

The next week the funny man was booked on the late, late-night show, the one that's watched by fewer people, and not so much watched, but something that's on in the background during sleep, or sex, or drinking oneself to death, but still, television! The funny man did a truncated version of the thing. At the end of his act the host came over to shake his hand before throwing it to commercial. "Great great stuff," he said. "Back after a break!" As the camera light clicked off, while still gripping the funny man's hand, the host, a former comic himself, leaned in and said, "Everyone else is going to hate you for this. You know that, right?" The host released his grip and patted the funny man on the back, the final pat feeling something like a shove off the stage. Once could be a fluke, twice begins to be suspicious, but a third time is, for sure, a pattern. The funny man was not going to be loved by the other funny men. His rise to comedy fame is to be a solo, rather than a team sport. This is how it always is, though. Even in ensemble situations, all for one and one for all means more for some. For every Rachel, there is a Phoebe. For every Chevy, a Larraine. He is comfortable with this because he has no choice.

~

WHEN THE PHOTOGRAPHER arrives he surveys the setup and asks if this is the architect everyone is talking about who designs the tiny homes, or is this the cancer survivor that hopscotched across the state, or perhaps the young author who everyone thinks is so rude? Is this the man who started a multimillion-dollar charity by banding the homeless together to sell chocolate chip cookies shaped like American presidents?

"Where am I, anyway?" he asks. "Can a guy get a latte?"

He looks at the llama and waves it away. The llama doesn't seem to care.

The production coordinator points at the tire. "Straddle it," he tells the funny man. "One leg down each side of the tire with the wife and kid sitting in the middle. Zany, but also precious. Beloved and unpredictable." This looks decidedly impossible to the funny man. The extent of his athletic prowess was a college intramural championship in Ultimate Frisbee. He is not flexible in any sense of the word. He suspects that his tendons are shorter and more rigid than average.

The funny man climbs to the top and gingerly stretches his legs around the tire. He feels a tug in his groin.

"Don't move," the production coordinator says to the funny man. "Tickle the baby," the production coordinator says to the funny man's wife. "Perfect."

A line of sweat leaks down the funny man's face. It seems possible that the muscle in his leg may detach from his knee. Did he not once see a show on one of the science channels that demonstrated how each muscle is a bundle of many fibers and that exercise is actually a form of destruction, where the muscle is damaged on purpose so that it may grow stronger in defense? But damage is different from destruction, which is what seems to be happening here. Damage is reparable, destruction permanent. For sure surgery, rehabilitation, a permanent limp or hobble. He breathes loudly through his mouth. His wife stage-whispers up at him through her smile: "Are you okay?"

"Ah, ah, ah," the funny man replies.

Putting down his latte, the photographer approaches the scene, squinting through one eye as he moves toward the camera. He squats down to his haunches and cups his hands around his eyes. "We'll fix that look on his face in post," the photographer mutters to the production coordinator.

"Shoot them," he tells the production coordinator. "Shoot them now."

Triggered by remote, the camera fires over and over and over.

⌒

A COUPLE OF weeks later, standing in the supermarket aisle, the neighbor tears through the issue of the magazine and there, on page 37 is her tree with the neighbors hanging from it. She always knew the wife was pretty and the husband is better looking than she'd thought, though up to that point she'd only seen him in sweatpants as he went to retrieve the morning paper. She did not know their names before, but now she does and she will never forget them again. They probably will not speak to each other because she does not want to be a bother, but she will wave when appropriate. Years from now she will tell stories about how she used to be neighbors with the famous funny man and his wife and how wonderful it was.

The picture is amazing to her. Every day for the past seventeen years she has looked out her front window at that oak tree. She has driven past it up her driveway, thousands and thousands of times, yearly she has ordered her husband into the yard to rake up its leaves, but here, in this glossy magazine, for the first time, she feels like she really *sees* it, you know? She buys ten copies.

7

Barry said it: "We're all monsters;" but if so, we aren't born this way. We become them. I figured the trial would tell that story, but the prosecution has presented surprisingly little of my sordid recent history, perhaps figuring the jury knew all that was necessary already ("untalented, successful, bad husband and father") and that to rehash things would appear to be piling on, bending the whole mood back toward sympathy. The tabloids have spared no ink on me over the years. Not that the additional humiliations would make a difference at this point. Ever since I shot the armed robber six times in alleged self-defense, my life has been a series of (probably well-deserved) humiliations, arrest, mug shot, detention, the whole thing the difference between laughing *with* and laughing *at*.

Like the location-monitoring device strapped to my ankle. Yes, I am in many ways fortunate to be out on bail and able to live and sleep in my high-rise apartment with the doorman and view of the park and access to take-out, but honestly, hasn't technology progressed to the point where the transmitter-receiver can be smaller than the brick-sized thing that I have to haul around everywhere save the courtroom? Mornings, when I shower, I have to dangle the leg out of the spray, which is difficult since my shower has six nozzles to provide full and constant coverage. If the device gets wet, the anti-tamper alarm will sound and a team of federal marshals will kick down my door and plant their boots in my spine, and they will shout things like, "What's doing here, smart guy?" And I want no part of that. Again.

When I raised this issue with Barry, he looked at me and said, "Please don't tell me you want me to bring this up to the judge." For a moment I returned Barry's look, incredulous, because of course I wanted him to bring this up to the judge, that's why I'd taken the time to mention it to him, but as Barry continued to stare at me and I saw the pity fill his eyes I realized that this was one of those incidents my therapist would point to in order to illustrate what he calls my "loss of perspective."

The only places I am allowed to go are the courtroom, my apartment, and the therapist's. I would like to quit the therapist because each session is more enervating than the last. This alleged "loss of perspective" is our only subject now. "Loss of perspective" is meant to suggest that I no longer have the capacity to see myself as others do, but I prefer to look at it different, that instead of losing perspective, I have gained one: My own.

"Loss of perspective" is only our latest subject following my struggles with "superfluousness," "indifference," and later, "free-floating rage." Personally, if you ask me, the start of my problems, or at least the start of my *real* problems, can be traced to starting therapy, as I had no real idea about how screwed up I was before. I would like to quit, but if I abandon the sessions I would miss the contact, the friendly greeting of the receptionist, Jill, her smile no less warm than ever even though I am now an alleged manslaughterer, and her offer of coffee and her assurance that my therapist will be free any moment, the mug now warm between my hands, the feel of it so comforting that I don't want to drink, and then her holding open the door to the therapist's office, smiling always, inviting me past with her free arm and the smell of her perfume on the way by. So many things have been taken from me (or I have thrust them away from myself) that I feel desperate to hold onto whatever I have left. This I will keep.

The fifty-minute hours themselves are exercises in futility. I'm pretty sure, anyway. I know what ails me now and in so knowing can self-identify the cure, but as the trial has dragged on, I have planned my weeks around those moments in the outer office and the thought of giving them up is like letting go a life-preserver mid-ocean.

What ails me presently, I am positive, is good, old-fashioned lovesickness and finally, this is what I told my therapist.

"It's not the trial, really, that has me so bent out of shape," I said.

The therapist made a noncommittal and nonjudgmental gesture. This gesture is encouraging without being approving. I imagine that he's practiced this gesture in the mirror for many, many hours. At conventions he gives seminars on the gesture, and after the seminars, at the hotel bar, other therapists ask him to do it, which he does, and he in turn critiques their gestures for them. "Go on," he said. *Gesture.*

"I'm in love."

"Oh?" Here the gesture failed him, the eyebrow lifting into skepticism. "With whom are you in love?"

I didn't want to get into it because I knew the pattern, we were on the route to "loss of perspective," perhaps after a detour toward "living in a skewed reality." "I can't really say much more than that," I said.

"And why not?"

"It's secret."

"You know I can't tell anyone about it, right? That our conversations are bound by confidentiality?"

"Sure."

"Then why won't you tell me?"

Why indeed? Because even to speak it is to relinquish some of its power. I'd said too much already. Some things just are. I sat stone-faced.

"Can you tell me where you two met?"

I intended to wait him out, but my face must have betrayed the answer.

"Oh," he said, "there."

"You have a tone," I replied.

The therapist threw his hands in the air, surrender-ish. "No tone, no tone," he said. "You know my feelings on that, we don't need to discuss it anymore."

I did know his feelings about the White Hot Center, where Bonnie and I met and fell in love.

His feelings were that the White Hot Center didn't exist.

His feelings were that what I described about what went on there was impossible to the point that maybe I needed some additional prescriptions or some time with a car battery and cables attached to my temples, whereas my feelings were that he was full of shit because I'd been there, my heart knew what it had experienced, what was real and not.

"We're not going to get anywhere, are we?" I said. My time at the White Hot Center where I was cured, at least briefly, demonstrated the almost three years of futility behind my conversations with this man.

A look that said "fuck if I know" flashed across his face before the mask returned. But the truth had been briefly revealed. I imagined that the therapist's mentor has always told him that therapy was as much art as science, but the therapist no longer believed this. He knows what I know, that therapy is neither art nor science, but something far more random. To his own therapist the therapist describes it this way: "It's like I'm holding some kind of machine gun while sitting on a spinning carousel and there's a target that flashes past as I go round in circles. When the bullets hit the target they're effective, for sure, but I'm spinning pretty fast and the gun really kicks around when I fire it, so while I *do* hit the target sometimes, I'm never quite sure where or why, and if you ever tell a soul that I said this, I'll have you killed and disbarred, probably in that order."

Or I could be making all that up. It passes the time anyway.

As PART OF the bail agreement, the only places I'm allowed to call out to are 911, Barry, my agent and manager, and the downstairs concierge, who will then place my carryout orders for me. The only people allowed to call in are Barry, my agent and manager, the downstairs concierge (to announce the impending arrival of my carryout) and my ex-wife, but she never calls.

Because Bonnie is also famous I can at least keep tabs on her, worship her from afar, if you will, since I now understand love is a form of worship, a true act of faith, and that distance is no impediment to the practice of it. Love always has been this way, it's just that I recognize it now.

Since the start of my trial, her game has gone into the toilet and there is tremendous speculation as to why—injury, illness, and (absurdly) aging—but I know the *real* reason. It is because she has been struck with the lovesickness also. We had plans and now those have been dashed. Do I take some pride in this, that my downfall ripples across the continents to her? I do, even as I mourn her misfortune. One of the great joys of being loved is having others feel your triumphs and pains, but at the same time, when they are feeling your pains, if you love them in return, you are then feeling their pain over feeling your pain and so on and so on and this is a difficult loop to pull out of.

I haven't mentioned this theory to my therapist either because I'm certain that it too would be chalked up into the "loss of perspective" column. He may not be wrong. My life as a famous person has altered me down to my DNA, my previous self a whisper, a sound you can't quite hear clearly. This is why I should not entirely trust myself on this front, but at this point, I'm too deeply invested.

So every time Bonnie double-faults or sprays a forehand return wide of the sideline, I believe I know why, I know that she feels it too. And we haven't even slept together yet! Or rather, we've slept together very briefly—the best night of my (second) life—we just didn't have sex. Imagine! As the camera bores in on her sitting on the sidelines between games, a towel over her head and a far-off look in her eyes where before there had been perfect focus, I'm not ashamed to say, my heart thrums. I am on life support and it is this that sustains me even it is just a few memories and a fantasy of an impossible future.

I have plenty of time alone in my apartment to contemplate these things. It is a nice cell, but still a cell. I leave the television on in the background as I wait for her next appearance and go to my big window, the first thing the real estate agent wanted to point out to me at the showing, even though at the time it mostly seemed like something I wanted to throw myself out of.

Now it, along with her, is my saving grace, a window to the world. I prefer the view at night when everything is reduced to shadows and lights, when the people can't really be seen and the cityscape is dominated by the neon in the store windows, the white domes on the top of the taxis that stack up along the park that snap off one by one as they are claimed. The slow-moving flashers on the horse-drawn carriages as they amble down the path. Brake lights sparking in sequence as cars roll up to the intersections. I open some cold beans and eat directly from the can as I stand at the window. I never wanted this view, meaning it wasn't a goal of mine, but all things considered, I'm glad to have had it, at least for a time. I have watched the scenes so often it's like I know what is going to happen next, the pattern and progress, and sometimes it comes in my head that these people below are at my command. It is both beautiful and peaceful and when we were last together I told her that I couldn't wait for her to see it.

8

THE FUNNY MAN and his wife ride a limousine to the big show. He drums his hands on his knees and hammers a leg up and down, nervous. At the house, the funny man spent half an hour peering through the curtains, certain the limousine would not arrive, that the big show in the city was a figment, a hoax, but there it was, five minutes early, an inky, rolling ship docking in his driveway, amazing.

The limousine is nice, not new, and not particularly long, but clearly this is *not* the limo for hyped-up prom-goers, with scratched leather, knobs twisted off of the television, crumbs in the seat crevices, grime along door handles, and a pine-tree scent freshener jammed in the divider between passengers and driver masking the stench of overuse. He would have ridden in one of those substandard limos if he had gone to prom, which he did not because of his abject terror around girls, but that is so far in the past as to barely exist. Since he started performing the thing he has had to remember is to throw out cocktail napkins with phone numbers scrawled in lipstick before he gets home.

No, this is the limo for the fairly famous, for the somewhat known, for a celebrity, of sorts.

"I am a celebrity," the funny man thinks. How many people would recognize him? Some, for sure. Many? Not many, but some. His name? No. Just that funny man, you know *that* guy with the *thing*. This show is officially "the next level" for the funny man. The moment he hits one level he is on to the next one, so thus far it has all been the same to him, but tonight the people in the audience will number in the thousands and they will be taping the performance for later premium cable broadcast.

The funny man looks at his wife. She looks good to him, very good. Her makeup is heavy around her eyes, but it is different and sexy. Her eyebrows have been trained by a professional into tapered arches that accentuate her truly excellent bone structure. Previously, if someone had asked him about his wife, he would have said she was "perfect looking," and meant it, but here she is looking *better than perfect*, which would've seemed impossible until everything seemed possible. How is it that the boundaries of the possible can move? It is not possible and yet it has been happening to the funny man.

Lately he has begun mentally listing those things that separate before from after: First the house, with its multiple floors and yard, as opposed to the apartment where they shared their bedroom with the child (the antiaphrodisiac, they joked) and where the kitchen and living room were one space, really; only formality and a two-stool breakfast bar designating them as different. There is now a car for each of them, new ones with six cylinders and leather, and of course, the true indulgence—the one thing he couldn't imagine he was buying, could not justify buying even as he read his credit card number over the phone to the toll-free operator—the chair that massages him with thousands of tiny fingers while he sits in front of the TV, which unfortunately also makes the TV look like it is jiggling, something that was not noted in the catalog description of the magic chair; which, come to think of it, specifically mentioned being able to watch TV while enjoying the massage and the heat. But no mind. How many people even own such a chair? Enough to make it worthwhile to put out a catalog filled with these sorts of luxury items, the funny man supposed.

And now this wife with professional eyebrows, not that they were a problem before (though she is half-Italian), but clearly, these are better—can he actually count the number of hairs left in the brows? He thinks he can. Yes, it is like they have been cut and combed, each hair the perfect length. There are people who excel at shaping a woman's eyebrows and his wife now goes to these people because of him and his success. Is this a source of pride? Sure. Of course. Just a year or so ago, before he'd met the clapping man, he was not even aware of these needs, but now, here they are, permanent and obvious.

And yet, every time he sits in the special massaging chair and tries to watch the shimmying television screen, rather than relaxed, he feels irritated, enraged even. Several times he has begun composing angry letters in his head to the chair-manufacturing company and the catalog that sells it. He added a three-minute bit about the chair to his act, pretending that he'd only tried one at a friend's house, a friend who was clearly the kind of asshole who would plunk down two months of the average American salary for a chair.

Seriously, though, had the chair company never actually tried watching television while utilizing both the heat and massage features? Seems inconceivable. They must have noticed this and suspected it was a fatal flaw, but chose to lie to save their own researched and developed hides. He should call. *"Hello, this is . . . Yes, that is me. What is my concern? Let me tell you my concern. . . ."*

Boy, is he nervous. He doesn't remember ever being this nervous. Not when he got married, not when the child was born. He had complete faith in the rightness of the outcome on both of those occasions, the bliss of ignorance. Both events were complicated, and one (the birth) was downright gory, but he does not remember any doubts. This time, there are doubts for sure, a sense that this could be it, that his career is a balloon that has been inflating from a tank of nitrous, with this gig as a giant pin of "fuck you, you're not fucking funny."

His wife wears a black dress cut above the knee that rides even higher when she snugs back, settling deep into the limo's leather seat. Beneath the dress, her dark nylons work in conjunction with her pressed-together legs and the soft, interior lighting of the limo to create a small, dark, inviting triangle at her crotch.

The funny man puts his hand there. He is thinking of a different kind of need. She puts her hand firmly on top of his and smiles at him.

"The windows are dark," he says. "There is a soundproof divider between us and our driver. No one could possibly see." The funny man runs his hand up the inside of his wife's dress, claws at the panty liner of her nylons. He has done some fine work there, in that space, with this hand, and the other as well, and sometimes even his tongue. When they first met, he knows he was pretty bad with all that, first shaky and unsure, then too rough and too quick, unskilled but eager labor, but she had guided him and he had improved. He is very good now, he thinks, you can't fake some of the things he's made his wife do (back arching, uncontrollable shudders, wetness) when he's working well down there, and what a night this is going to be. Shouldn't this be bracketed by some limo sex? Before and after the performance? This isn't even daring, rather the kind of thing expected—nay, demanded—of a celebrity. And he is a celebrity. Millions have seen his picture in the magazine, and then the performance on the late-night show. (Okay, the late, late-night show.)

His hand retreats, drawing a small circle with his index finger inside her knee, first gently, then more forcefully, trying to part her legs. He is sly, his touch perfect, impossible for his wife to resist. Soon her lips will part, her breathing will both quicken and deepen and they will finish this business he has started just as they arrive at the theater and emerge from the limo panting and rumpled, and the dressing room attendants will notice the sleepy look on his face for what it is, the look of a man who can have sex in a limousine.

But his wife's knees stay locked together, very firmly. She works out, sometimes with weights. She pats his hand. "Not here, I don't want to get messy." Her look is not unkind, and the funny man removes his hand, strokes his chin. She makes sense, of course. This is not only his night, but hers as well, a partnership, an equal partnership. She has made sacrifices too, and he should honor her wishes on this. Of course she makes sense. She has always been the sensible one, had even warned him off the massage chair before giving in, admitting that he deserved an indulgence. He should have listened then like he's listening now.

The funny man turns to look out the window and rests his chin on his hand and he sulks. He doesn't think of himself as a sulker, but he is, he is, always has been. His mother would say so and his wife as well. He tries to banish the limousine sex images from his mind.

No! the funny man thinks. She does not make sense. She is absurd! Look at her! She is hot! There should be limousine sex! Images of his wife's legs thrown over his shoulders dance through his head, her feet thumping against the window glass. With all these things he now has, with the massage chair, with the heated floor in his bathroom, with the part-time (okay, one day a week) personal assistant (who is actually the babysitter most days) who will pick up his dry cleaning without complaint (not quite true, he has to add a tip to the total), is he really being denied limo sex?

Seriously?

On the way home, when they reprise this limo sex, when he is triumphant, he envisions his wife pouring champagne down his back as she rides him, giggling together at the waste. When they exit the limo, finally back at home, he will wear her torn panty-hose as an ascot and tell the driver that the manager (there is now a manager in addition to the agent) will take care of everything, which is true! That's true! His manager would take care of everything! This is almost tragic, he thinks. How many times does this happen in a person's life?

From behind! He will take her from behind! He will open the window so her head is part of the way out of the car and he will take her from behind! She will rock and squeal and whoop! They will speed pass the cars of the non-famous on the way from the city, and they will know that something is really going on in that limo. *Who could that be?*

Me. Me. Me. Me, the funny man thinks.

The funny man presses his forehead to the window and clutches the leg of his pants in his hand. Where do these things come from? He's never seen anything like these things he is imagining.

There is a sunroof! (A moonroof; it is evening.) His wife could strip her top and whirl it around her head, as she rides torso-bared halfway out of the sunroof!

He feels feverish. Could he really be getting sick? The funny man smoothes his hands along his legs and tries to breathe deeply and shifts a little trying to relieve some of the pressure building in his pants. He tries to think of baseball. He tried to play baseball as a kid because he loved and still loves baseball, watches it all the time while sitting on the special chair, because the slow pace of the game makes the jittering less infuriating, but he was bad enough at it that the only way he ever saw the base paths was to screw himself up and let the ball hit him. He was not adverse to this, though, because he liked running—and what's this?

His wife's fingers tiptoe across the arch in his pants and work the zipper down. She smiles at him as her hand works the goods free.

Limousine head, the funny man thinks. Of course. Better than limousine sex? Not better, no; but good, very good. Very very very very very good. This woman is a genius, the funny man thinks as they ride toward the big show.

THE SEATING IS theater-style. No tables, no drinks, no drinks with swizzle sticks to absently twirl around fingers or crunch between teeth while the funny man delivers his material. People will not be drinking. If they are drunk, they did it to themselves prior to arrival. There are to be no distractions. The funny man will be the sole focal point of the entire room. The steamer trunk full of props waits for the funny man on stage. They have paid to see him, not to cover the two-drink minimum. This is not the first time for that, but it is still a relatively new thing.

The dressing room is beneath the auditorium and the funny man can hear the rumbling above him as the audience files in and it feels to him as though the temperature is rising by the moment. They are treading on top of him and don't even know it. He is holding them up, supporting all of their weight. This performance will be filmed, and he has blocking to remember, spots to hit during his "thing" to ensure the best camera angles. Something extra to worry about. He has rehearsed his routine infinite times. When he wakes in the mornings he often finds his mind has been working the routine over in his sleep and when his wife smiles at him, he imagines it is in response to one of the jokes running in his head. The material, he knows, is good; not great, but good, but the thing—*his* thing—is great. The thing is outstanding.

The funny man never knows what to do with himself in the last moments before it is time to take the stage, so he is shadow-boxing, flicking his fists into the air, bobbing from foot to foot. The stagehands look at him a little oddly, but surely they've seen stranger. As he nears the entrance to the stage, the houselights go dark and the audience whoops and whistles. The funny man listens to their cries.

I haven't even done anything yet, he thinks, but still, they love me.

9

F OR SOME REASON there is a ten-day hiatus before the start of
my defense. Ostensibly it is to allow Barry time to prepare,
but Barry is spending at least part of the interim in the Barbados,
leaving me confined to the apartment, special, hiatus-scheduled
twice-weekly visits to the therapist my only escape.

At least it leaves me some time to catch up on my "work." It is not
that the money is *gone*. That would be ridiculous, impossible even,
but there is for sure much, much less of it, primarily thanks to the
divorce, a fiscal cleaver leaving two halves, one of which I no longer
have access to. The trial is proving to be spectacularly expensive and
the offers hadn't been rolling in even prior to the incident.

Not long before Beth and I were to get married, my father made
us both scotches and took me aside to the porch and we sat together
and my father raised his glass in a toast and said, "Son, I'm going
to tell you the key to happiness." He wanted to tell me about the
importance of "the nut."

I was surprised. This wasn't our kind of relationship. Oh, there
was love there. I felt it in the way the man knocked himself out for

my mom and me, traditional-father-role-style, but it was almost all
backstage, coming out from behind the curtain only on occasion,
like once when I was around eight years old and the entire town
had been buried in a blizzard and Dad couldn't get to work and
instead clomped down to the basement and dragged back upstairs
with an armful of cross-country skiing gear that I'd never seen
before.

We set off down our empty suburban street, everything doused
with snow so high that even the hydrants and mailboxes at the
curbs were covered. The plows hadn't come through yet, and my
father blazed the trail while I followed behind, mimicking his
swinging arms and kicking legs as we made our way to the golf
course, a perfect, almost untouched expanse of white save for the
tiny paw prints of squirrels and rabbits. As we entered the course
I could then see the undulations of the ground, little hills to chug
up and slide down. At the top of one, the tallest one we'd encoun-
tered, my father paused and waited for me and said, "This is really
something, huh?" before schussing down into a depression and
coming to a quick stop, hockey style.

The way up the hill had been a gentle climb, but at the peak, I
could see that the way down was rather steep and that my father
had generated a pretty good amount of speed before slamming on
the brakes. I hesitated. I'd never been on skis of any kind before
and as far as I knew, cross-country was limited to flats only. These
skis weren't designed for this sort of move. But my father smiled
up at me, eager for us to go on, and held his arms out, the poles
dangling from his hands and said, "Come on, boy!"

I pointed my skis down, directly into my father's tracks. Because
the snow had been tamped down, I gathered speed very quickly.
I tried to bend my knees to absorb any jolts and this caused me to
go even faster and as my father grew in my vision I realized that
I didn't have the foggiest idea how to stop. Looking up, I saw my
father's eyes go wide and his hands push forward to brace for a
collision. At the last instant, I did the only thing I could do: Fall
heavily into him. My face filled with snow, numbing my nose and
lips and I felt the tip of my father's pole jab my leg.

"Ow," I said.

"What?"

"My leg."

My father tore his gloves off and started pawing his hands over my body. "Oh. Oh. Oh. Oh. Oh," he said. He was obviously and instantaneously terrified, and seeing this terrified me and I began crying. "Oh. Oh. Oh," he said. "I felt it. I felt the tip go in. It pierced you. I felt it. Oh. Where? Your leg?"

I shrieked now, my head bobbing frantically. This looked like the end of the world to me, the stoic man who stood on the sidelines of my baseball games and refused to scream like an idiot as did so many of the other fathers; the man who much later would look at a report card with two C's and not yell, but instead shake his head sadly and say only two words, "wasted potential"; the man who brought me to the porch to give me advice and wisdom as I was about to embark on a marriage was melting down in front of my face.

He slapped the snow away and pulled up the legs of my pants and his hands searched my skin for wounds, for bleeding, and I couldn't remember being touched like this by my father. When I was younger, my mother bathed me. When I got sick it was her hand that pressed to my forehead or rubbed menthol on my chest. She insisted on hugs and kisses, but not my father, never my father. Would he have liked that sort of thing? The hugs, the kisses? I'll never know. "Here? Here? Here?" my father said. I could only shake my head because I had no answers. If this man did not know, who could?

Eventually, we figured out that I was fine. That I had not been pierced by the ski pole, that it had been a glancing blow and all our terror was overblown, a mutual misunderstanding. My father laughed halfheartedly as he plucked me upright out of the snow and placed me back on my skis. As we made our way home, I stared at my father's back and willed my trembling legs to keep going because I did not want to let him down again by scaring him further. Neither of us said anything about the incident to Mom, but boy, did it make an impression. I mean, obviously because there it is all over again, and maybe that's also because when faced with my own responsibilities to protect my son, I was an abject failure, but I'm not talking about that yet.

ON THE PORCH my father sipped his scotch and gazed out at the dying light of evening. My father was definitely not a drinker, but I'd counted this as the old man's third cocktail. We had a little time before Beth and her parents were to arrive for a "get to know you" dinner that would actually go incredibly well as our mothers bonded over their mutual belief in their children's stupidity and drown their disappointments in a mid-range Chablis.

"They key to happiness," my father said, "is keeping your nut small."

I spit my sip back into my glass. I didn't care for scotch then. "What?"

"Your nut, your expenses. You've got to keep them under control, and I'll tell you why it's important. It provides flexibility."

I stirred my finger inside my glass, trying to induce the ice cubes to melt and cut some of the harshness of the liquor.

"How long have we lived in this house?" my father asked.

"My whole life."

"And six years before that, which means in eighteen months I own this thing outright."

"And how many kids do we have?"

"Just me."

"You know why?"

I sort of hoped it was because my parents had only had sex once. I just shook my head.

"Because I did some calculations that on my salary we could afford to provide completely, and I mean completely, for one child, so we had one child. Believe you me, we could've had more. Your mother is a sexy woman."

"Dad, please . . ."

"Tell me, have you ever wanted for anything?"

I shook my head. I had not had *everything*, there were others with more, but there was no doubting that I had plenty, more than my share.

"And how long do I keep my cars?"

I pictured the American-made sedan in the garage. No one would call it stylish or contemporary. "Long time."

"That's right, seven years minimum, which is how long they're designed to last without major issues. And where do we go on vacation?"

A slide show played in my mind, lots of miles in the back of the latest sedan, sunburns, costumed tour guides . . . "Let's see, Grand Canyon, Mt. Rushmore, Colonial Williamsburg, Disney World, Santa Fe . . ."

"Right again, all in the good old U.S. of A., because I'll tell you something, we've got a lot to see right here and Europe *costs*."

I ventured another sip. Watered down, the scotch wasn't so bad.

"Let me tell you something," my father said. "I'm still south of sixty and eighteen months from retirement and if I wanted, I got enough dough to buy a boat, and when I get that boat, if I decide I want one, I'll take it on the water where there aren't any roads. Who can beat that?"

My father leaned forward, elbows on thighs, and looked down at his scotch. "Flexibility, son. It's the key. Nobody owns me. Yes, I work for the man and I live in the suburbs and have a wife and a kid, but because I've kept my nut small I'm beholden to no one other than my own conscience. They think they have me, but they don't. I've got them. They talk about the American Dream and this is it. What most people don't understand about dreams is that they can look a lot like reality. I've lived my whole life this way and I'm the happiest motherfucker in the world. And I want to say that I'm proud of you."

My father drained the last of his drink and smacked his lips and squinted at the sunset and then clapped me on the knee as he stood. "Time to face the music, son."

I'VE LONG AGO lost control of my nut. My nut is like Godzilla, a baby reptile irradiated into a rampaging monster. The only person who could even guess the size of my nut is my accountant, who has been using words like *belt-tightening*, *reining in*, and *constriction*, which all mean the same thing. There are, of course, the residuals, the steady trickle of money tied to what I've done in the past, and there's a standing offer of six figures plus for a "no-holds-barred" interview with British television, but Barry has forbidden it, and if I manage to get acquitted there are endorsement deals from Japan and Scandinavia stacked up like planes trying to land during peak travel hours. Turns out infamy might pay almost as well as fame as long as I'll take it in yen or kroner.

But all of these possibilities are reserved for after, so for now, I sign things. Each week, a delivery, a giant rolling mail hamper filled with pictures and objects and unmentionables and it is my job to sign them. I receive twenty-five dollars for each signature and if I'm really humming, I can sign upwards of 150 items per hour. Ironically, this revenue stream was not open to me prior to my arrest and trial. In fact, I used to gladly give my signature away for free. (Almost always gladly, anyway, save the one unfortunate "elbowing" incident that was blown entirely out of proportion as an example of my "violent" nature during the prosecution's case.) But now, suddenly, my signature has significant value, at least as long as it's dated postarrest, which slows down the process a little, but not much.

I've been letting the shipments stack up, because, let's face it, it's not exciting work, but with nothing but idle time for the next ten days I dig in and get busy with a permanent marker. My signature has devolved into an illegible scrawl, but each scrawl is the same, so it is known to be mine. Each item has been previously opened by an assistant, the payment removed and verified. I'm almost certain the assistant steals some of the cash payments, but whatever. If I lose the case, he'll be out of work, so maybe he's just planning for the future. I sign dozens of pictures, concert T-shirts, CDs, commemorative posters, DVDs, all items I've produced, many of which I barely remember doing, making sure to keep them with their return addresses so my assistant can get them repackaged and sent. When I grow bored, I start to personalize each item at first with individual words chosen from the dictionary:

> *Hey Garth:*
> *Logorrhea!*
> *(Signature)*
> *(Date)*

. . . and then with nonsense (non)rhymes:

> *Janet:*
> *Roses are red*
> *Violets are blue*
> *Monkeys share 98% of their DNA with humans.*
> *(Signature)*
> *(Date)*

On a lampshade someone has sent, I begin a story, writing around its perimeter:

> *Gene:*
> *A long time ago in a village far, far away there lived a man with enormous testicles. The man's testicles were so large that he was forced to cart them around in a wheelbarrow. Over and over he goes to the doctor and says, "Doctor, why are my testicles so large? Can't you please give me something that will make my testicles smaller because I'm in love with a girl and I'm afraid she will never love me back because of my enormous testicles . . .*

I enjoy my own story. It's both silly and juvenile, my stocks in trade, and every time I write the word *testicles*, I giggle. I enjoy it so much that I work on it through the night and into the morning, covering the entirety of the lampshade in the text, the letters growing smaller with each revolution until there is no room left to even finish the story, let alone for a signature and date and I decide that I might as well keep this particular item and that it is probably now worth much more than twenty-five dollars anyway.

I consider sending it to *her*. I could do it anonymously, but surely she would know who it's from. I can picture her opening it, the dawning realization on her face, like a flower opening to the sun. I see it like it has actually happened. I would like her to see my creative powers, such as they are. She is too young to know what it was like during my prime years, the phenomenon of me and yeah, it's my ego talking, but I have regrets about that. But on second thought, isn't it even better that there's love there in the absence of that, that it's not part of the equation? Isn't it purer that way?

Of course, contact could land her in trouble as well. She has many millions of endorsements at risk that any association with me would surely taint. I am incompatible with her brand.

Even when there is not a tournament currently going on, I can turn on my television at any random time of day and within forty-five minutes she will be there on-screen urging people to buy something, something that she dearly loves and believes in. My favorite is the commercial for the hamburgers where she is on the court, smacking balls over the net with all of her power and grace on display, when suddenly, in midair, one of the balls turns into a half-pound "chunk burger" and she drops her racket and grabs it out of the air, gripping it so the condiments (ketchup, mustard, grilled onions, jalapeño-jack cheese, roast beef bits, Parma ham, sautéed mushrooms, avocado, and a single pineapple ring) are clearly visible, bursting from beneath the bun. The soundtrack kicks in, seventies soul, seduction music, organ and wah-wah guitar, and as she opens her mouth and takes a bite, the condiments spill down the front of her pristine white top, leaving a trail between her modest, pert breasts, but she does not care, no sir, she is under the spell of this hamburger. For the moment, her life revolves around this hamburger; she is the chunk burger's captive and she loves it. She simply can't get enough of this chunk burger. If an asteroid from space impacted the Earth, threatening the extinction of the human race, she still would not be distracted from this burger. If piranhas were working their way up from her toes, she would not pay heed because of this burger. If fire were threatening to consume her, no sweat, got the burger. You can tell by the way she licks the lingering grease off her lips.

The commercial ends with the tagline, "can't live without it," and her performance is convincing. The commercial is so good that millions of people seek it out and pass it on to their friends, telling them that this is something to see.

Even though I could do this too, it's more fun, more meaningful when it happens organically, without design, so as morning comes, I turn on the television and idly scratch at the monitoring device as I wait to see what I can't live without.

10

THE FUNNY MAN and his wife are embarrassed by the ritual,
would never tell anyone else about it, but first they'd come to
love it and then they'd come to need it. In the beginning it was just
weekly. One of them would look at the other across the breakfast
table and say, "Do you want to call?"

"Should we?" the other would say.

"Why not?"

"Didn't we just do it the other day?"

"A week ago two days from now, actually."

"Really?"

"Really."

"Okay."

And the funny man would stand and get the cordless phone and
bring it back to the table and invite his wife from her seat onto
his lap. He would cradle her across his legs as she steadied herself
with a hand draped across his shoulders. They both had the number
memorized, but it was also on autodial, and the funny man would
hit the button and listen to the ten-note tune and once he heard

the ring and entered the account number and pass key (their wedding anniversary) at the appropriate prompt, he would place the phone between him and his wife, holding the speaker up near their pressed-together ears.

What they had discovered is that at a certain point, money makes money and then it makes more money and after that, still more money. At that point there was only one account and the money flowed in automatically and grew as if by magic, and the phone number was a special automated system where one could call and get the account balance for that day recited to them by a pleasant sounding computerized woman. Even though they continued to pay their bills: mortgage, utilities, diaper service, cleaning help, meal delivery, etc. . . . the amount was larger each and every time.

After hearing the number, the funny man and his wife would look at each other wide-eyed, astonished. How does one have more money despite still spending money on things like nonstick pans and a pool table and a convection oven and that one weekend in the mountains where they rented the cabin and each cabin had its own outdoor tub fed by the natural springs and the cabins were strategically placed in relation to each other and the natural foliage and no two people since Adam and Eve had spent more time naked.

Usually after the ritual one of them said how "lucky" they were and the other nodded, offering their lips to seal the agreement with a kiss.

At some point, it became daily, something they both needed to get started, and sometimes it was done in the bathroom as they brushed their teeth, or over the kitchen sink as the breakfast dishes were rinsed, or as they worked together to stuff the child into that day's clothes.

On one day, a fair bit down the road after they'd moved into the second house, where even the closets were like rooms, it was the wife's turn to declare themselves lucky.

She is in the bathroom and because the funny man is in the bedroom, sitting up in the bed flipping through channels on the television, she says it loudly into the mirror as she clamps a device on her eyelashes.

"We sure are lucky," the funny man's wife says.

"What?"

"I said, we're lucky."

"What?" This house is large enough that a person in the bathroom cannot be heard in the bedroom without shouting.

"Luc-ky!"

"I can't hear you," the funny man says, muting the television.

His wife appears in the bathroom doorway. "I said, we sure are lucky."

"What do you mean by that?"

"What do you mean, what do I mean?"

"I mean, do you really think we're lucky or are you just saying that?"

"We say it every day."

"But do you believe it?"

"We're pretty fortunate, I think, considering," she says, turning back into the bathroom.

The funny man jumps from the bed and follows his wife into the bathroom, fishing his penis from his fly and relieving himself as he speaks. "Considering what?"

"Considering everything," she says, still looking in the mirror. "Can't you wait until I'm done?"

The funny man extends the show of peeing, swirling the stream around the bowl, grunting out the last few squirts before giving the works a vigorous shake and tucking it back through his fly. "Not really," he says. "Are you interested in my prostate exploding like the *Hindenburg*?"

"That's not funny," his wife says.

The funny man follows his wife back into the bedroom where she searches through the closet for the right pair of shoes. "What if I told you that I don't think we're lucky?" he says.

"What do you mean?"

"What if I told you that luck has nothing to do with what we are?"

The funny man's wife bends over to place her shoes on her feet and he steals a glance down the front of her blouse, which makes him want to forget the argument he is for sure trying to have. "What do you mean?" she says.

"I mean, I think our circumstances are not so much due to luck, but to hard work and vision."

The funny man's wife steps toward him and runs the front of her hand gently down the right side of his face and then the back of her hand across the left side of his face. "I've got to go. Let's talk about it when I get home."

THE FUNNY MAN spends the day preparing to talk about it when his wife gets home.

First he looks up *luck* in the dictionary and sees that it has to do with *chance*. He looks up *fortune* and sees that it means pretty much the same thing as *luck* and that essentially they both mean things happening "without design," things that are "fated." Things that were meant to happen *no matter what*.

The funny man decides to break down the issue. He goes to the office supply store and purchases an easel, a large pad of white paper, and three different colored markers.

At the top of the first page in black he writes *money*. He asks himself, Is the steadily growing account growing because of luck? No, it is growing by design as a function of sound fiscal planning rooted in the deep traditions of capitalism. Is contemporary American capitalism a matter of luck? Definitely not. It is a matter of having proved itself a superior basis for commerce. Just ask the *former* Soviet Union. Below the word *money* he writes *not luck* in blue.

He turns the page and writes *the thing* at the top. What about the thing, which is what has produced the seed money that is now growing on its own and continues to provide ongoing employment in front of sizable crowds for which the funny man is paid handsomely? Is this lucky? The funny man thinks on this for awhile, remembering back to the moment it came to him, and no, this was not luck, inspiration perhaps, but inspiration is 90 percent perspiration and perspiration implies work, which is not luck.

Because he sees that he could easily run out of paper, rather than turning the page, beneath *the thing* he writes *the boy*. His son had inspired the thing—he's said that in the interviews. Is that lucky? Not really. Perhaps if the boy had been adopted it would be a sign of luck, pure chance handing them just the right little baby boy, but no, this is *his* son, product of his loins and his wife's loins, or his loins and some other part of his wife, the female equivalent of loins. This is not luck so much as good planning, or maybe chemistry, which is in the realm of science, and is, therefore, not luck.

What about the boy's general good health and well-being, that he had been born with a hand that he could try to shove in his mouth? This is not luck, the funny man figures. Sure, people with retarded children with flippers instead of hands might be unlucky, but the rest who don't, like him and his wife, aren't lucky, they are simply some word that means what has happened is what should happen under normal circumstances. Call it "the odds."

Now, he was wearing a condom when the boy was conceived. That's true. Generally, society would hold that condom failure as unlucky, a bad break (ha ha ha), but the child is undeniably a good thing. Wouldn't that then be a stroke of luck?

The funny man stands in front of the easel, chewing on the end of the marker as he looks at *condom failure*. He writes a question mark in red next to it. After a time, beneath it he adds *wife's sexiness*. It was the wife's sexiness that led to the initial encounter. Perhaps this ingredient was necessary to understand the true nature of the condom failure.

Come to think of it, he remembers the moment the condom failed, or not failed so much as slipped off, because they were standing and he'd had to crouch down to lift her on to one of the library's shelves for a superior angle of attack, and in the moment, if he really thinks about it, he felt the condom pull free and if he asked his wife—she probably felt it as well—but neither of them did anything to put the brakes on the moment. He had wanted her from the instant she'd stamped his books, and apparently she felt the same way, and if anything, things got a bit hotter, and even afterward when the condom was removed and clearly not filled, there weren't any recriminations, just shrugs and, believe it or not, a sequel.

The funny man draws a circle around both *condom breaking* and *wife's sexiness* and in blue writes *prob. not luck.*

For some reason that time he and his friend Binder were on spring break in Vegas and decided to take peyote and drink wine and go to the desert and watch the stars pops into his head. They'd pulled to the side of the road and walked into the scrub brush and scraped a little clearing with their shoes and laid down and tweaked out for hours until the wine had overwhelmed them. They did not wake up until a state trooper nudged his boot into the funny man's ribs, which was somewhere around noon the next day, but not before he and Binder had gotten enough sun to cause second-degree burns, which swelled their faces to purple masks. The state trooper said it himself at the time: "You goofy assholes could've died if not for me. What do you think of that?" The funny man and Binder couldn't reply because their lips were too swollen and blistered, but as the funny man writes *not dying in desert next to Binder* on the easel, he thinks that he might've escaped thanks to a little luck that time.

Though aren't we all entitled to a little luck here and there, enough to balance the scales at least? Surely there were times where misfortune befell the funny man with equal weight. And just how fortunate was he to be discovered by a state trooper on a routine patrol who had probably found college kids sleeping one off in a desert gully while their flesh was fried and the buzzards circled overhead millions of times?

The clapping man telling the funny man's future agent about him before he died. Was that luck? What about the clapping man not dying before he even had a chance to see the funny man?

At some point, does the sheer weight of these probably non-luck-based coincidences have to add up to some luck, the way that change in a jar can turn into real money, given enough time?

The funny man turns the easel to a blank page and retreats to his chair. He has opened up a can of worms. He has thought of these things in passing before, the barest of glances before turning away with disinterest, but now he can't stop thinking about it, the endless chain of events that led him to this particularly charmed time and place, how any of the links in that chain could have been broken in any number of ways.

He sets the massage feature to "shiatsu." He has given names to the settings. Shiatsu is Tomoko. Swedish is Inga. Shantala is Joan, because he cannot not think of a female Indian name. He gives himself over to Tomoko and tries to forget that time when he was seven and fell off the skateboard, his head bouncing off the concrete like a basketball, the lump just off his temple bigger than a golf ball and his mother cried all the way to the hospital yelling at him, "Don't you sleep! Don't you go to sleep!" slapping him on the shoulder with one hand while the other twisted the wheel. "Don't you dare fucking go to sleep!" she yelled. It was the first and maybe only time he'd heard her say "fuck."

Or at eleven, when he was having his tonsils removed and they gave him a shot of something meant for the kid the next bed over and his heart accelerated and his vision went static and then he woke up what seemed like (and actually was) three days later.

Tomoko lays into his neck, digging right into the vertebrae. Digging in between the vertebrae, digging into his marrow like she may come out the other side. Sometimes the funny man thinks that Tomoko and maybe Inga are the only people who understand his needs. (Joan is too rough.) The funny man grunts a little under her touch and refuses to think about swim class, the near drowning that put him off water forever, or that time just the past winter, on the way to the airport from his wife's parents when he *knows* he fell asleep at the wheel, knows it because his eyes were closed and then opened and he'd sweated through his clothes in an instant.

He dozes lightly as Tomoko eases back to level 3, and the funny man fights off the thought that his wife just might be right about this luck business, because at this point, luck isn't going to take *him* anywhere.

When his wife arrives home he decides that he doesn't actually want to talk about it, which is lucky because she doesn't want to hear it.

THERE IS SURPRISINGLY little to do in the funny man's day-to-day life. There is now significant demand for the funny man, but the demand is not daily, or anything like that, certainly not even always weekly. It is somewhere between occasional and frequent. Recurrent? Persistent? He couldn't even tell you what he does on the days he is not needed. Work? Can he really call it work?

There are demands from the funny man's wife (she would call them requests) since he is around the house most of the day while the funny man's wife is at her charity work, which she enjoys and has embraced since it is fulfilling in ways that are hard to articulate. These requests from the funny man's wife seem very simple *to complete* when they are written on the dry erase board that hangs on the pantry door, but they are surprisingly difficult *to start*. He will look at the dry erase board and see an item half-smudged at the top, something like *sort clothes for Goodwill* and standing there, he will tell himself, *Let's get going to that closet and find the clothes that we never wear and give them to people who will wear them. When we decide on the discards, let's write our name on the labels with a black marker so maybe the new owner will get a kick out of owning a shirt that was once owned by this famous person.*

Still standing in front of the dry erase board, the funny man will scratch himself roughly underneath his boxers and continue to think. *These are both excellent ideas, the giving away of the no-longer-used clothes and the writing of our name on the label. We should do this right away, without delay, because there is absolutely nothing in front of us until the week after next and the casino gig.*

After this thinking and scratching, the funny man will move from the dry erase board to the refrigerator and open it and survey the contents and then close it and then he will go to the pantry, glancing sidelong at the dry erase board as he swings that door open, poking boxes and cans to the side to see what lays behind.

(Beans. Always cans of beans, different varieties, garbanzo, great northern, light red kidney. The funny man doesn't even know how one would prepare beans.) Then the refrigerator, open-close. Pantry, open-close. To the drawer underneath the phone with the carryout menus that he will leaf through until finally he will shut the menus back in the drawer and take something like a banana from a bowl on top of the refrigerator and he will shuffle through the house and flop into the special massaging reclining chair, one leg hung over the arm and he will peel the banana with his teeth as he flips on the television and decides he should watch one of the movies that is presently showing because he is in the entertainment industry and it is a smart move to know who is doing and has done what.

On these days, the funny man's wife comes home and asks what the funny man did that day. She stands in front of him, hands on hips, occasionally, but not unreasonably often, with a shopping bag looped over an arm, and he replies, "work on my material," which is a joke he used to use when he had to use the bathroom, i.e., "I'll be right back, I've got to go work on my material." In truth, though, most of the time, when he is asked this question by his wife, the funny man blinks up at her with eyes saucered from staring at the television and realizes that he has no idea what he's done that day. He does not even realize the day has gone, never to be back again.

THERE IS A nanny now for the child. She's been in their lives for awhile actually, but it is only at the new new house (as awesome as the first one was, it was bought under a different, lesser set of circumstances and needed replacing) that she has a room (more like a wing) of her own, but still the funny man has time with his son every day without fail, like clockwork, except for those days when there is no time or when he's on the road, of course. Each new thing the child does is a genuine and delightful surprise all the way from pretty much sleeping through the night to not shitting his diaper a dozen times a day.

All that is in the past. The child walks and talks now, which is for sure fun. Entertaining, even. He has diapers that are underwear, or perhaps underwear that double as diapers. On the days the funny man spends in his special chair he envies his son's diaper/underwear.

There are phases, one of which was the boy pretending (or maybe not pretending) to run into the doorjamb and falling into a giggling heap over and over.

"Not bad," the funny man thought, writing the idea in his notebook.

His son now cries instead of laughs when he sees the funny man shove his entire hand inside his mouth. He runs from the room, arms outstretched, legs stiff and stamping towards Pilar, who scoops him into her arms and rubs his hair and whispers *"mijo."* This is usually the signal that father-son time is done for the day.

Shoving his entire hand in his mouth is now very easy for the funny man to do, physically, but growing increasingly difficult to do psyche-wise.

For example, there was that show at a theater that sat many times more people than had seen him be funny up until he developed his thing. On stage, after thirty minutes or so of material, the funny man says, "good night, you've been great" and walks into the wings without having done his thing, only to be met by the theater owner-promoter who places a large hand in the middle of the funny man's chest and says, "Where the fuck do you think you're going?"

"Show's over, that's it," says the funny man, trying to brush past, which is not possible because this man is large and the passageway small.

"It doesn't sound like it's over," the owner-promoter says. The audience stomps the floor and hoots through cupped hands, demanding . . . more.

The funny man feels suddenly angry, and flushed with anger slaps the man's hand off his chest. "I'm not a fucking trained chimp. I'm not Shamu. I don't own cymbals that I clap together. I don't eat fucking halibut at the sound of a whistle and when I say the show is over, it's over."

The owner-promoter raises his hands in a we're-just-talking-here gesture and smiles and then squeezes the funny man's shoulder in a friendly/intimidating way. "Look, let me tell you what's going to happen if this continues like you say it's going to continue. I'm not going to punch your lights out, no. No, I'm not going to twist your thumbs off of your hands, no. I'm not going to clap my palms simultaneously over your ears and rupture your eardrums. No. First, I'm just going to send that limousine waiting for you behind the theater home. That's my cousin's boy behind the wheel, so for all practical purposes, he works for me. Next, I'm going to take that check with the five figures and turn it into four, but I'm still going to go on that stage and tell those fine people who are hooting and hollering out there that you've earned more than most of them make in a year for thirty minutes of 'work.' Then, I'm going to shove you out into the alley where your limousine should have been and I'm going to go on my public address system and I'm going to tell those people where to find you. You will have maybe a forty-five second head start. You've got some nice shoes there, leather, expensive I'm sure, but they don't look like running shoes to me, so my recommendation is that you take a shot barefoot." The owner-promoter pauses for a moment as the funny man looks down at his shoes. The funny man raises his eyes a hair and sees the blue-ink tattoo of an anchor on the owner-promoter's arm.

"Now, I got no problem with making them wait a little bit. In fact, making them wait is probably a smart thing, since they're sitting there wondering if indeed it's going to happen, if this funny guy with his thing is going to do his thing, and in that waiting there's a tension. Do you feel the tension?"

The funny man cocks an ear to the crowd. Their stomping and clapping is rhythmic now, timed together, like inmates before a riot in a prison movie clanking their cups against the bars, organized, angry.

"Tension is a good thing, a necessary thing. It's where doubt lives. Even when we're pretty sure something is going to happen, we wonder if that thing is *really* going to happen. We know that the guy in the hockey goalie mask is going to drive a pitchfork through the virgins. We *know* it. We're *sure* of it, and yet when it does happen, it surprises, delights even, because of doubt. Where would we be without doubt? Without doubt we would, no doubt, do some very stupid things, and what I'm saying here is that I'm trying to keep you from doing what is for many reasons, a very stupid thing. Do you doubt what I'm trying to say?"

The funny man looks into the owner-promoter's eyes and sees that there is a small chunk out of the gray-green iris in the right one and that come to think of it, that eye drifts just a bit to the side as well. The funny man realizes that without a doubt he does not doubt this man. He turns and walks back to the stage from the wings, a single arm raised with a fist at the end clinched so tightly the knuckles blanch.

He's never heard such a roar in his life.

FOLLOWING THAT GIG, when he pours from the limousine in front of his house, he looks at it for a fleeing moment of rare self-awareness and wonders if it is a palace or a prison. As he approaches the front door a motion-sensitive light snaps on, causing him to blink and shade his eyes, and once inside he must deactivate and then reactivate the alarm. He doesn't think about these things at the time because he doesn't want to.

11

H ER PACKAGE ARRIVED amid all the other junk, three feet deep in the mail cart, a small padded mailer, hand-addressed to the PO box. I don't know why I gravitated to it among everything else. Now that I believe in fate, I'm going to call it that.

Inside was a picture of me and a letter like every other letter, telling me to be strong, wishing me well, asking for the privilege of my signature. Her name was not on it, of course, because she could not risk it being seen, but what caught my eye was her insignia in the top corner of the paper, a small pink rabbit (her nickname is "the bunny" for her ability to cover the whole court). I brought my nose to the paper and it smelled salty but clean, just as she did that last night we spent together at the Center. Turning it over, I held the paper up to the light and I could see that certain letters stood out in greater relief that others. I quickly transcribed them onto a sheet of paper and found the message contained within them.

I have been thinking of you and of how we can be together regardless of the outcome of your trial. I am out of room, but I'll write more soon. ♥ *B.*

I wished for more, but perhaps this is all she had time for, particularly because she had to also encode the letters. I imagine she is being watched fairly closely by her handlers. She had, after all, disappeared not just from the tour, but the face of the planet for better than two months, returning without a single answer to any of the questions about her whereabouts at her first press conference. This was before my walk in the rain and the attempted robbery. I watched live on the sports news channel. I had not seen her since I'd left the Center and she looked great, rested, tan (as always). She smiled for the cameras as she made her brief opening statement: *I'm back and I intend to win a couple of major tournaments and then I will leave tennis and live happily ever after.*

The press crowd chuckled lightly and there was an awkward pause when they realized she had nothing else to say. Flashes popped as she looked left and right, grinning. Finally a hand went up:

Q: Where have you been?
A: I'm not talking about that.
Q: Why not?
A: I'm not talking about why I'm not talking about where I've been.
Q: Why not?
A: Because I can't talk about it.

This went on for a couple additional minutes until they tried a slightly different tack.

Q: Can you tell us *anything* you've been up to lately?
A: I've been getting into music.
Q: What kind?
A: Old stuff. Classic rock.
Q: Like who?
A: Oh, you know, the usual suspects, Beatles, the Doors, Hendrix, Joplin, that kind of thing.
Q: What turned you on to that music?

Here, as I watched the television I could see a brief, faraway look come to her eye before she refocused and answered.

A: I heard some of it performed live and it just really spoke
    to me.
Q: What do you mean live, like a cover band or
    something?
A: Sure, or something.

I hoped, I trusted that the "happily" ever-after part of the equation was a reference to me. To us. But then, I shot an armed robber six times in (alleged) self-defense and blew it.

But now the messages are coming and the hope is rekindling. I search each new arrival of signing items frantically for her latest missive and there isn't one every time, but often enough to make each search worthwhile.

This arrived today, on a postcard, symbols hidden in a panorama of the Eiffel Tower, invisible to others, bold as neon to me:

We're going back, somehow. Some way. The day after our country's independence. That's the day. ♥ *B*

So she has given me the when, but we still need to figure out the how, a not inconsiderable task considering that by her deadline, my trial won't yet be finished and my ankle bracelet keeps me tethered to very few spots, one of which is not where she and I met.

The hurdles are high, but for the first time since my arrest and the start of my trial I have something I have lacked for quite some time, a sense of purpose.

12

THE FUNNY MAN sits in the manager's office, splayed along a couch across from his manager and his agent, who share a different couch. His agent and manager are both dressed in suits, but the funny man no longer bothers shaving or dressing for these occasions. His pants could even be mistaken for very elaborate pajamas, though they are not because they cost better than two thousand dollars and were fashioned from the beards of billy goats. The funny man is still not entirely sure why he needs both an agent and a manager or what their respective duties are, though he is most assuredly aware that certain percentages leak off of his total into their pockets. The total is large enough that these sums do not particularly matter to the funny man, they are not missed, but he also knows that the sums are large enough that he matters very much to his agent and manager. For that reason he knows that he can wear these pants that look like pajamas and not sit up straight and absently scratch at the three days' growth that sprouts in patches across his face.

His career has become stagnant, recursive, endlessly looping back on itself and what was once fun now looks and feels suspiciously like work. Fewer people come to see him than in the past and recently, prior to a gig, he walked the streets of the city and asked a hundred people, "Do you know who I am?" and only fifteen of them said yes. Of those fifteen, the funny man then asked, "Who am I?" and only twelve of them were correct. The funny man wants to get to the next level before he slips from his present one. He has come to recognize that celebrity has its privileges, that he can do things like drink for free or pay cash for expensive luxury items. The funny man has insisted that they install a commercial-grade deep fat fryer in the new new home and he recently spent most of a day making and eating doughnuts. His wife (mostly jokingly) accused him of having a second childhood and the funny man scowled and said, "What's wrong with that?" Still, even as he has grown more and more famous, he senses himself devolving. Tasks that previously seemed inconsequential, easy, like say, swishing the cleaner around the toilet and scrubbing the ring of mung, now look Herculean and he wonders how this nanny-housekeeper can bear to do it. He has come to see his agent and manager because it is time to shake things up.

"We have some offers," the agent says.

"Offers with an *s*?" the funny man replies.

"A commercial, for one," the manager says.

"Voice-over?" The funny man arches a hopeful brow. Voice-over is cherry. Voice-over is big-time. Stars do voice-over. Voice-over is an afternoon's worth of work for a lifetime of checks.

"Acting," the agent says. The funny man's brow deflates.

"Doing what?"

"You play a guy trying to rent a car. You're at the airport trying to rent a car and you go from counter to counter but they can't understand what you're saying, can't fulfill your car rental needs until you get to the client's counter and they know just what you want and you're off on your way, happy as anything. Totally fulfilled. Job well done," the manager says.

"Why can't they understand what I'm saying?" the funny man asks.

The manager and agent look at each other, each nodding for the other to spill the beans in more and more exaggerated ways until finally the agent is forced to speak up, because, after all, he earns 2 percent more of the funny man's money than the manager.

"You've got your hand shoved inside your mouth," he says.

The funny man slips deeper into the couch, burying his head under one of the throw pillows. He screams into it, feeling the mist of his breath bound back into his face. He would like to scream at these two that they're a couple of fucking assholes with this shit, but the funny man is not the sort (not yet, anyway) who calls his people fucking assholes, even when they are clearly behaving like fucking assholes.

It's not that he's tired of the thing, not at all. The thing is great, and every time he performs it, it kills. No matter which celebrity he does with his hand in his mouth (and he's now done them all, trying new ones all the time), the people laugh and laugh and laugh. The thing is the nuclear fission of comedy, self-renewing, inexhaustible.

Except that it exhausts *him*. It really does. He hasn't tried to get away with not doing it again because the first owner-promoter has apparently spread the word about his bout of recalcitrance and the funny man is routinely pre-threatened before he even hits the stage. Recently, at a show in Pittsburgh or Portland, he's not sure which, while doing the thing the funny man contemplated shoving his hand down into his windpipe, even knowing as he contemplated it what the likely outcome would be. Would he be dead before the audience realized it wasn't part of the joke? Like all creative people, the funny man's politics are liberal so he doesn't throw these words around lightly, but he feels it wouldn't be an exaggeration to say that he is "enslaved" by the thing. It has gone from blessing, to blessing and curse, to just curse.

After awhile, from underneath the pillow because he thinks that if he looks these two in the face he might leap and try to poke their eyes out, the funny man says, "What's the other one?"

"Movie," the manager says.

The funny man removes the pillow from his face. "Movie?" he says. "Or film?"

"Movie. Road comedy, a bunch of high school friends accidentally rob a bank and go on the lam. Hijinks ensue," the agent says. "You know the drill. The kid with the music videos is attached to direct."

"Role?"

"Buddy number three out of five."

"My own subplot?"

"Mostly comedic, with a pinch of romance," the agent says.

This is an interesting proposition for the funny man. It is the next logical step for a person with his career profile. Actually, television is the next logical step, which means he is actually skipping a step. It will mean three months or more on a movie set, grueling days of sitting around and doing nothing while being away from his wife and child whom he loves dearly, of course, but who will be increasingly well-provided for, thanks to his sacrifice.

"What's the catch?" the funny man asks, putting the pillow aside and sitting upright, elbows on thighs.

"Catch?" the manager says, moving a piece of paper across the table toward the funny man.

The funny man leans a bit more forward and looks at the paper, which has a number with lots of zeros on it. He's never been good at math, so he counts them, with his finger, just to make sure.

THE DIRECTOR YELLS, "Cut, take five!" and the funny man removes his entire hand from his own mouth and walks over to the chair with his name stenciled on the back. He assumed such chairs were a myth, but no, just like grade school, chairs on a movie set are indeed assigned. He figured that other things about making movies were a myth as well, for example, the director saying "take five," but no, he really says it, says it rather often, though "five" (minutes) is usually closer to forty-five minutes and once extended to three days.

They are somewhere in the Midwest, not Midwest like Chicago or even St. Louis, Midwest like Kansas or Nebraska, the parts where no one goes and hardly anyone lives. They are driving through flyover country, but are presently parked in front of an abandoned drive-in restaurant whose exterior has been made up to look brand new, while on the inside a massive colony of rats basically runs the place. The cinematographer has noted that occasionally, when they are shooting toward the restaurant, rats perch in the window, visible in frame and may have to be removed digitally.

The funny man will spend 85 percent of his screen time in the film with his hand in his mouth, something his agent and manager (the fucking assholes) neglected to tell him before he signed the contract. But that number. The funny man knows that as long as he lives like a semi-reasonable human being he will never have to work again, that the number represents a figure more than he had earned up to that point and his earn-ings up to that point were nothing to sneeze at in the grand scheme of things.

The funny man's movie love interest sits next to him doing word searches to pass the time. She is ungodly beautiful and yet only the third most beautiful woman on the set. In between takes she drops to the ground and pumps out twenty Marine-precise push-ups. When the funny man asked her about this she raised her arms, Christ-style, palms up, and waved them forward and back. "When they start to flap," she said, gesturing to her triceps, "you're playing someone's grandmother."

She is also crushingly stupid and dull and the funny man long ago gave up trying to talk to her beyond the barest pleasantries. She is so dull he can't even muster any sexual interest in her, not that he would cheat because he promised that he wouldn't, not only on his wedding day, but before he left for his shoot when his wife dropped him at the airport, kissed him on the cheek and said, "Don't stick your dick in anyone else," which she meant as a joke, but in a serious way.

Once, when the funny man's movie love interest got up to do a scene, the funny man looked at her word search and noticed that most of the circled strings were not even words, or at least not the kind of words that utilized vowels.

The love interest looks up from the word search and the funny man realizes he's been staring.

"What?" she says.

The funny man turns away and looks back at the director, who is being talked to by the cinematographer. The director is nodding his head, which the funny man has come to know is a bad sign, a sign that they're going to try something different, something not found in the script.

When the funny man first met the director, the director described his style as "freewheeling," which the funny man has come to understand means "making shit up as you go along because you don't know what you're doing." The director is as malleable as one of the funny man's college buddies whose nickname was "Dummy," as in "Dummy, go up and tell that girl that you love her," or "Dummy, fill this cup with your urine so I can pass this drug test," or "Dummy, spank that cop and see what happens."

Some things have surprised the funny man about making a movie. The first thing was that the movie is not shot in order. In fact, it's not shot in anything close to the right order. In one of the funny man's very first scenes, just about his first moment of acting in front of a camera, he was told to face his love interest, look into her eyes with a passionate fervor and kiss her as ardently as he could muster. He had been led from his trailer by a walkie-talkie-wielding assistant who said they were "on route" into the mouthpiece as the funny man closed the trailer door behind him. Thirty-five seconds later they were there, the set, a small clearing that overlooked the Grand Canyon, the backdrop for the big scene. The funny man had visited it as a child, bumping down to the bottom on the back of a burro, wondering why vacation always had to be so boring.

In the movie the characters are traveling east to west, but the production is doing pretty much the opposite, leaving from their Los Angeles headquarters as a money-saving measure. His love interest stood next to a bit of tumbleweed, brought in by the prop master to give the foreground some perspective. A rubber snake sat off to the side of the tumbleweed, coiled as if to strike.

The funny man had met his love interest once before, briefly, at a read-through of the script where they sat around a table and recited their parts in turn. The director brayed like a llama at every alleged punch line, but the funny man got the biggest laughs of everyone because of course his hand was always in his mouth and that shit's just funny.

The arc of the funny man's story in the movie is this:

1. While pulling the robbery, the funny man is pressed into service to boost one of his compatriots up through a hole drilled in the bottom of the vault. In order to keep from yelping at the pain as his buddy steps and then jumps up and down on his head as he tries to get all of the way into the vault, the funny man shoves his hand in his mouth to stifle any noise.

2. Following the heist, where the semi-hapless gang gets away with the loot, but not without triggering an alarm and pursuit by the authorities, the funny man finds he cannot remove his hand from his mouth.

3. Hijinks ensue as each member of the gang in turn tries unsuccessfully to pull the funny man's hand from his mouth while they flee in a conversion van, weaving this way and that to avoid the SWAT-team bullets. At one point, the funny man's arm is (thanks to special effects involving prosthetics and camera angles) shoved into his mouth up to his elbow.

4. They eventually get away from the hottest pursuit, and as they travel across the country, heading toward Mexico, and presumably freedom to spend their stolen wealth, more hijinks as the funny man looks longingly at his buddies every time they eat or drink and he tries to cram a road cheeseburger past his knuckles into his mouth.

5. At some point, he drinks a Coke through his nose.

6. Ultimately, the van breaks down and the boys are forced to hole up for a few days in the canyon, waiting for repairs, where the funny man falls for the beautiful Mexican maid who cleans their cabin. She expresses sympathy and worry over the funny man and they talk for hours, sort of, since she speaks mostly Spanish and the funny man can only scribble notes on a pad.

7. Finally, the funny man approaches her at the canyon edge as she looks wistfully across the divide, a symbol for her separation from her family, and she thinks about how much she'd like to go home, back to Mexico, but only once she can earn enough money to support her and her eleven brothers and sisters. Desperate to finally speak to her, in a heroic act, the funny man yanks his hand from his mouth and declares, "I love you, Graziella, and I have three million dollars in the van," after which they kiss passionately and weep tears of joy.

8. After which the rattlesnake uncoils and bites the funny man in the junk.

9. Because the movie is PG-13, they will only imply that, thinking quickly, Graziella sucks the poison from the wound.

10. With her mouth.

11. Near his penis. (Get it?)

12. The rest of the movie, they periodically cut to shots of the funny man and Graziella in the back of the van, she holding a bag of ice over his comically swollen crotch as she leans in to kiss him on the cheek.

She was beautiful, and her mouth was eminently kissable, but he still could not manage to do the act with anything approaching passionate fervor no matter how many times he tried, which was many. He even imagined he was kissing his wife, which did not help. Ultimately, the director gave up trying to get a convincing kiss and ordered a take where the special effects guy triggered the snake into the funny man's crotch before the kiss could be consummated, which everyone agreed was funnier anyway.

And so the production lurched eastward, each state line confirming what the funny man suspected from the initial table read, that the movie was terrible, that his first filmed role would be in a terrible, terrible movie, the kind of movie where everyone wonders how such a movie was conceived, let alone completed and then released. In his previous civilian life, the funny man would go to these sorts of movies and wonder this very thing: "How could this happen? How could they have turned out such a steaming heap of shit?" And now he knew, except there was still no explanation for it. It was just one of those things that happens.

The latest scene in front of the rat-infested drive-in has ceased to make any sense to the funny man. If the love interest is present, it must belong close to the end, but it is not in any script that he's seen. He has no idea where it fits in the movie and is pretty sure it doesn't matter anyway. The director shouts the dialogue to him off camera bit by bit, different words each take, and the funny man has found it harder and harder to stay conscious, and after a take where the funny man stands and stares blankly for a full forty-five seconds the director shouts, "Cut, we can use that!" and walks off, clapping his hands together like a cheerleader trying to psych up the team. The love interest wanders back to her chair and recommences her word search.

The funny man had recently called his agent and manager and spent a lot of long-distance roaming minutes telling them how absolutely terrible the movie is. They tried to convince him that sometimes there are miracles in the cutting room, that a skilled editor can weave something passable out of just about anything, but the funny man told them that no one can make a fine tapestry out of rotting garbage, out of entrails, out of fetid, worthless crap. The funny man tried to express to his agent and manager that he thought he was probably not going to make it through the entire shoot, that he was willing to do something crazy to get booted off the film if necessary.

This is when the funny man's manager explained some parts of the contract to him that the funny man hadn't bothered reading, things like he was not only obligated to finish the movie or risk his salary plus unspecified "penalties," but he was also to be available for up to three weeks of promotional responsibilities, one of which may be outside of the continental United States, at times and places to be determined by the producers.

"What you're saying," the funny man said, "is that not only do I have to finish this movie, I have to go talk about how good it is afterwards?"

"Yes," the funny man's manager replied.

"You're fired."

SINCE HE DISCOVERED there's no escape, all the funny man can think about is escaping. He must disappear like people in the witness protection program. If they can't find him, they can't make him do these things. He will go somewhere and send for his family, and they will live quietly on the considerable money he has already earned. He will take a job with parks and recreation where his job is to drive a modified golf cart going from trash can to trash can, changing out the bags. He will wear heavy work gloves and a small circular name patch on his uniform. Sometimes the bags will leak and spill on the funny man's overalls, but he will accept this as simply part of the deal, his small sacrifice for keeping the public spaces clean. It is a life of sacrifice he envisions for himself, a life of service.

He gets out of his assigned seat and starts walking toward the road, the first steps toward his new life. The sound of the director and cinematographer arguing fades, replaced with the whiz and rumble of traffic. The funny man stands, watching the cars and trucks zoom by, then closes his eyes, raises his hand, and extends his thumb. Nothing happens other than the funny man swaying gently on his feet until he hears a car slow and pull over, tires crunching the gravel on the side of the road. The passenger-side window goes down. The funny man opens his eyes and sees a middle-aged man with a shitty comb-over leaning across the seat. He can smell the alcohol of the man's aftershave waft toward him.

"Hey," the man says. "I know you."

SO BECAUSE HE cannot escape, he resolves to take as many others down as he can. But even this plan is quickly thwarted when at the outdoors store he asks to buy a gun, but because of the meddling federal government, they will only sell him something that shoots paint, so he buys the one that the clerk claims has the greatest stopping power.

"What will it stop?" the funny man asks. It is shaped like an assault rifle and sits heavy in his hand, the metal dull and unreflective. It feels real except for the giant plastic bin for the paintballs jutting from the top.

The clerk scratches his chin. "Guess I've seen it put down a woodchuck, or maybe a grackle, starling, that kind of thing."

"Not a person?"

"No sir, can't kill a person with that weapon. It's for sport, you know? Competition? It's got professional leagues and everything. Could take an eye out, maybe, which is why we recommend protection." The clerk holds up a face mask that looks like a cross between something a hockey goalie and a snowmobiler might wear. The funny man tries it on and looks at himself in a mirror and sees that he is scary and unrecognizable.

The clerk looks at the funny man more closely. "Do I know you?"

"Nobody knows me."

"That some kind of riddle?"

"Just the truth." The funny man points the paint gun down the aisle and sights some of the other customers and mimes pulling the trigger.

"Bang, bang, bang," he says.

"So you know," the clerk says, "if'n that was a real weapon, I'm not sure I'd sell it to you, given your look and behavior and all."

"But it isn't real, right?"

"Right."

"So, if I said that I'll take all of it, you wouldn't stop me," the funny man says.

"Nope. I'd ask how many rounds you need?"

"How many you got?"

FOR ABOUT NINETY seconds, the funny man has never had more fun. The eyes of the rats glow red in the funny man's headlamp (also purchased at the outdoors store) and as they turn to face him, he unleashes a stream of automatic paintball fire their way. They scatter throughout the abandoned diner, diving over booths and under tables, their hard nails scrabbling along the front counter. For the most part they're far too quick for the funny man to hit, but once or twice he hears a squeal as one of the pellets connects. After the initial burst he stands still and soon the squealing stops as the rats regroup and return to the open. There must be hundreds, maybe even thousands, little pairs of devil eyes flashing wherever he turns.

The gun has an impressive rate of fire and during his second assault he quickly learns that if he leads the scurrying rodents enough, he can usually score at least a glancing blow. His breath is hot under the mask and he hears someone laughing and then realizes he is the one who is laughing in a borderline-crazy way. The funny man knows he's not crazy, not really, because if he was really crazy he wouldn't think about being crazy. He would simply be crazy. Still, he feels crazy, or maybe he feels like what it might feel like to be crazy without actually being crazy.

As the first load of pellets drains out of the bin, the funny man reaches for the spare to his side and clicks the ammo into place, but the pause has already leaked much of the pleasure of the adventure out of him. The mask has delayed the smell, but now it oozes around the gaps, an aggressive musk of decay that is so bad he must sniff more deeply to confirm how truly bad it smells. As he turns his head to survey the room, the headlight illuminates a handful of rat near-corpses. Some of them have clearly shattered spines, dragging their useless hind parts behind them as they go for cover. Others lay on their sides, gasping, trickles of rat blood flowing from their noses. None of their unscathed compadres appear willing to lend assistance, which figures. One stares at the funny man, its rat nose twitching, an eye replaced by blue paint that turns purple in the light of the funny man's halogen lamp. The funny man has an urge to apologize, but that seems really crazy because they're fucking rats after all.

A group of them have massed near the door and as the funny man heads their way, rather than dispersing they seem to grow tighter, more of them joining the mass. It looks like they are pulsing. They appear to now realize that they have the funny man outnumbered big-time, that if this is the Alamo, they are the Mexican part of the equation. The funny man fires a burst of paintballs into the ceiling.

"Beat it! I don't want to hurt you. Not any more than I already have anyway."

The rats stand strong, their numbers increasing by the moment. The funny man levels the gun and fires another burst just above their heads. This separates them momentarily, but in short order they are re-massed. They appear to be stacking on top of each other, a rat pyramid, growing in height, as tall as the funny man, taller even.

"So that's how it's going to be, huh?"

The funny man fires directly into the crowd and because they are so densely packed, most of the pellets strike home. Still, the larger population does not budge and in fact, appears to start advancing on the funny man, climbing over each other in their eagerness. He shakes the gun and the container rattles with the final handful of ammunition. Out of options, he turns and sprints away from the rats toward the front window. Earlier in the filming, during the bank heist sequence, he saw a stuntman do what he's about to do and after watching the scene, the funny man asked him how he did it, and the stuntman replied, "There's no particular technique or anything. The key is that you've just got to commit."

The funny man accelerates and as he approaches the window he crosses his arms in front of his face and leaps and the window shatters and he is outside. The stuntman did not lie. After a barrel roll across the graveled parking lot, the funny man is on his feet and sprinting toward the motel, assuming the rats are in pursuit.

WHEN HE RETURNS to his room at the motel reserved for cast and crew, he opens the door to find his love interest stretched across the bed. She wears short shorts and lays on her stomach facing the television, the omnipresent word search in front of her. She lightly chews the butt end of her pen. She has cranked down the thermostat on the wall-unit air conditioner and the funny man can feel the sweat evaporate from the back of his neck. She looks up at the funny man framed in the doorway and makes no note of the mask and goggles pushed up on his forehead and the empty paintball gun dangling at his side. She is beyond incurious, a blank slate. The funny man thinks that he would actually like to climb inside her brain for awhile, just to, you know, have room to stretch out and relax.

The funny man comes fully inside and leans back against the door. He is tired and sweaty and his clothes are splattered with paint and rat blood. He has come through his window-smashing leap miraculously unscathed except for a slight twinge in his back. The rats have not followed him back to his room.

"I was thinking," the love interest says, "that we should just go ahead and screw."

The funny man slides down to the floor, his back still against the door. The coldest air has sunk to ground level. It is like a mini-fog covering the bottom four inches of floor. "And why were you thinking that?"

"Well, you know, because the movie's almost over."

"Exactly," the funny man replies.

"Exactly," she volleys in return.

"Wait," he says. "Why are you saying *exactly*?"

"What do you mean?"

"I'm saying *exactly*," he says, "because it doesn't make sense to sleep together now. Why would we want to start an affair when the movie is almost over?"

"And I'm saying, *exactly*," she says, "because now is the best time for us to screw because there's no danger of having an affair. It would just be a notch in our belts, a deposit for the future."

"I don't know what that means."

The love interest sits up on the bed, her nipples taut against her shirt. They are like scouts searching for targets. "Think of it this way," she says. "It's like insurance. Odds are, one or both of us is going to get famous, or more famous than we already are. If we sleep together, at some point in the future, we'll be able to tell someone about it and when the story comes out, we'll be linked together and each of us will get a little boost in the press."

"What?"

"Okay, it's not really like insurance. I just said that to keep it simple. It's more complicated than that. It's more like celebrity arbitrage."

"I still have no idea what you're talking about."

The love interest says it again, slowly, *arbitrage*. French-sounding, vaguely dangerous, a Bond villain. "Arbitrage is when you have two markets of unequal value. Think of fame as a market. Right now, admittedly, you're more famous than me, no doubt. You've got some heat behind you with that thing and honestly, you're the only interesting part of this crummy movie. At the moment, your celebrity value is higher. However, I'm on the rise. My agents say my look is coming into vogue, which is important for an actress. I'm still young, I'm single, and I haven't done any nudity yet. I've got a lot of weapons left in my arsenal. We have every reason to believe that my celebrity is on the rise."

"You're not as dumb as I think you are, are you?" the funny man says.

The love interest closes the word search and smiles. "I'm smart about some things."

"Go on."

"So, right at the moment, your value is higher, but there's reason to believe that someday, my value will be higher because honestly, that thing, how long is that going to hold up? This is a classic arbitrage situation. Because you're more valuable at the moment, I'm offering you a premium, namely, you can just lie on your back and I'll hop on and do all the work, and I won't care if you don't get me off."

The funny man reaches down and pushes himself up from the floor. He feels each vertebrae click into place as he rises. The back is perhaps more scathed than he initially figured. It takes a good thirty seconds to stand fully upright. He twirls the wedding ring on his finger and thinks about how sleeping with this girl is the kind of thing he should do. It is what a celebrity does and a celebrity is what he is. This not-as-dumb-as-she-seems girl just said so. Why should he not do what is expected of him? Since his marriage he had never taken his ring off until he began filming the movie. It has been one production assistant's job to hold it while he does his takes. When the director says "cut" the funny man beckons the production assistant back and retrieves the ring and places it where it belongs. He believes in that bond, of course he does. He has long ago ceased to notice the ring's presence when it's on, but even in the middle of live action on camera, part of the funny man's brain would think how weird it felt in its absence.

The funny man puts his hands on his hips and levers back at the waist, trying to stretch some of the stiffness out of his back. "Look. You're a lovely girl, very alluring, and what you say makes a lot of sense—in the kind of world you describe, anyway—but something I'm realizing is that I want nothing to do with that world, so I'm going to take a pass." He is proud of himself. This may be the highlight of his life, an act of heroism even, since this love interest will go on to truly incredible heights of fame and is widely considered one of the most desirable women on the planet. The thought that a heterosexual male would pass on sex with her is sinful, criminal even, but at this moment this is what he does, which is about the least believable part of this stupid tale.

Here he starts walking toward the bathroom and a final phrase from his childhood rises in his brain. At that time he thinks it is hugely clever, but he will later come to regret this to the very marrow of his bones. "Tell you what, let's not, and say we did," he says, and with that he shuts himself inside the bathroom.

"It's your funeral, pal," the love interest yells through the door.

The funny man hears her leave the room and he curls up in the bathtub and goes to sleep.

13

BARRY HAS RETURNED from Barbados and called an "urgent nonemergency meeting." One of Barry's philosophies, as he explained it to me, is that there is no such thing as an emergency, just varying degrees of urgency. "If you think about it," he said, "emergencies don't really exist." He even said the word like it tasted bad on his lips.

"Break it down," he continued, "look at the root, *emerge*. Now, *emerge* means to come forth, to come into existence, but why should that be a cause for panic? If you plant a seed in the ground, eventually a stalk with *emerge*, but this should not be a surprise, since after all, you knew the seed was down there and it's a seed's job to grow, so when the stalk appears it's simply an expected arrival. Or babies. Often, when a baby is on the verge of being born it is treated as an emergency, a cause for panic and worry, but again, the root, *emerge*. The baby, along with some very explicable, very natural goo, is going to 'emerge' from the birth canal. Unless you're talking about one of those self-deluding high school girls that drops the kid behind the Dumpster during lunch, everyone knew the damn thing was in there, right? And at some point it's got to come out. What is so goddamn surprising?"

"You don't have kids, do you," I said.

Barry frowned. This was early on before he had agreed to take me on as a client and for a moment I worried that I'd fucked up the audition. "You don't choose him," my manager warned. "He chooses you."

"My belief," Barry continued, "is that with proper planning and vision and foresight and vigilance, there will never be an 'emergency.' All events are foreseeable. Everything is predictable, not for everyone, but for me."

"Like a psychic?"

Barry frowned even deeper this time. "No, nothing like a psychic. There is nothing mystical about it."

"Sorry."

"Even when you see an ambulance, siren howling, lights blazing, zooming through traffic, all appearances to the contrary, that is not an emergency."

"No?"

"Look at what's probably inside, some fat ass who for forty years started his day with a rasher of bacon and half gallon of coffee with cream. Not even half-and-half, cream. That his coronary artery exploded like a sabotaged Iraqi oil pipeline shouldn't be *surprising*, should it? Or maybe it's one of those bike messengers who refuses to wear a helmet and when he flips over a taxi, whoops! There go his brains all over the street. Who could've seen that coming?"

Barry had worked himself into a pretty good lather. He wiped the back of his suit sleeve across his chin. Frankly, I liked the passion. I was in a pickle.

"These are not emergencies, they are *eventualities* and that's not no voodoo."

During the months of my trial I've spent a lot of time thinking about Barry's little philosophy, about how it manages to reconcile both free will *and* predestination. In Barry's world, there are two categories. Barry types who embrace their role as agents of change, influencers of events, controllers of destiny. Then there are others

who allow themselves to be nudged inexorably toward their preas-
signed fate, their *eventualities*.

And yet, because he had agreed to take me on after that first
meeting, by implication, I was being invited to the other side.

BARRY'S OFFICE IS expecting me and I am shown into a conference room with an even better view than my apartment. The
carpet is thick and springy enough for a floor exercise routine
and on one wall I see a buffet that would embarrass the Sunday
brunch at the Ritz. There is a carving station with steaming
rounds of ham and prime rib, a shrimp tree, and at the end,
after a full array of sides of both the starch and green vegetable
variety, what looks to be a fully outfitted sundae bar. I am alone
in the room.

At first I figure the spread is for some kind of office celebration
they're having later, but when Barry walks in followed by a guy in
whites topped with a chef's hat, I realize what's going on.

I'm in a pitch meeting.

In entertainment, whenever two parties meet, one of them is
empowered to say "yes," and because that yes turns into action they
are very important. That person is the one who is being pitched.
On one's way up the ladder, you do the pitching and when you
do the pitching it is necessary to prepare the proper tribute prior
to delivering of the pitch. Sometimes this can be dispensed with
using mere flattery over a recent creative endeavor, or small tokens
like cigars or especially good prostitutes. Other times, you prepare
a sumptuous feast like the one in this conference room. I have to
say, this is a surprise, because even as I am on trial for my life,
Barry has had the final say-so on all matters of tactics and strategy.
Until now, apparently.

Barry is clearly excited, pacing the room as our chef prepares
and then places a plate in front of me. I am not particularly hungry,
but I thank him and Barry gestures him from the room.

"I had a vision," Barry says.

"Vision?"

"I was on a reef dive, really beautiful, like two-hundred-million-year-old coral there, thinking about your case and it came to me, the perfect defense."

"I thought we already had the perfect defense."

"We did, but now this one is more perfect."

I feel one of our Abbott and Costello routines coming on. "How do you get more perfect than perfect?" I ask.

"The old thing was perfect, the new thing is better, therefore, more perfect. The perfect defense . . . plus."

I decide to let it drop and try a bite of the mashed potatoes. They are warm and buttery and agreeably lumpy with just the right hint of chives. Judging from the way my suit hangs I have not been eating all that much, and as I try the beef (succulent, tender), I realize I have no real memory of any recent food ingestion. It is, in short, hitting the spot.

"Now, it's a risk, which is why you've got to sign off on it, why we've got to commit, but I've been thinking about it nonstop. I couldn't even enjoy the magnificence of the giant sea turtles. I think it's a risk worth taking. I think it's at least precedent-setting, if not history-making."

Barry and I share a dramatic pause that only one of us is interested in.

"Not guilty by reason of celebrity." When he says it there is a pause between each word and he spreads his arms apart, like he is viewing it on a marquee from across the street.

"I don't get it."

Barry doesn't seem surprised at this.

"Okay, you've heard of being not guilty by reason of insanity, right?"

I can only nod because my mouth is full of perfectly pink beef. The food appears to be stoking my appetite like I didn't know I wanted it until I tried it. It's just a little better than a cold can of beans.

"This is like that, only it's not guilty by reason of celebrity."

"It sounds like you're saying that being famous is some sort of disease, or defect."

"I'm not *like* saying that. I *am* saying that."

"I don't know if I like the sound of this."

"I can't believe I didn't see this before," he says. I am super-fluous now. He is an avalanche making its way to the bottom of the hill. "It's practically already in the law. It's just that nobody's put it quite so plainly. I've got some clerks working on the briefing, but I'm pretty sure it's going to fly. The judge is no-nonsense, but she's fair, and she's got to really take a hard look at this. The law is allowed to recognize a de facto affirmative defense ex post facto its establishment. Look at the precedents. If an average person took a nine-iron to some dude's car in the middle of the road, what would happen to him? Criminal mischief? Felony property damage? When Jack does it, what happens? Nothing. If Bob Smith saws three quarters of the way through his wife's neck and takes out an innocent bystander to boot, what happens to him? Life? Death? O.J. . . . . nothing. Ergo, not guilty by reason of celebrity."

Barry goes on and on, citing case after case: Michael Jackson, Mel Gibson, Kobe, Rush.

"The one or two times one of you actually did go to jail, pretty goddamn quickly everyone realized it was a big mistake and they got her the hell out of there."

"Paris Hilton? Lindsay?"

"*Exactamundo!*" Barry says.

"Fonzie."

"What are you talking about?"

"Gary Coleman, kind of," I said, "but you've to say it differently. It's more like, *what chu talkin' about?*" Barry looks like he wants to break me over his knee. I take a moment and gather my shit.

"But what about Martha?" I said.

"I've thought of that," Barry says, rubbing his chin in contem-plation. "But it's an aberration. I made some calls and looked into it. Number one, that was federal; federal is different. Number two, because she thought it would look tacky, they were ordered to play down the celebrity thing. She wanted to be treated like everyone else. It killed her. Terrible strategy."

"Sounds like you've got it all covered," I say.

"Think about it," Barry says. "Celebrity *is* just like a disease. You can catch it, so it's communicable like a disease. It can also be hereditary like a disease. And I know I don't have to explain to you how it does its damage. The world is fundamentally different for someone with celebrity, an honest-to-god alternate reality. An irreality, even. Also, celebrity is tenacious, incurable. Once it has you in its grasp, it will not let you go. At the very least any celebrity by definition has a prima facie case of diminished capacity."

"What does that mean?"

"It means you're never wholly responsible for your actions. There will always be some mitigating factor."

I polish off the last of my meal. "This sounds crazy," I say.

Barry waves his hand in front of his face like he's swatting a mosquito away. "Think about it," he says. "All we've got to do under this theory is first prove that you're a celebrity, which they'll basically stipulate to. After that, it's just a matter of illustrating what we all know to be true, that celebrities are not like the rest of us."

I could've pointed out that Barry was himself pretty famous. Self-awareness was not his forte. He continued.

"The judge may not go for it, in which case we'll stick with plan A, but I'm telling you, the briefs look good, very convincing, and I think she'll see a little lasting legacy juice for herself in this. If we get this through, we're talking permanent history in the annals of law, real *Plessy v. Ferguson, Brown v. Board of Education, Roe v. Wade* stuff here."

"So why do you need me to decide anything?"

"Because of the risk. Either way, win or lose, it's going to appeal, maybe even all the way up to the Supreme Court. We're talking years before this case is resolved. Years and years and years. This is going to hang over your head forever and beyond. This is your obituary. This is your tombstone. The good news is that win or lose, you'll be out on bail. If we win, you'll be as free as anyone else who can't go anywhere without being stared at and generally loathed. If you lose, you're looking at more home confinement."

I do some of my own contemplating. "You said the original plan is perfect, right, that if we do that, we'll win."

"That's right."

"And you're sticking by that?" I say. "That's still a winning strategy."

"Of course." He looks offended that I might think otherwise.

"So why would I sign off on this new strategy, this strategy that's going to paint me as some kind of defective?"

Barry smiles because he has foreseen this, just as he promised. He has directed everything right where he wants it to go, true master-of-the-universe style. "Because I'm going to waive all of my fees."

This is the most interesting thing Barry has said to me and I chew slowly as I consider it. Bonnie's wristband missives have made it clear that one of the prerequisites for a successful execution of our plan is a pile of money. My pile is severely depleted. Barry is offering me a way to rebuild it. It won't be enough, but it's a start.

I do the only thing I can. I say, "You've got a deal," and make myself a sundae to go.

14

I N THE IMMEDIATE aftermath of the movie things got a little
dark. The first night back the funny man crawled into bed and
wept into his wife's shoulder until he exhausted himself into sleep
and when he woke to her worried face he declared that he was not
having a breakdown, he just needed some space to figure some
shit out. It will take several months to piece what was done into
something that will be shown to test audiences, besides, if he is
lucky and/or the studio has any sense, the movie will be quietly
euthanized in the editing room.

He did not know what was going on with his mind. He was
simultaneously overjoyed to see his wife and son and deeply
ashamed about so much and grieving for what he was certain was
the end of his career, and so he was having a hard time facing them.
From the massage chair, his "throne" (his wife's sarcastic term) he
saw a household that seemed to operate just fine without him, as
though his absence while filming illustrated that *he* was the gunk
in the gears holding everything back. The child looked good,
walking more steadily, making eye contact and asking for things

in multi-word sentences. The funny man counted the boy's age on his fingers, almost needing his thumb, and couldn't believe it. As the boy passed by the chair the funny man would beckon him closer, like one would a dog, and the boy would stand just out of arm's reach and say, "Daddy's sad," (this came from the wife as well) and sprint off to somewhere else.

At the insistence of just about everyone he started seeing a therapist and one of the first breakthroughs was that one source of the funny man's discontent was his feeling of "superfluousness."

The first session with the therapist was his first foray outside of the house since the end of the filming and he blinked hard at the sun as he made his way toward the car. He'd chosen the same guy everyone uses because he's the best and most expensive, or maybe he's the most expensive because he's the best. Whatever. He specializes in "performers," which was made to sound like an affliction to the funny man, even though it was (probably) not meant that way. Pilar was tasked with the driving since no one was going to trust him with that, and she jacked the seat as far up as it would go and still it seemed like she had to look through the space between the top of the steering wheel and the dash to see out. On the way to the therapist's office the funny man punched the radio presets and all of them connected with Spanish-language stations. He had no idea there were so many. He settled on what was either a soccer game or stock market report. The therapist was all the way in the city because people said that suburban therapists are for teenage girls who like to cut themselves, so the drive took awhile and he laid his head back and waited for the inevitable crash that never came. When they arrived, Pilar said, "right here, one hour," like it was a command and then disappeared down the street leaving the funny man wavering on the sidewalk.

The therapist started the session the way he would start every session from then forward by asking the funny man what had been on his mind lately and the funny man talked about the film and the child and Pilar and the radio stations in the car and he did not stop until his time was up. The therapist asked how he was feeling now and the funny man said, quite honestly, "better." At the third session, the therapist introduced the "superfluousness" thing and the word lodged in the funny man's head like a puzzle piece locking into place and he asked the therapist what he should do about it and the therapist said he should make himself "useful," that this would bolster both his self-esteem and his self-worth.

The therapist also gave him a prescription for some pink, ovoid pills that he said should help.

And boy, did they.

In fact, he is now considering firing Pilar. He has not told his wife this because she and Pilar are pretty friendly; not just friendly, they appear to be friends, chuckling over coffee in the kitchen mornings. His wife majored in Spanish so when they chat the funny man has no idea what they're saying, save the stray word here or there, but this is not why he is considering firing Pilar, no way. It is because she is no longer necessary, more anchor than buoy to the good ship of his family.

The household goings-on had previously looked to the funny man like a category 5 rapids rushing by him with no safe point of entry, but three weeks to the day after the third therapy session, having ingested a sufficient loading dose of the pink, ovoid pills, as Pilar and his wife discuss who will take the child to the toy store in order to buy a gift for a little friend from kindergarten's birthday party, the funny man announces confidently, "I'll do it." The two women stare at him, but he stands resolute and his wife looks at Pilar, who nods, and his wife says, "Okay."

The trip to the toy store proves to be simultaneously triumphant and horrifying, a real turning point in the story of the funny man. Where he grew up, the toy store was just that, a storefront in a small downtown strip, next to the clothing store, two doors down from the hardware store, in the same area as the grocery and stationery stores. The toy store he is sent to with the child is easily the size of all of those stores combined, much more like a toy warehouse. The funny man had, of course, known of the existence of this kind of store, but they were indigenous to the late-blooming suburbs and during his time there, the funny man had always had enough money and people to ensure that he did not have to go inside them.

A pneumatic burst of freezing air blasts the funny man as he crosses the threshold of the store, sapping the fluid from his eyeballs, and he gazes at the extra high, girdered ceilings and the layout like a maze, where each aisle must be traversed in order to make it to the payoff of the registers and he feels very small. There appear to be thousands of everything in the store, enough of each item that every child in the world could have one if they were just willing to pay for it. Surely, not all of these sell, the funny man thinks. What happens to the leftovers? The less popular? The castoffs?

The child is of the age where his walking is perfectly sufficient, though obviously he is much slower than a full-sized person. The funny man would like to toss him into the cart and wheel the boy around to speed things along, but the boy walks until he gets tired and reverts to a younger, more helpless self in which case he will beg to be carried, but he is heavy enough that carrying the boy for anything other than short distances is a chore, a real catch-22. Because of the shelves' height, the child can only see maybe one-eighth of the merchandise and he is predisposed to inspect almost each and every item in his viewing range. Doing a quick calculation the funny man guesses that at this pace, it will take better than a day to navigate the entire store, so he makes an effort at moving things along.

"Whose birthday is it, buddy?"

The child inspects a plastic unicorn with a rainbow mane where when you push a button the head bobs up and down mechanically and the unicorn plays a seven-note scale, up and then back down. "Nico's."

"And what does Nico like?"

"Nico likes cars." The child presses the button again, satisfying himself that the head bobbing and music are the limits of the unicorn's powers.

"So maybe we should look at the cars, then?" The child looks at the funny man with a face that says "duh" before edging down the aisle and picking up a hyper-muscular dwarf doll that has long rainbow-colored hair and is apparently a companion of the unicorn's. The arms rotate at the shoulder and the legs at the hips and the child works them back and forth, first like the doll is hammering something with his fist and then like he's walking stiffly in the air. The child takes the dwarf and straddles him across the unicorn's back, and even though the figure is a dwarf, in scale, it would surely break the unicorn's spine.

"I think the cars are somewhere else, pal." The funny man gently puts his hand on the child's shoulder while reaching with the other for the dwarf figure but the child shrugs him off and pulls the figure away and works the limbs some more, his face focused in concentration. The boy is careful, knowing they are not his. He has been well-brought up. The funny man considers heading to the car section and coming back with some choices for the boy to peruse, but it's several aisles over and he doesn't want to leave his son unattended.

There is a small commotion behind them and the funny man sees a woman pushing a shopping cart with one hand while the other grips a girl, a year or two older than his boy, underneath the arm, pulling her up and along high and fast enough that the girl's toes touch the ground only every other stride. The woman is thin, sinewy, dressed in a workout tank top and tight, three-quarter-length pants elasticed just below the knee. Her calves are knotty, hard, and her bicep tenses at the effort of holding the girl just off the ground. The girl's face is a mask of fury, her features crowded together in the center and as the woman weaves around the funny man and his son, the girl grabs an item off the shelf and hurls it to the ground. So quickly that the funny man can barely register it as happening, the woman releases the girl from her grip and swats her on the behind hard enough to cause the girl to jump. "We don't have time for this shit, Margie," the woman says, low and menacing, one eye sliding to look at the funny man as she speaks.

The girl works herself into a cry. The funny man has seen this kind of thing before in his own child, a situation where the boy knows that crying is plausible, but not imperative—say following a fall and a glancing blow from an end table—and there's a beat before his eyes scrunch and the wailing starts.

At first, the girl is unconvincing. The crying tones are too shallow, an obvious force, but as she warms to the task the tears appear genuine enough and as the mother finishes replacing the item on the shelf, she turns deliberately and slaps the girl across the face, hard and quick, and when the girl doesn't stop crying, she does it again and then again, *whap whap*. The funny man looks down now and sees blackened circles marring the gray-specked linoleum, and he recognizes them as spots where gum has made itself a permanent feature of the floorscape. The girl, now having been silenced, her mouth a perfect, stunned *O*, is re-gripped under her arm and dragged away from the funny man and his son. The girl touches her hand to her cheek where the funny man is sure it must be red before her fingertips again brush the toys, grasping. "Please stop," the funny man thinks.

His son, engrossed in a mermaid figure that is part of the dwarf and unicorn group, has registered none of it. Crying children must be a regular feature in the life of a preschooler. Slapping as well, though usually of the child-on-child variety. The funny man looks at his boy and tries to imagine slapping him, or grabbing him by his plump forearm and twisting it until the boy feels his skin burning, or kicking his legs out from under him and knocking him to the ground, or later, when the boy is older, pounding his knuckles into the boy's nose, mashing the cartilage in on itself, and the blood pouring into the boy's shocked, open mouth, quickly coloring his teeth red, and the funny man is pleased to realize he can't imagine such a thing, that it just wouldn't and couldn't happen, that he would *never* do that.

For several hours, the funny man follows his son around the toy warehouse as his son inspects seemingly every item, or at least every item in his sightline, before settling eventually on what looks like a briefcase that when you open it holds thirty different toy cars, each with its own slot. "It's a good choice," the funny man tells him. On the way out he asks the boy if he wants anything for himself, and he replies, "Mom said it was just a trip for Nico's present," and the funny man's eyes fill with tears. Such a good boy.

When they arrive home, hours past the expected time, dinner congealing on the stove, both his wife and Pilar look at the funny man disapprovingly, but the funny man waves them off, a fresh confidence to his bearing. "It took awhile to get the right thing," he says. The boy stops to show the women his choice while the funny man exits the room, leaving the women's mouths hanging and because he is enjoying the drama of the gesture, he goes to the massage chair and with a mighty, sweating effort shoves it toward the door and out into the yard and to the curb, slapping his hands together as if to say, "that's enough of that."

The funny man marches back inside and tucks into dinner and even though it is well past prime, he eats quickly and ravenously, plunging a fork into the spaghetti while the opposite hand grips a large wedge of garlic bread that he periodically chomps from, chewing with his mouth open because he is smiling at every other person at the table in turn.

Pilar and his wife aren't talking, so the funny man converses with his son, though the dialogue is more like a monologue, punctuated only by the boy's nodding agreement and the sound of the funny man's own chewing.

"We killed that store, didn't we, buddy? I mean, we laid that place to *waste*. There was nothing left when we got out of there. We crushed that mother." (Turning to his wife now.) "You wouldn't have believed it, honey. I think we took a look at every last toy and game and action figure and puzzle and doll in the entire place and this boy here," (gestures at son) "this magnificent little shit—sorry, hon, I'm just so goddamned proud—he found the *best* choice. Nico likes cars and he picked out cars. Damn. And I want to tell you something." (Here he raised his fork and used it to point at his wife and then Pilar.) "I realized something today, something important, which is that I am a fucking good father. There's some real maniacs in this world, some real monsters and I'm. Not. One. Of. Them."

That night, for the first time in what seemed like forever, the funny man gives it to his wife, hard, and because in those moments he has the intellectual capacity of Australopithecus, as he climaxes he shouts, "Making babies!"

After the toy outing, the funny man inserts himself more aggressively into the day-to-day household goings-on and upon close inspection, he finds some things lacking. Much of Pilar's day consists of talking to the funny man's wife or drinking coffee while watching *telenovelas* in the kitchen. Yes, the boy loves her, his face lights up when he comes home from his half day of school, and no doubt, her food is good, she's got a real flair for spices, and no, he does not know how much Pilar costs because his wife had commandeered the finances after some unfortunate lapses on the funny man's part, so maybe as a housekeeper-nanny-buddy she is a bargain, but the general slow pace of Pilar's work rate, the deliberate, methodical way she folds the laundry or wipes down the counter or vacuums bothers the funny man. "This is sloth disguised as industry," he thinks.

For a week he begins preempting her tasks, intercepting the towels out of the dryer just before cycle's end, or having the boy's snack prepared and stashed in the fridge for his return home, pulling it out with a flourish even as the child disengages from his hug with Pilar. The pills have both clarified and energized his brain and in the sessions with the therapist the funny man has raised the possibility of cure, even suggesting that nothing had ever ailed him. Pilar circles behind him, inspecting his work, re-tucking a corner on a perfectly straightened sheet or swiping at some nonexistent dust. The language barrier keeps them from having a direct confrontation, but he can tell Pilar gets the subtext, she is no dummy. He is trying to derail her gravy train. To rub it in her face, one afternoon he goes outside and reseals the fence and then spreads a mound of ground cover over the dirt around the bushes, work normally reserved not even for Pilar, but the lawn service. Pilar watches him through the front picture window and he strips off his shirt as he works and each shovelful says, "You can't touch this, bitch."

He does not want to overplay his hand, so in bed with his wife one night several months into his reemergence he suggests a vacation for Pilar.

"Let's send Pilar on a cruise," he says. "Or home, I'm sure she doesn't get home enough. On me, I mean . . . us, we'll pay."

His wife wears just a T-shirt and panties, a look he finds far sexier than any bustier or lingerie. She is sitting up, her legs straight in front of her, reading a magazine focused on exotic travel, picking out somewhere they will go together now that he has come out of his alleged "crisis," and equilibrium has been regained. The funny man squeezes her leg just above the knee, making sure he has her attention.

"Who will take care of the house? You know the big fund-raiser is coming up and I'll be pretty tied up for the next few weeks. I'm even staying in the city two nights," she replies.

The funny man is a little hurt that she does not get it, but he plows on. "Me. I will take care of the house."

His wife snorts from behind her magazine.

"What?" The hurt in his voice is now on full display. "Seems like way back when, I did it fine."

She tents the magazine over her thighs and touches him on the cheek and he sees love in her eyes, but it is a patronizing kind of love, a *you-poor-delusional-sucker* kind of love. He knows that the "breakdown" (if they want to call it that) after the movie scared her, but his recovery is impressive, even the therapist says so (though he gave the funny man a similar patronizing look—sans the love—when the funny man brought up the idea of being "cured") and the funny man thinks this deserves some recognition.

"I've been practically doing everything already, anyway," he says.

Her look changes only slightly, the eyes narrowing as if to say, *it's your funeral, pal.* "Sure," she says. "We owe her some time off, knock yourself out."

HERE'S THE THING: The child gets sick.

For awhile, with Pilar gone, everything was great, just two pals hanging out, playing games, watching some television, running through the big house in their tube socks, playing tag and hide-and-go-seek and a game of their own invention called "pillow

grenade" that's too complicated to explain, mostly because the
rules seem to change constantly in the boy's favor. It was like old
times, except even better because now the boy could talk and run
and shout and had a full head of hair and spontaneously says, "I
love you, Daddy." Every time the funny man catches or finds his
boy he grabs him up and turns him upside down and tickles him
and the boy squeals and it is the best.

While she is home, the wife looks on approvingly. Nights his
wife leaves out her diaphragm, and after rough, athletic sex followed by a session of sweet and tender love they talk about whether
or not the seed for another one has been successfully planted.

"I wonder if Pilar is enjoying herself," the funny man says over
perfect flapjacks prepared by him that he flips in the pan without
the aid of a spatula, by which he means: *She does not need to come
back. We don't need her here.* He thinks he may see agreement in
his wife's eyes, along with the love and admiration for a man who
has been so successful, yet remains truly grounded, a rock, just
like his father before him, but with a larger bank account and the
ability to do domestic duties that his father wouldn't have even
considered.

When she prepares to leave for her overnights to administer the
final preparations for the charity event, he quizzes her on what she's
packed, making sure she is properly outfitted and accoutremented,
and she says she wishes he could be there with her and he says, "I'll
be there in spirit," and before she leaves they do it one last time on
top of the clothes that haven't yet made it into the suitcase.

Under previous circumstances, the boy becoming ill had not
been a problem. Back when they still lived in the apartment and
the funny man had significant caregiving responsibilities, he had
dealt with child sickness often, as for a time the boy had an undiag-
nosed food allergy that produced projectile vomiting as reliable as
Old Faithful, which was followed by several hours of inconsolable
crying from the pain of cramps and an empty stomach.

But back then, it was shift work, handing the boy back and forth
as one of them would head for the bed and a blissful couple of hours
of rest and sleep. The knowledge that it was a team effort, that

there was relief coming, made it seem possible, even as the boy's screams turned his face from red to purple and the doctors in the emergency room swore that they could offer no solution but were pretty sure the child was not in any serious danger. Some children just "fuss," they claimed.

Oh, what a load of bullshit that was! What a crock of slimy horseshit these jerkoffs with their degrees and their white coats with the pen protectors were trying to feed them! And the funny man said so, making a spectacle, pointing his finger and over-turning some equipment as they stormed out with yet another prescription for baby Pepto. As he and his wife returned home, the boy hugged between them in the back of a taxi, the funny man looked at his wife and he could tell that she saw him as he was, a warrior, a tiger who would not relent when it comes to the well-being of his child.

Together, they got through it, thanks to a new pediatrician who diagnosed the allergy in minutes, and once they were on the other side of the exhaustion and worry, both the funny man and his wife saw it as strengthening. A real trial-by-fire bit of survival. Forged steel.

But even with his recent flurry of domestic activity, the funny man is rusty and the boy is larger than before, which means a greater volume of sickness that is coming out both ends and it's fucking impossible to keep up with the laundry like this, and goddamn if the little guy doesn't look like he's suffering, wrig-gling around the bed, not even wanting to watch a video. The temperature is only 101.5, high, but tolerable, not dangerous in any real sense, but he's just so miserable. The incidents when he was a baby come back to the funny man not as a source of strength and experience, but more like post-traumatic stress disorder, distant memories reawakening in him, feeling like they happened minutes, rather than years before, and Pilar is whale watching in Alaska and his wife is in the city. His wife would race home in less than a heartbeat, fuck all those victims of whatever it is she's volun-teering for, let them find their own cure for dysentery/clubfoot/malnourishment/sickle-cell/drought/nonspecific ennui/school bullying/eczema/media bias, but the funny man is not ready to admit defeat.

The pink, ovoid pills seem to be helping—not the boy, who has the flu—only time and the body's natural defenses can help the boy. The pills help the funny man, so he takes a couple extra. Even when the boy's insides are out of ammo he sweats through his pj's and whimpers in his sleep. Any time not spent washing and folding is at the child's bedside, urging him to take spoonfuls of broth or sip juice through a bendy straw.

When his wife calls in to check how things are going he is nonchalant, describing the boy as "peaked," but okay. She asks right away if she should come back, but he says, "No, of course not."

And okay, he was unfamiliar with some of the nuances of the front-loading washer. Perhaps Pilar has been a kind of safety net there, coming in behind and averting disaster. She could have told him that he was doing it wrong. This is sabotage. The front loaders are supposed to be superior to the traditional top loaders that the funny man knows from the coin-op models in the basement of the old apartment. Such a great place, that apartment, where magazines didn't fit in the tiny lobby mailboxes, so if you were home first, or just often (as in the case of the funny man) it was like a well-stocked lending library. Oh, and they'd laughed so many times over the stairs, how the landlord had carpeted each one in a different colored remnant, one more nauseating than another. The machines in the basement were big, Laundromat-sized, and if they overflowed (which happened once when the funny man used too much detergent) it just went to the drain in the middle of the concrete floor, no harm done.

Should the front-loading washer even turn on if the door is not shut and latched? Shouldn't there be some sort of fail-safe there? Isn't that a design flaw? Yes, he could have noticed the water streaming down the hallway sooner, but the boy had mercifully gone down for some semi-peaceful rest, and the funny man was trying to snatch some sleep for himself and why wouldn't such a high-end machine know when enough water has been pumped, rather than having some sort of fill trigger that will never get triggered if the door is left just barely ajar, allowing the water to escape. Just barely.

It takes longer than it should to recognize that using a push broom to sort of schuss the water out of the front door and into the yard is better than trying to sop it up with paper towels. Sure, finding the shutoff valve for the water first would've been a better call as well, but hindsight is twenty-twenty and all that. Not thoroughly drying his hands before making sure the 115-volt dryer plug had not been compromised by the mini-flood also was not well thought out either, but at least the child—even through his sickness haze—got a kick out of how the funny man's hair stood on end.

Running while the wood floor is still slick with soapy residue is a mistake as well. The funny man knows that the pink, ovoid pills are not designed specifically for the muscle spasms that radiate the length of his spine with occasional forays to his rib cage in order to constrict his breathing and drop him to his knees, fetaled over and crying, but they are the only ones he has, save the round blue ones that look like they have a poorly rendered heart carved out of their middles that the therapist gave him after the first session and said to take "only if things get unbearable."

Well, things are pretty damn near unbearable, so the funny man crawls to the bathroom and yanks out drawers in the vanity until he finds them and swallows them dry, followed by three aspirin and one more of the pink, ovoid jobbies just for good measure.

LATER, HE WISHES that his wife could've seen the effort it took to rise as the boy's cries wash through the halls down to the funny man's ears as he lays curled on the bathmat.

"Daddy?" Faint, questioning.

"Daddy?" Louder, more insistent, a tinge of urgency and worry.

"Daddy!" A demand. A tractor beam pulling the funny man upright, knuckles white on the bathroom counter, arms trembling, spine screaming, but now, thanks to those blue ones, feeling like the pain is coming from a distance. It is loud, undeniably powerful, but it is not all that near, a thunderstorm already passed. Each step toward the boy is easier than the last, floating on love, compelled by duty, lubricated by pills. In the apartment, he would've been with the boy long ago, no more than six or seven steps necessary to get from one room to another; so tidy, so perfect, a masterpiece of efficiency in design.

He should have moving walkways installed, like they have in the airports. He can afford that, you know.

"I need to go, Daddy." Of course, the child has been "going" on his own for some time now. No assistance needed, other than the occasional reminder to wipe thoroughly, but the child is sick, scared, a reversion to something smaller, helpless.

"Sure, buddy, let's go."

He looks better, his skin dry, eyes clearer. As the boy sits on the toilet, the funny man touches his forehead and finds it cool. The worst has clearly passed, but back in the boy's room, as he climbs under the covers, the elephants from the circus-themed wallpaper lift free and begin to dance on their thick hind legs. The boy seems unbothered by this development, so the funny man plays it casual, tucking the comforter under his son's chin and giving his boy a reassuring smile.

But why are the elephants playing jazz out of their trunks? And are the stars shooting from their eyes dangerous to him or the boy? Have the clowns always had those fangs? Should walls really undulate like that?

WHEN THE FUNNY man's wife arrives home, the boy is fine. The sickness has passed and as she breezes in, dropping her suitcase at the door, she finds her son in the kitchen trying to retrieve the gallon container of orange juice from the refrigerator, arms stretched over-head, grasping blindly for an upper shelf. She swoops in and rescues the boy before he dumps it over his own head. There is a bit of a musty smell in the air and no sign of her husband, the funny man.

"Where's Daddy?" she says.

The boy shrugs and she takes the juice from the boy's hands and bends to kiss him on the forehead. "You need a bath, pal." The boy nods in agreement, which is unusual.

The funny man's wife installs the boy at the counter with his juice and some dry cereal and goes in search of her husband, calling his name. The carpet in the living room squishes under her feet, foam rising to the surface. She tries different tones with her calls—laughing, urgent, bemused, angry—all with no response. She searches everywhere on the first and second floors, yells into the multicar garage, scans the yard, and still, no husband.

She is pissed. She is terrified. Her husband had been erratic for a time, but that is done with, and even at his most erratic he would never jeopardize the boy.

Surely not the basement. The basement is unfinished, a concrete slab used exclusively for storage. There is talk of tricking it out once the boy is older, if they still live here, as a place for him and his pals to hang, play video games, shoot pool, karaoke if they don't think that's too dumb. The funny man and his wife have the resources to make it the coolest spot in the neighborhood.

But now, months pass without either of them having occasion to go into the basement. More often than not when they go down, whatever they thought was there wasn't anyway, likely having been discarded as they moved from one house to the other.

All the reasons an erratic-acting person may go into a basement flash through the funny man's wife's head as she descends the stairs, plain pine boards, unsanded at the edges, purely utilitarian. She feels as though she should rush but cannot will herself to do more than tiptoe into the gloom. The single bulb with the dangling chain is on, 60 watts, and she knows he must be here somewhere, and she begins trembling and she gasps when she sees a body, huddled in the corner on its side, its back to her, curled in on itself. Perfectly still. She is about to run upstairs and dial 911 when the body raises its arm and she gasps and runs to the funny man and uncurls him and turns him over on to his back, which makes him tense and moan.

The funny man smiles up at his wife and reaches a hand toward her beautiful face. "I got sick," he says. "I ran out of pills."

15

T HIS IS THE first time I've seen any crack in the judge's composure. Barry and me and the prosecutor are in her office, the two of them standing before her desk, me off of Barry's shoulder a step and a half back, my usual subservient spot. She has Barry's brief and the prosecutor's response spread in front of her. There are Post-its tagged in half-a-dozen spots. Eight-inch thick law books bound in calfskin are open on the floor surrounding her chair. Looking down at the briefs she flicks her glasses to her face and then off again and looks up at Barry.

"I can't believe I'm saying this, counselor, but I think you've got a point here."

Barry stays perfectly still, but the prosecutor slumps in his place and groans audibly. I can see that his collar is imperfectly rolled down over his tie. "Come on," he mutters under his breath.

The judge shakes her head. "I hear you, Mr. State's Attorney, but we're in a real bind here." I see Barry suppress a grin. "If I deny this, you're looking at an appeal for sure. Hell, he's going to appeal anyway, am I right?"

Barry refuses to give anything away, standing stock-still, his expression unchanged.

The judge continues. "But if I deny it and he appeals, you're looking at pretty much a full retrial. The appeals court may even just send it back here and we start all over completely, new jury, everything. That's what I'd do if I was them, anyway."

The prosecutor apparently concedes the point, ducking his chin to his chest.

"So what I'm thinking," the judge says, "is that we just bite the bullet and get it over with. Let's lay all the cards on the table and see what the jury makes of it and we'll let appeals come in and clean up the whole mess rather than sweeping some of it under the rug for later."

The prosecutor nods in a way that makes it look like someone is pulling a string on top of his head. Barry allows himself a grin.

I want to tell him that it's never good to laugh at your own jokes, but as we leave and hustle back to the town car, I decide not to piss on his parade.

"The one regret I've always had," he says, "is that I wasn't born a woman so I could experience the miracle of birth."

"I can think of a few million women who might trade with you," I reply.

"I'm totally serious. It's why I don't have children. Being the father is an inferior substitute. But here, with this, I feel like I'm actually birthing something, that what I'm doing here will be permanently woven into the tapestry of the American experience."

"Your legacy," I say.

Barry frowns. "Are you listening to me? I'm not talking about something as simple as that. We're at the DNA level here, my friend. A legacy is the thing people remember about you. What I'm talking about is marrow-level permanence. This will forever be of the world, even if people don't know it. It's like, when we . . . when I do this act, where others are bound to a generally agreed-upon reality-based community, I am capable of creating my own reality, and others will come behind me to study what I do and comment, judiciously, if you will, but there I am creating newer realities that others will live by. I will be one of history's actors."

"Like Hitler?" I say.

"We'll see," Barry replies. "We shall see."

16

PILAR RETURNS FROM her vacation with presents for everyone, a beaded necklace for the missus, a stuffed polar bear almost as large as a real one for the boy, and even something for the funny man, a hand-carved pipe shaped like a whale's body. "Eskimo," she says as she hands it to him, kissing him on the cheek. The funny man watches her back as she wheels her suitcase down the hallway to her room and he admits to himself that he is glad to see her small, sturdy carriage. When she returns to the kitchen and ties the apron behind her back and switches the television from the sports channel to the Spanish-language network, it appears as though their domestic universe has been restored.

To the funny man, the term *accidental overdose* is a complete crock of shit. First of all, it makes him look like an addict and while he knows that "a doctor prescribed them to me" is the oldest excuse in the book, in this case it happens to be true. Right, hindsight says the amount of the pink, ovoid one in his system was truly horrifying, but he blames that on the little round blue ones, which caused him to forget that he'd already had his allotment of the pink, ovoid ones. Sure, he could have refrained from working some of his shadier connections made on the road to score some additional little round blue ones, but they seemed to be the only thing kept the dancing, jazz-playing, stars-shooting-out-of-their-eyeballs elephants from attacking.

And the pain. The pain was so real, like it had become part of him, like he *was* pain. No one should doubt the pain. The MRI *proved* the pain was real and would probably follow him around for some time, maybe even forever. "Significant narrowing," the doctor said. "Stricture." "Impingement."

He knows finding him in the basement like that scared his wife, but it was the only place the funny man could get any real relief because the elephants didn't like to go downstairs and the concrete felt so cool and inviting. He couldn't have been there more than ten or twelve hours, if that.

There is still some lingering pain, but his wife and Pilar control the blue circular ones so there is no danger of overdoing it there. Pilar is also a help with the doctor-prescribed stretching and strengthening, working the hamstrings by levering the funny man's foot toward his head as he reclines on his back on the new living room carpet.

Some other things are lingering as well, like his wife's resentment. He knows it is resentment born out of fear, born out of a worry that she'd lost him or could lose him, resentment from a loving place, but it makes it no less painful when he looks up and sees those brief flashes of hate in her eyes.

Though he has been deemed untrustworthy, probably permanently, he has not been completely neutered. It is his task daily to retrieve the boy from school and if he informs someone ahead of time they are allowed to go out for ice cream on the way home. On Pilar's night off he makes dinner, something he is getting better at, progressing from carryout to food preparation (opening of cans, combining of no more than three ingredients, heating) to actual cooking (recipes, chopping, basting, dry rubs, etc.). He is not superfluous, but neither is he vital. The money continues to flow, even as he does nothing, refusing all bookings and projects presented by his agent and manager. Been there, done that, he thinks. When he signed the contract to do the horrible movie he said to himself that it was a lifetime's worth of money and he was right. He has left a mark, a small one, but it is indelible. He may not get his hourlong biography, but when they get around to doing the "Remember that crazy shit back in that decade that just passed" shows, he will be in there, forty-five seconds' worth, maybe even a whole minute of being made fun of by funny men who would kill for even a fraction of that kind of success. Now that's irony!

He is chronologically very young, but he feels so old, so maybe it is time to retire. He has achieved his goal. He is a comedian, not a great one, maybe not even a good one, but he has made many people laugh. More than many, actually. If you stacked the number of people he has made laugh on top of each other he imagines they would reach the moon. The only question left is whether or not a press release is even necessary, if anyone would bother taking note.

But then his manager calls. The movie is done and they would like him to see it. The funny man thinks that he experienced it, why does he need to see it? But thanks to a little time and necessary perspective, and the pink, ovoid pills at a reasonable and safe dosage, the thought of watching this abomination fills him with more curiosity than dread.

The showing is scheduled for a private screening room in the city, and the funny man expects to be reunited with everyone from the movie: The easily swayed director, the cinematographer, his costars, the love interest, but when he arrives, while there is room for thirty or so attendees, the only people present are his agent, his manager, and two guys in suits expensive enough that they must be executives, one of whom looks a bit on the young side.

Handshakes and introductions all around confirm what the funny man has suspected about the men in the suits. They are from the studio, and one of them is really, really young. They offer him popcorn, which the funny man declines, and as the lights dim, the funny man tosses back one of the pink, ovoid pills and settles in.

"I think you're going to be surprised," the older-looking suit says. "And we hope you're going to be pleased."

As the movie plays the funny man is unsurprised about at least one thing, and that is that the movie is truly terrible. It is unoriginal, unfunny, poorly paced, wretchedly shot, and unbelievably (blessedly) short, with a sixty-six-minute running time. Much of the footage used is outtakes that the funny man assumed would be buried deep in the DVD extras (if there even was a DVD release), moments where someone broke character, or a boom mic bobbed into the frame, or when the getaway van burst into flames too early, or when the funny man had pulled his hand out of his mouth in order to yell at someone. (He doesn't remember doing this and feels some shame over it.) Five minutes in the middle appear to be cell phone–filmed footage of two extras having sex behind one of the production trailers and the climax utilizes cardboard cutouts of the funny man's and the love interest's faces with human lips pushed through—*Clutch Cargo*–style—to deliver the dialogue.

However, there *is* one extremely surprising thing about the film. He is now its star, the undisputed lead. Rather than being a footnote to this disaster, he is out front, *the* name on the marquee. He is all over this movie from the first frame to the last. As the final names of the credits scroll up the screen the funny man turns to look at his agent and manager and the two suits who sit behind him and he says, "How did this happen?"

"It's a hit," one of the suits says. As the lights rise in the theater the funny man can see that the expensive suit masks the fact that this executive is indeed no older than fifteen. His cheeks are hairless and pimples dot his forehead. His wrists below the cuffs are small and bony.

(The funny man only learns this later, but the studio has hired this kid because, for the last year, on his blog, he has predicted the box-office gross of every major theatrical release within three million dollars. He simply knows what will and what will not be popular with mass audiences, often without having to see the movie. If he actually views the movie, the prediction is within decimal points. In the industry, he is known as "Peoria" because he always knows what plays there.)

"How old is he?" the funny man asks his agent and manager.

The second suit jumps into the breach. "We were surprised too," he says. "But once we got rid of that jerkoff"—everyone in the room knows he is referring to the director—"and took control of the footage, it's like the movie just announced itself."

"But it's terrible, right?" the funny man says, still looking at his agent and manager. Surely these two owe him the truth since he relented on his promise to fire them, and on the advice of his therapist, even apologized for his harsh tones. "I mean, it's really, really bad, isn't it? We're looking at a career-ender for everyone involved here, aren't we?"

"It's a hit," Peoria says again.

"In fact," suit number two says, "we're moving up the release. It's going to be our comedy tent pole for the summer."

"Tent pole?"

"The movie that holds everything else up. Our rock. Our anchor. Our sure thing," the executive says.

"But it's hardly a movie," the funny man replies. "It doesn't make any sense. It's not even long enough to be a movie."

The executive smiles. "That's the beauty of the thing. Thanks to the tight running time we can cram in an extra showing per day. Multiply that by five thousand screens seven days a week and you're talking real money, my friend."

"It's a hit," Peoria says again.

It is at this point that the funny man begins looking around for the hidden cameras. In an instant it becomes clear that his refusal to take any work has resulted in a desperation move by his agent and manager to book him on one of those shows where celebrities are lured into unsuspecting situations and secretly filmed embarrassment ensues. *You've Been Played, Sucka!* the show is called. At least they didn't crush his car with a piano falling out of window, or make him believe he'd murdered a prostitute in an Ambien haze, like they've done to others. He would like to shout "well played!" because it is. The funny man used to love a good prank as much as anyone and the lengths they've gone to here with the screening room and the kid in the suit, and even cutting something together that looks sort of like a movie is just brilliant stuff. He imagines this is a little payback from his agent and manager for their temporary firing, and it is hard to begrudge some harmless revenge, and there's got to be a few bucks in it for him when the show actually airs. The funny man stands fully ready to blow the lid off, to invite the hidden crew and show host in from the wings, but looking at his agent and manager, he thinks better of it. Now that he is aware of their little game, the con has been reversed. This is like *The Sting* and he is Redford, or even better, Newman! This is *Ocean's Eleven* and he is Sinatra *and* Clooney depending on which era one prefers. He has the upper hand and there is no harm in continuing to play along, to have a little fun of his own and besides, they won't be able to show any of it because he'll never sign the release. Who will get the last laugh then?

The funny man notices a small, circular pin on the lapel of his agent's suit, which he figures must be a camera because who would wear a lapel pin that ugly. "Oh, this is going to be fun," the funny man thinks.

"Fantastic!" the funny man says, leaning into the lapel pin for his close-up. The funny man has just seen incontrovertible evidence that he is a shitty actor, so he hopes that he is not overplaying things. "This is going to put me on a whole new level, right?" His agent and manager nod enthusiastically. They are better actors than the funny man by far. Their obvious relief that the funny man has decided to rejoin the celebrity race is palpable. They should get out of the agenting and managing business, they are so convincing. More handshakes and promises of meetings for marketing and strategy, all of which the funny man heartily agrees to. He doesn't know when they'll break the illusion, when they'll burst from the wings shouting "you've been played, sucka!" but he knows he's not going to do it himself because *they're* the ones who are getting played. Suckas!

"This is going to be great," the funny man thinks.

WHATEVER THEY'RE DOING to him must be the longest, most elaborate con in the history of televised prank shows.

The screening-room showing was one thing, and it's easy enough to cut a trailer once you already have the fake movie. It probably started to get a little expensive when the marketing campaign kicked into full gear with the television commercials and fast-food tie-ins. (Anyone willing to try to order their foot-long sub with their hand in their mouth gets 10 percent off.) Taking the time to negotiate his contract for a sequel was a nice touch, very subtle, very attention-to-detail. That they gave in on his salary (eight times the original) and profit-sharing demands (significant percentage from dollar-one gross, plus full share in merchandising) and his increasingly ridiculous rider for the upcoming "shoot" (private jet transportation home at the end of each shooting day, regardless of location or end time) only confirmed that the con was continuing. He didn't bother reading it, but he assumes that the script for the sequel would've passed believability muster. They even gave him final cut. "No one gets final cut," they said, right before giving it to him.

He does not tell his wife about his theory, saying, "fine" and "progressing nicely" whenever some movie-related question was posed. He does not want to be talked out of his delusion because it is what allows him to get up in the morning and live his life. Isn't most everyone's life the product of delusion, a delusion that things are progressing, that they are prospering, or if not prospering presently, will be prosperous in the future? It's just that the funny man's delusion is a bit larger than average, which is fitting since he is more important than the average person. His delusion is sized to scale.

The movie-related activities are barely a blip in the humming-right-along daily household goings-on. Talk of more children has stopped—the diaphragm back in place—but with the boy and Pilar, the house feels full enough. He is afraid if he shares all of his machinations because his wife is good and kindhearted, she will force him to pull the plug on his prank and he's now thinking of his prank as a nice swan song to his career, if it is indeed a prank.

The press junket is a real coup. He has to admire the effort there. Bravo. The funny man was more than happy to agree to three days sitting in a hotel room while the nation's media come to him to ask about the film and return home with their blurbs and video clips. He was contractually obligated to do so, after all, and by saying yes, he forced the prank show into pulling it off.

And boy, do they.

He convinces himself that as he's shown into a hotel suite decked out with a small, two-person interview set that this is where everyone will burst out of the bedroom saying, "You've been played, sucka!" But no, as he sits in his assigned chair a woman comes and dabs some makeup to take the shine off his chin and forehead and another clips a small microphone to his jacket lapel. Not wanting to give away that he knows what's what, he has gotten dressed up for the occasion, strategically distressed jeans, button-down shirt, stylish sport coat. On his way out, his wife cupped his buttock over his jeans and wolf-whistled. He hasn't looked this good in years. His agent and manager are there, nibbling on the snack spread and drinking bottled water, giving thumbs-up whenever the funny man looks their way.

The funny man doesn't need to look for any hidden cameras because there is one right there in front of him recording each and every answer to the "questions" that these "journalists" have to ask him. They ask so many of the same questions. He's not sure why he needs to do so many individual interviews, but perhaps it is all part of the gag. Yes, that's it: The prank has become a war of attrition. They weren't counting on the fact that the funny man has nothing better to do. Every seven minutes with twelve-minute breaks every three interviews, a new person is sitting in the chair across from him. The funny man imagines they are pulling people off the street to come in and pose as, for example, "Jennifer Hoffkiss, of KMBC, Channel Nine, Kansas City, Noon News at Eleven AM."

Like the rest, "Jennifer" enters the room with an armful of swag, posters, CDs, drink koozies all emblazoned with the film's title or a picture of the funny man with his fist shoved in his mouth. She is pretty without being beautiful and wears too much makeup. There is a reason she is Jennifer Hoffkiss, Kansas City, and not Jennifer Hoffkiss, Los Angeles, or even Chicago. The interviews are as formal as kabuki. As the video technician changes out the tape they begin with the ritual introduction (i.e., "Jennifer Hoffkiss, of KMBC, Channel Nine, Kansas City") and handshake, followed by the insincere praise ("the movie looks great") and acceptance of said praise ("glad to hear it"). Following the preliminaries there are the questions, which are drawn from the following:

1. This was your first movie. That must've been a fun change of pace from performing solo.
2. What's it like performing for the camera when you've spent so much time working with live audiences?
3. Tell me about working with the director.
4. Do you see yourself doing more movies in the future?
5. What's your favorite comedy of all time?
6. How was the on-screen chemistry with (the love interest)?
7. Who would you like to work with someday?
8. You did some filming in our fair city? How did you like it?
9. Is it hard to shove your hand all the way inside your mouth?
10. What's next?

And there is Question 11, which every Caitlin, Ben, Ashley, Kelly, Jeremiah, Elizabeth, Ian, Amy, Bradley and Jennifer from Ann Arbor, Syracuse, Mendocino, Nashville, Tulsa, Boise, Corpus Christi, Des Moines, Indianapolis, Sioux Falls, and Kansas City ask: "Real quick, can you put your hand all the way inside your mouth and say 'hello' to our viewers back home?"

IT IS WEARING on the funny man, but he plays along. He has the grit to persevere. He has the pink, ovoid pills as the Tonto to his

Lone Ranger. They are raising the stakes, these prank-show shitbirds, but the only way for him to lose now is to give in. He is fully invested in the charade, and there is no turning back, no matter the frequency or intensity of the warning signs in his path. They are sweating, these fucking, prank-show motherfuckers. They are huddled in the closet, sucking on the stench of their own body odor, sweat pooling in their ass cracks as they watch their monitors, waiting for him to get flustered, to give up the prank-show money shot, but he will not do it, no way. He answers the questions thoroughly, dutifully, semi-consistently. He slathers praise on one city's barbecue and another's crab boil. One has the best cheese he's ever tasted. Another he found to be remarkably free of potholes. It doesn't matter if any of these statements are true. Each city will receive the flattery with gratitude. *Hey, he really knows us.*

The funny man expresses a deep-seated desire to work with every name actor and director of the last quarter century. He is so appreciative of the director that he can't imagine working with anyone else ever again. His love interest is "a doll," "a major talent," "on the verge of tremendous things," "capable of more and then some."

He shoves his hand in his mouth and waves hello to every bored, television-watching mouth-breathing asshole from coast-to-coast.

At the end of the last interview he steps out into the hotel hallway and finds himself face-to-face with his movie love interest.

"Hey," she says.

"Hey." He is both surprised and not that they've roped her into the scam, but if they've gone this far, why not go all the way? The film is likely a career-ender for the love interest as well, so maybe this is the only work she can get. The two of them are apparently alone in the hallway. She is dressed in what the funny man would call "demure sexy," a summery dress that doesn't look short until she sits and crosses her legs, at which point the crease where ass cheek meets upper thigh is no longer left to the imagination. There is a small pendant resting in the cleft of her breasts. This is where

the camera must be. There, plus fish-eye lenses in the peepholes
on the hotel room doors.

"These things are *sooooooo* boring," she says.

"You bet."

"You just get tired of saying the same thing, over and over and
over."

"I hear you." The funny man knows he is so close to the payoff.
Just a few more seconds and everyone will be his "sucka!"

"So," she says. The funny man's movie love interest twirls the
toe of her high-heeled sandal in place, like she is nervous, bashful,
searching for the right words. "Remember when I said we should
sleep together and you said, 'let's not and say we did'?"

The funny man nods. He feels what he's pretty sure is a grin
form on his face. He is the Cheshire cat who ate the canary and
shit out the canary and then re-ate the shit. He stares directly into
the pendant just above her breasts. He sees his own eyes twinkle
in the blue gemstone.

"I took your advice."

Still, the funny man grins, though his eyes shift to hers.
"Huh?"

"I took your advice. I told someone in one of those interviews
that you and I, you know, had an affair thing, on the set. I said
it only lasted for the film, and it's over, but that it was super-hot
at the time. I even said you broke it off because of your wife
and kid. It's probably going to hit right around when the movie
comes out."

"Oh, ho, ho, ho, ho." The funny man feels the laugh rising from
deep in his belly. So deep that he smells the pretzels he had for
lunch many hours ago on his breath. He swings around, making
sure each of the cameras in the peepholes gets a good shot before
leaning down, pressing his face right into the camera at her breasts
that smell of talc and sunbeams. They got him. The tears of mirth
stream from his eyes and collect in her cleavage. Goddamn if they
didn't get him after all.

"This is just too much," he says. The laughing feels cathartic,
purgative, medicinal. He backs off from the movie love interest

and hunches over, hands on knees. His sides hurt. "Ho ho ho ho ha ha ha ha ha ha ho ho ho," he laughs and laughs.

The movie love interest edges further away.

"So you're okay with it, then?"

The funny man cannot speak because he is laughing so hard, doubled over, falling to his knees. He waves a hand at the girl as she backs further away, an I'm-fine-you-go gesture.

"Great!" she says, far enough away now that she needs to shout. "See you at the premiere! Can't wait to meet your wife!"

Alone in the hallway the funny man continues to laugh for some time. He feels the muscles encapsulating his spine start to seize like a closing fist and lowers himself all the way to the ground, back flat, knees raised to relieve the pressure on the lumbar area just as the physical therapist has shown him. Giggles still ripple through his frame, sending the pain coursing along. "Guys!" he yells, his voice echoing through the empty hallway. "Come on out! You got me! This is too much! It's just too much! Too much, I say!"

17

WITH OUR STRATEGY change now officially accepted by the court, and a little time granted for the prosecution to recalibrate anything they deem necessary, I have nowhere to go except to my therapist. I feel light and free as I breeze past the ever-smiling Jill into the office. I'm not sure what there is left to talk about, having achieved very little progress over the years. Sure, he has seen me through my phases, I suppose, escorting through the superfluousness, helping keep a lid on the flee-floating rage, but now, supposedly, we have "loss of perspective," and, particularly when looked at from his perspective—a movement from one unsatisfactory state to another—it's hard to see how our time together can be called "progress" on any level.

We have mutually agreed that Bonnie and the White Hot Center are off limits, "not a productive area," according to him. His goal, it seems, is to bring me back to firmer ground, space and time we can agree upon, which means he wants to talk about my childhood.

Like all therapists, mine is obsessed with this, despite my insistence that there is nothing there. I did not devour an unborn twin in the womb. There was no greasy uncle in a stained tank top with wandering hands, or a babysitter that locked me in a closet. I was not left behind in a department store. I did not walk in on my parents doing it doggy-style. I wasn't even spanked, my father always preferring the rational road to problem-solving as opposed to blunt force. My therapist says at the roots of any problem there is also some fear, something that sticks, a "psychic stain."

I settle into the couch, sitting upright because it is poorly padded and uncomfortable, though stylish. I suppose its lack of comfort serves a function as well, no one really wanting to spend more than fifty minutes on it.

He, as always, leads with the gesture, his encouragement for me to set the terms of our conversation. I asked once why he couldn't even inquire into my general health, or even just how my day was going and he said that if he did so, we'd start talking about my general health, or how the day was going, and he had no idea if that's what we should be talking about.

"What *should* we be talking about?" I ask.

"Whatever you want."

"So right now, we're talking about what I might want to talk about."

"That's right."

"How do we know if that's what I want to talk about?"

"Because you brought it up," he replies.

Because I know we'll sit and stare at each other for a near hour, I tell him about how from ages five to seven I slept on one side of my single bed, my back always turned to the window.

"Why did you do that?" he says.

"I was afraid of the monsters."

"What monsters?"

"The ones with giant heads and big teeth that would come through the window."

"Why were the monsters after you?"

"They wanted to eat me."

"And how did turning your back on the window help? Did it keep the monsters out?"

"No, the monsters came in, but if my back was turned I couldn't see them, which meant that they couldn't get me."

"You're talking about denial," he says.

"Not really."

"Why don't you think so?"

"Because there weren't any monsters. You can't be in denial over something that doesn't exist. Only if there were monsters would I have been in denial. The whole thing was my own invention. I was delusional, not in denial."

The look on his face tells me I've scored, a rare occurrence. I wish for someone to high-five. "So what changed?" he asks.

"I figured out there was no such thing as monsters with giant heads and big teeth."

"So you don't believe in monsters?"

"Not of the giant heads and big teeth kind."

The look on his face indicates that he sees this as progress. I have made an admission, monsters exist, but that's not really news.

"What kind of monsters are there?" he asks.

"According to my lawyer, we all are," I say. He gives me the gesture, but it doesn't work on me anymore. I make him ask the obvious question.

"And do you agree with him?"

"It seems about right."

"Why do you say that?"

"Seems like we've all done some pretty shitty things, doc," I say.

"Even you? You're a monster?"

"Especially me."

"Because you killed someone?" To be quite honest, up until this moment, the idea that this act that I was on trial for is what made me a monster had never occurred to me. It had felt like the right thing to do in the moment, and even afterwards as it went horribly wrong with the arrest and trial. It is one of the few things I do not regret, right up there with allowing the condom to slip off as my ex-wife and I had sex in our college library, or allowing a funny-looking harpist to play my father to his death.

"Actually, no," I say. "I'm good with that."

"Really?"

"Really," I say, and I know my answer makes him believe the monster part is most definitely true.

18

H E SKIPS THE movie premiere. He uses a trick remembered from his childhood, heating the thermometer on the bedside lamp lightbulb while his wife's back is turned.

"A hundred and nine!" she says. "That can't be right."

"Regardless," the funny man replies, "it's a fever, and honestly, I feel like shit. Is it okay if we don't go?" His wife sits on his side of the bed and pushes his hair clear of his forehead.

"You don't feel that warm."

The funny man chokes up a cough. "Maybe if I sleep a bit I'll feel better and we can go." He can see the disappointment in her eyes. She has been saying for the past week how much she is looking forward to the premiere. So exciting and glamorous, an excuse to dress up, real show business, not all the nastiness in the clubs with the drunks. The studio has reserved a suite in the city and they would stay overnight and order pancakes and waffles in the room in the morning and not worry about it because Pilar is taking care of the boy. At the same time the funny man knows she is worried about his fragility, the potential for events to tilt him off course. He would like to tell her that they won't be missing anything anyway by explaining the whole crazy prank, but in the moment, even though he wasn't sick in any real sense of the word, he doesn't have the energy to get into it.

"No," she says. "I'll call, say we can't make it."

Forced into staying in bed all day by his ruse, he is unable to check any news reports to see if the event actually goes off without him as its target. The next morning at first light, with his wife still asleep, the funny man makes a show of stretching and rubbing his eyes as though he's emerging from a hibernation before easing out of the bed to retrieve the paper from the front porch. There it is, front cover below the fold of the arts and entertainment section, the love interest throwing her head back, showing all her teeth as she pauses for the paparazzi on the red carpet. The article makes no mention of the movie itself, just the event attendees, including the "notable absence" of himself.

"They could've faked the paper," he thinks. If they were being especially clever they could dummy up a copy and replace the real one at his door with this one. People did that kind of thing all the time for birthdays and anniversaries. Excited at his theory, he rushes to the computer and searches the news and there's more than thirty stories about the event. Surely they couldn't all be faked. But looking at each article closely he notices that they are basically the same, the kind of thing a computer program could generate from an initial template.

So tricky they are. They would be one step ahead of him if he weren't one step ahead of them.

Wearing only his boxers and a T-shirt, the funny man drives to the nearest convenience store and scrounges enough change out of the ashtray (he never carries a wallet anymore; it's someone else's job to worry about that stuff) to buy copies of every paper he can find, some of them not even in English. In one of the papers he finds an actual review of the movie, someone claiming to have seen it. The funny man recognizes the name of the reviewer. Surely this person would not compromise their professional integrity just for the sake of a television prank show. The words seem to swim around the page, making it hard to read and grasp the full context, but phrases like *brilliant stupidity* and *sidesplitting idiocy* float up and into his brain. He is pretty certain that the review is positive, that the movie is being recommended.

"Impossible," the funny man thinks.

He drives home, scattering the newspapers out the window as he goes, and upon arrival splashes down into his bed next to his still-sleeping wife. This time, he really is feeling ill.

Throughout the week there are near-hourly texts from the funny man's agent and manager updating him on the "expected gross" for the movie's opening weekend. They tell him to get ready to "blast off" because he's heading for the "stratosphere." Each text reports a higher number than the last until the funny man flushes his phone down the toilet and that is the end of the reports. His wife (wrongly) reads his obvious distress as nerves. He wonders how they can be so out of sync, how she cannot detect the soul dread that is creeping through his body, threatening to consume him. There was a time where they were linked perfectly, where one could read the other and deliver the exact word, the exact touch, the exact gesture necessary in the moment.

He is thinking of when his father died. As the baby grew inside of his wife, the funny man's father seemed to shrink. Right after the wedding, his father thought he'd thrown out his back taking the garbage to the can, but the X-rays showed something more serious, a tumor eroding his spine and another in his lung, the likely original culprit. His father had never smoked (not good for the nut to spend so much on cigarettes), but there it was. "Sometimes we don't know why these things happen," the oncologist with the beard that went too far down on his neck said. No shit.

Through the chemo his father had to wear a hard, plastic, clamshell brace because the wrong move would snap his spine. There was almost no bone left. They called it a miracle that he even walked into the hospital for that first X-ray. What a dumb use of the word *miracle*. The brace ran from his groin to his chin and cinched down with Velcro in front and back. It took two people to assist him into it and it was only tight enough once the breath grunted out of him. When people would ask how he was doing, invariably the funny man's father would say, "I can't wait to get rid of this brace," his only complaint, and the funny man's mother would make agreement noises; what an improvement that will be, and all the while the funny man is thinking very loudly, so loudly that his thoughts seem to be screaming around the inside of his brain, that that brace is *never coming off.*

The funny man was right *and* he was wrong. The brace came off, but only once his father was in hospice, a well-tended mid-range hotel room for the imminently dying. They'd been moved there from intensive care after the oncologist showed them the three-dimensional image of his father's torso on the computer monitor. The doctor used a track ball to scroll from head to bottom, each image a slice of his father, collectively producing something with space and volume. The tumors scattered through every organ started as specks, then swelled in size as the technician scrolled through the body, before receding again. The chemo had had no real shot. Liver, pancreas, one of the kidneys, spleen, both lungs, all "compromised."

His father was unconscious throughout his hospice stay. The funny man's wife was in her eighth month with the boy, constantly uncomfortable, but still she was there, with the funny man and his mother in the hospice room, monitoring his father's death. The caretakers at the hospice were lovely, like angels on Earth, knowing exactly when they should or should not do something, keeping them informed on the progression of things, having hot or cold beverages ready at just the right time, and still the funny man had the urge to punch each and every one of them in the face. His father's head had been shaved bald for the chemo and blue veins traced across the skull. His skin was a sack for his bones. Dry, white crud collected in the corners of his lips. His breath smelled rich, earthy, elemental. All of the hospital monitoring machines were stripped out at hospice so the only sound was his father's breathing: slow, shallow gasps.

Until the girl with the harp knocked softly and introduced herself and explained her purpose, how she was both a harpist and a researcher investigating the effect of music on the terminally ill. She looked like a harpist to the funny man. Odd. Harpists are odd, because what kind of person chooses to play the harp? Impractical, flaky people. Harps are both gigantic and fragile. Only people with station wagons or cargo vans can play the harp. People who burn too much incense in their crummy apartments, annoying their neighbors who do not enjoy the smell of hippie, play the harp. And additionally, what kind of person chooses to play the harp for dying people? Absurd. The moment you make a fan they are meeting their maker. No percentage in that.

She had long, impossibly thick hair that hung like black ropes and wore a dress that looked almost medieval, bunched and gathered velvet. She wore heavy wool stockings and flat, elaborately strapped sandals. She explained that she recorded the pulse and respiration of the dying person before and after she played and even though they were almost always unconscious and seemingly insensible, the vast majority of the time the music brought beneficial effects.

"We find," she said, "that it brings them ease."

The funny man was ready to send her on her way, to tell her to get the fuck out of there with her stupid instrument and her dumb clothes, when his wife gripped his wrist and said, "that sounds lovely."

And it was. Boy, was it. The woman started by introducing herself to the funny man's father, using his name and explaining what she wanted to do for him. She touched him softly on the temple and then the slack skin at his arm before laying two fingers on his wrist to gauge his pulse.

Who knows what she played? The funny man had not heard harp music before and has not since. The funny man and his wife sat together on a couch near the window, his mother next to the bed, opposite the harpist, holding her husband's hand. The notes sounded so warm to the funny man, soft and tangible, and he laid his head back and shut his eyes and the tears streamed from beneath them. But this was not sobbing. The funny man's breaths remained easy, regular, slowing even as the music continued. It's just that his eyes would not stop unleashing the tears like they had been made for this very purpose. After awhile the harpist began singing along with her playing. No words, just sounds. The word *contralto* emerged in the funny man's head and he knew it was right in describing her voice and that felt like a little miracle because no way did he know that word. His wife reached for his hand and held it and he had no idea how long the woman played and sang, but it felt endless and too short both, this overwhelming feeling of peace, and when the woman finished the music still seemed to linger in the room as she touched his father again at the temple and chest and wrist and finally wished him "farewell."

His father died a couple of hours later, peacefully, the blue veins on his head flushing red briefly before going pale. It was the worst thing that had ever happened to the funny man and his wife understood, letting it be what it was: terrible, earth-shattering, not minimizing or reducing, even though their child was due imminently and he was going to have to pull it together for that. She trusted he'd be there and he was.

That was really something, the funny man thinks.

On the eve of the movie's worldwide release, the funny man looks at his beautiful wife in their beautiful kitchen, spreading peanut butter on stalks of celery, a snack for the boy. He can hear Pilar bustling upstairs, running the vacuum in the hallway. There is a window above the sink that overlooks the back yard, where there is a creek that gives up little toads for the boy to collect. They are no bigger than a man's thumbnail and their colors blend with the mud, but the boy is patient and therefore good at catching them and placing them in shoeboxes with holes punched in the top. Come evening he always releases them back to the wild. The yard is so spacious it takes half a day for a team of three to tend it. Light comes through the window and strikes his wife's hair, making it shine. They are surrounded by abundance. He is rich in every way imaginable. He should be the happiest motherfucker in the world.

PART II
The Fall (The Rise)

19

ONCE THE MOVIE opened, things progressed very quickly, very strangely, very, very badly for the funny man. He snuck into a showing of the movie opening night. He came in after the previews and saw a theater full to bursting with middle-school to college-age kids. The movie was even worse than the funny man remembered from the screening, but oh, did they howl at every last shitty joke. (It's not even like there were jokes, at least in the traditional, setup-punch line sense.) In some cases, half the crowd inexplicably recited punch lines along with the actors, shouting over the audio as though they'd been there before, many times. Afterwards, as the theater emptied, the funny man stayed in the back, pressing his face to the wall and watched the seats refill with a carbon-copy audience of the last showing.

His agent and manager had left thousands of messages at the house, some of them just the sound of them shrieking with excitement into the voicemail. They sounded like teenage girls listening to The Beatles on Ed Sullivan, shrill, fainting-prone. The funny man's wife asked him how it was going and he had to force himself to hold back the tears as he said, "It's a hit." The gifts started arriving shortly thereafter. Constant deliveries of congratulations and well wishes from those who had been enriched by the film as well as those who wished to work with the funny man in the future because of his potential for someday enriching them: Flowers, candies, candies sculpted into the shapes of flowers, baskets stuffed with nuts and crisps and cheese and exotic spices that made the funny man sneeze when the packages were opened. Pilar practically ran out of room trying to find places for all of it. The coup de grâce was his-and-his sports cars sent by the studio, one for the funny man, and one for the boy (at one-fifth scale).

"Holy shit," his wife said.

They had been thinking that the funny man's rise to his previous prominence was something of a lightning strike, but in reality, it had taken years of quasi-toil in the crummy clubs, being indifferenced to death. This latest move was quantum, logarithmic, hyperspacial, like his first level of fame was akin to traveling to the moon by train and this one was like being faxed to Glaxo-23 in the Rglyplyx Nebula.

MONDAY AFTER THE opening weekend the funny man is in his manager's office with his agent also in attendance. Their greeting hugs are closer to tackles and they can't seem to stop smiling. The funny man has come resolved to explain everything, how it's a misunderstanding. How he thought it was all a gag and that he never intended anything to get this far, that he is prepared to stand astride the madness and yell "stop."

"You," his agent says, pointing at the funny man.

"You," his manager chimes in, also pointing. "You are a genius. That's what they're saying, you know that."

"Really?" No one has ever said this word in conjunction with the funny man, most likely because it isn't true, but that doesn't mean it can't feel good.

"Hell yeah!" his agent says, picking up a stack of newspapers and brandishing them like a weapon. "They're calling you 'the savior,' the 'box-office slump buster.' Before this weekend industry gross was down eleven percent year-to-year. After this weekend, *up three percent,* and that's all you, buddy."

The funny man knows that the movie is doing well, but he had no idea it was doing this well. He wonders if there is some utility in letting them continue with whatever it is they have to say, just to, you know, see what's what. Once invoked, genius is not a word to be casually dismissed.

"It's a wave," his manager says. "It's a tsunami and you're riding it . . . *we* are riding it, but we've got to strike immediately because once a wave breaks, it's nothing but foam and seaweed and a bunch of dead shit left behind. Now, we've got the sequel locked in and that's got to start soon. Brilliant move insisting that you direct this one, by the way."

"I'm directing?" The funny man has only the vaguest memory of the negotiations. He was just throwing out random thoughts to see what would stick. Why should he remember something that was all supposed to be pretend?

"Uh, yeah," his agent says. "Shooting starts in three months, remember? Remember how you approved the script and we hired the director of photography and everything? How the whole cast is returning? They've been scouting locations for weeks. If it was possible, we'd try to push it up, but since we can't we've got something else planned."

"Oh?"

The funny man's manager takes the handoff. "Now, the window is tight, but we think we can do a full-court blitz stadium and arena tour up and going, forty shows, twenty-two cities, in forty-three days."

His agent hands him a sheet of paper with several columns titled *Date, City, Venue, Capacity, Estimated Gross, Net Proceeds.* The estimated gross for each spot is a truly grotesque number. The net proceeds is pretty obscene itself.

"Just sign here, and here, and here," his manager says, handing over additional papers.

The funny man is aware that he is at a crossroads, perhaps for the first time in his life. No, this is not his first crossroads, just the first time he is aware of it at the time of the crossing. Knowing the condom had slipped off and continuing to have sex with his future wife in the library, that was a crossroads. Doing the thing for his agent for the first time, crossroads. Signing up for the movie, crossroads. Deciding not to jump from the top of the tornado slide at fifth grade recess, crossroads. But in each of those instances only hindsight has identified them as such. In those moments he existed in a state of blissful ignorance as to the likely consequences of his choice. Even with the tornado slide incident, he didn't exactly think he'd shatter his ankle like Tommy Rodman did when he called the funny man a wussy and nudged him aside and made the jump himself. The funny man wasn't hesitating at the apparent danger. He was just thinking how it didn't look particularly fun.

In this moment, he knows what's what, that to sign where his manager is telling him to sign is an irreversible choice with significant and lasting implications, most of them probably bad.

He is a genius. Everyone is saying so. They are offering him the GDP of a developing country to perform in basketball arenas and football stadiums across the country. He knows the schedule is backbreaking, particularly for someone with a balky back. He signs the papers without glancing at them, knowing that this is the wrong thing to do, but he does not care. The wave has crested the dam of his denial. He's spent many hours of his life dreaming about this eventuality. He thought that perhaps the terrible movie would be the end of his quest, but it is more like the beginning. His life is a fairy tale (of sorts), a story not entirely in his own control, and who is he to say it should end, even if it ending right at this moment would mean living happily ever after?

THE HOUSE IS empty; no wife, no Pilar, no child. It feels oddly similar to the day they moved in and each room was bare, someone else's home that they were just visiting. The gifts of the weekend have been cleared away. Everything smells very clean.

On the kitchen counter beside a supermarket tabloid is a note from his wife. The cover of the tabloid displays two photos: The funny man in the movie's promotional poster, eyebrows arched, hand shoved all the way in his mouth; and his love interest stepping out of a limousine in a black suit and oversized sunglasses. Her head is ducked, but not so much that the camera doesn't recognize her. It is all very Jackie O in mourning.

I NAILED HIM! the headline shouts above the picture. *Steamy on-set romance heats up summer blockbuster*, it says in smaller type beneath them. The story inside quotes a lot of anonymous crew members saying they never suspected, nor saw anything. *"Duh,"* the funny man thinks.

"I thought they hated each other," one of them says. *But the on-set chill gave way to a behind-the-scenes inferno, according to the lady love herself*, the article continues.

The funny man yells at the ceiling as she shreds the paper into confetti before reading the note from his wife. His hands tremble as he holds it, making it hard to read. Fortunately, it is short, handwritten, the same writing she uses for the grocery list or the Christmas cards. It is as familiar to him as his own.

> *Shitbag—*
> *I can't believe it, but then again, I can. You've been acting weird ever since you got home. I thought it was stress. Turns out it's guilt. I need some space to think this through. We've gone to Mother's.*
> *Love,*
> *(Signature)*

"Love." She has signed it *love*. This, plus the fact that he really does have the truth on his side, means there is hope. He knows his wife is a woman of substance, of conviction, someone who cannot be purchased or paid off, and her views on infidelity are (rightly) inflexible, draconian even. She said as much before they were married, before they knew she was pregnant with the boy even, not long after they had de facto moved in together after only a couple of weeks of "dating." They were in bed together, listening to the radio and the disc jockeys started talking about a story of a woman who affixed her unfaithful husband's penis to his leg with Krazy Glue. The man needed surgery and skin grafts and even after all that, he sported a distinctly leftward tilt.

The funny man chuckled at the story. "That sucks," he said.

"He got off easy," his wife, who was not yet his wife, replied.

"What do you mean?"

"I would do worse, ten times worse. A hundred times worse."

The funny man was sure she was kidding, that they were joshing around. "Like what?" he said, smiling.

She told him in enough specific detail that it seemed as though she'd spent some time thinking about it before, had maybe priced out some of the specs, done a couple of napkin sketches regarding the logistics. Rather than using a hypothetical, she kept saying, "you," to funny man, as in, "If you were to get a blow job from a disgusting whore, I would . . ." The funny man was both horrified and deeply turned on. He did not know it at the time, but it was the crossroads moment when he decided that they would be getting married or at least that he would ask. She had such spirit that he was fairly sure she'd say no, and he was sure he'd love her for it.

But *he* has *not* been unfaithful! Flaky, unreliable, wayward— yes, guilty as charged—but not unfaithful. He has been filled with faith. He is bolstered by this truth. He also has the tremendous news about his impending megastardom to share with her. He is now a planet with increased gravitational pull. His agent and manager have made it clear, he is mighty. In fact, they bowed toward him as he left his manager's office.

He dials his mother-in-law's number and grovels his way past the bitch (she *never* warmed up to him, even after the thing succeeded and all those worries about his abilities as a provider were proven to be for naught) and gets his wife on the phone and pours out the whole sorry story, the encounter with the love interest, how she propositioned him (there was an audible intake of air on his wife's part here), and her whole theory of celebrity arbitrage, but that he turned her down, flat! He slept in the bathtub! And how the bimbo took his flip little comment literally and that he was sure the movie was one big prank, and now how it not only wasn't a prank, that he was the newest and hottest star in the celebrity universe and if he could successfully navigate eight to ten brutal months of spirit-crushing cashing-in/selling-out, at the end of it, they'll have enough money to buy their own island, just as they've always wanted. No, he knows she's never said that she wanted an actual island, it's more of an understood thing because who doesn't want an island with brown-skinned, loinclothed servants? No, that is not racist, because he is talking about naturally tanned people, not some sort of native tribe subjugated to the will of the white man thing. No one would possibly turn that down if it were offered, which it is. It is in the offering for him now, for them. For them!

It doesn't take nearly as long to say everything as he thought it would and when he finishes, his wife says, "I'm having a hard time believing this."

"Me too," the funny man replies.

20

THERE WAS A time, at the brief peak of my fame and popularity, that I fantasized about being martyred, Lennon-style. I was thinking that I would attract the attention of some lunatic and then be cut down in my prime, a permanent beacon of untapped genius. Even at my most recognizable, I would walk the streets, head down, but not too far down, letting passersby grab a glimpse and I could sense their bodies seize with recognition, but even as they were saying, "hey, isn't that . . . ?" I was past them. At some point I hoped an obsessed fan who smelled like the inside of a crayon box would emerge from the shadows and ask me to sign something before knifing me in the gut. I would look dramatically skyward as I sank to my knees, eyes on the heavens and as someone else recognized me and realized what had been done, they would wail in their surprise and grief.

Or a plane crash, or a safe falling out of a window and crushing me, something that would snuff me out without me seeing it coming.

Now, thanks to the unveiling of Barry's strategy, the judge's prediction has come true. I am widely viewed as the biggest shithead on the planet. Before, just a shithead, now the biggest. There are protestors outside my apartment almost twenty-four hours a day. I have been protested before, but this is bigger, angrier. They push petitions into the hands of pedestrians that urge a retroactive change to the law to make manslaughter punishable by death. They chant obscene slogans. Using a bedsheet and black spray paint they made a sign held up toward my view that just says, *DO THE WORLD A FAVOR AND JUM!* I'm assuming they ran out of room for the *P*. Most of the time I leave my blinds drawn now, but when I do make an appearance, or my silhouette shows up against the curtains I can hear the boos and jeers from my many floors up.

When I look at the gruesome truths of my life coming out via the testimony during my defense—what I have done to my wife, the incident with my child—it's hard not to be sympathetic to the protesters' position. Today was the therapist's fourth on the stand. Because of my "not guilty by reason of celebrity" defense I had to waive doctor-patient privilege over certain events, and every last morsel has poured forth. Barry says it's all necessary, as part of our celebrity-as-sickness strategy. I don't remember saying or doing lots of the stuff, but it's all in the man's notes, dated and timed, so it's hard to dispute. I mostly watch the jury watching him. If they weren't sequestered, I could imagine them joining the protestors in front of my apartment. The prosecutor just sits there, I'm sure wondering what the hell Barry is up to. I'm the only one tempted to stand up and say, "I object!"

The sheriff's deputy who will recount fully the incident with my son is scheduled soon, and his testimony, plus the associated video, will only further harden their hearts to me. It was and is inexcusable, inexplicable, unbelievable, and if I wasn't rather cowardly, I would've killed *myself* right after it happened. Like I told the judge, I deserve every bit of what's coming to me.

But that doesn't mean I want to go to jail because things have changed and I now have something to live for. Her messages continue to arrive disguised in more and more elaborate ways. Yesterday it was in a news story about her preparations for the upcoming major season. The first letter of each word in her quote, removed, arranged into *thinking of you.*

I'm looking forward to the Grand Slam season, for I will be able to see her much more often, matches in their entirety instead of highlight snippets here and there. Her seed is low, but her game has been looking up, a newfound sense of purpose and resolve apparent in her groundstrokes, at least according to the experts that pretend to know these things.

Barry will not admit to any miscalculation, that he may have overshot the target. On the contrary, he sees it as merely the ultimate fulfillment of his original strategy. "So now we know you're the villain, which is great."

"How can that be great?"

"Villains are compelling. We love villains. Tell me, who's the greatest villain of all time?"

"Hitler?"

Barry shakes his head for the thousandth time. "No. Hitler was evil. Evil people aren't villains, they're just evil. Are you evil? No, you're hateful, but not evil. I'm talking movies, television, that kind of thing, pretend villains."

"But I'm not pretend, I'm real."

"I thought you'd been paying attention," he says. "The whole point is you're not real, you're a celebrity. Anyway, the greatest villain of all time is Darth Vader."

"If you say so."

"And at the end of *Star Wars*, George Lucas makes a very big show of making sure we know that Dart Vader is saved, that he will be back. Do you know why he did that?"

"Because he knew there was a sequel?"

"No, because he knew, deep down, we don't want our villains vanquished. We need our villains. Why are we always worried about some half-assed dictator five thousand miles away armed with rockets that a seventh-grader could outdo in his backyard, getting his hands on nukes? I'll tell you why, because then we don't concentrate on the shit happening under our noses. Villains are there for us to pour all of our baggage into, all that fear and hate, making us believe that we're nothing like them. Villains become indispensable. We can't live without them. Think of it as your public service."

Following the incident with my son, I was at my lowest. I went caveman. I went feral, holed up in the apartment alone. My pits crusty, mushroom-scented. My skin moist, mossy. I pulled the drapes off the rods and wore them like a loincloth. At times I may have scrabbled on all fours. I itched, often. I scrounged old take-out from the fridge for food. I'd come to like Scotch by then. I'm sure there were pills, but I don't remember any of the specifics. I may or may not have been trying to kill myself. If so, it was going to be slow, painful, because that's what I deserved.

I left the phones off the hook and shunned visitors and it didn't take all that long for people to stop even trying to see me. I was being left alone just as I said I wished. This is when I became a tennis fan, because every other channel and show for some reason made me cry. For awhile I tried animal shows, but when a family of meerkats was wiped out by a fox and the lone remaining meerkat howled piteously under a glowing orange moon, I felt my legs collapse out from under me, so I went with the tennis. The matches were hypnotic, transporting, all that geometry on the screen. I liked to hold up my hands to cover the players in my sight so it looked like the ball was hopping back and forth on its own. Of course, some of the time I must have been watching Bonnie, she being the most popular player in the world, but I made no special note. I also made no special note of sleeping or waking or anything. All of it smeared together. It seemed both instantaneous and endless, permanently trapped in a single moment.

Which is why I don't remember how or why the card appeared. It wasn't there and then it was.

I was staring out the window wondering about the strength of the glass, rapped on it with my knuckles and felt the glass wave in its frame. Glass is actually a liquid in suspension, you know. Always flowing, just very, very slowly.

The card was actually glowing. I saw it reflected in the glass, pulsing from my coffee table. I went and picked it up and saw that it was made out of the thinnest paper stock possible. It was like vellum, but somehow still rigid. When I held it to the light it glowed even brighter. On one side of the card was just an insignia, a phoenix rising out of the ashes and a phone number. On the other side it said *In case of emergency*. I thought it might be vibrating in my palm.

The last thing to enter the apartment had been dim sum three or four days previous, judging by its state of decomposition resting on the table. I put the card next to the take-out container and foraged some pistachios out of the creases in the couch and rested back on my haunches, shelling the nuts as I stared at the card. I shut my eyes and opened them and it was gone. I shut them again and reopened and it was back. I puffed out my cheeks and blew out the air and the card flipped once before settling back down. If I looked at it long enough, I thought I could see the phoenix wings flapping. I picked it up and tucked it into the folds of my loincloth and went back to my window.

That evening I woke in my bed and realized I was clutching the card in my hand. It should have been wadded and wrinkled, but when I unfurled my fingers it sprang back into pristine shape. I thought I could maybe hear it humming. I found the phone and dialed, my fingers trembling over the keypad on the headset.

A recording answered on the second ring. A computerized female voice said, "Are you ready?"

I was silent, breathing heavy, and it repeated its question, "Are you ready?"

"Ready for what?" I replied, or maybe that was in my head, I'm not sure. I felt like I could hear a hard drive whirring on the other end.

"Are you ready?" the voice repeated itself, with a little edge this time like there was only one possible answer, so I gave it, and the line went dead.

21

WHILE THE FUNNY man's marriage teetered, his career entered what he later came to think of as "the Midas period," where he would turn many things into gold and they glittered briefly before they became useless shit. Because the house—sans wife, child, and Pilar—was empty and echoing and he was lonely, he hired an assistant, Langley, but when he quickly realized he had nothing he needed assistance with, the assistant soon became something closer to servant, which is actually how these things usually go. The funny man was now not just a funny man, but a movie star, *the* movie star of the moment. A possible franchise, even, the foundation upon which many other things rest. He now appeared on the covers of many magazines simultaneously and as he watched television, which he was doing a lot of again, sometimes—no, not sometimes, but often—there'd he be, large, highly defined, not so bad looking for a guy who doesn't need his looks to make money. The funny man would lean forward or stand and walk toward the screen to look more closely. It was as though somehow his television had turned into a mirror and he was looking at, not himself exactly, but maybe a twin; a cooler, more accomplished model, Funny Man 2.0, if you will. He started to realize the truth about television, which is that the images on screen were far more real than reality, since these were the things that everyone could share: Our collective spirit. There was no objective truth outside what some critical mass of people believed. No one could *really* know the original funny man, not even himself, but Funny Man 2.0 was everywhere simultaneously. He should have seen this before, but it took becoming one of the people inside the television to recognize the truth of it.

The funny man recognized this other funny man as himself, but deep down, he knew he was not him and that he would need to work hard to fulfill this image. Langley was his first effort on that front. He called his manager and said, "I should probably have an assistant, right?"

"Do you want an assistant?" his manager asked.

"I have no idea."

The funny man could hear the manager humming softly on the other end. The humming was new and the funny man recognized it as the manager's verbal tic as his brain calculated the "proper" thing to say. Not the "right" thing, as in the thing that would be the best possible advice and counsel for the funny man's well-being, but the proper thing, the thing that greased the wheels of his relationship with the funny man.

"You know what I always say," the manager said, "better to be safe than sorry."

The funny man had never heard his manager say this, but never mind, six assistant candidates were waiting on his doorstep the next morning. The funny man had never had occasion to hire anyone (his agent had chosen him and the manager simply seemed to appear one day), so he had no idea how to go about such things. In the end, he selected the candidate that most looked like Morgan Freeman in *Driving Miss Daisy*, Langley.

Langley was installed in one of the guest rooms and became a lingering, frankly creepy presence about the house. But Langley already had a month's worth of pay in his account and there was that Funny Man 2.0 in the television that he was supposed to head toward, and so the funny man simply started having Langley do anything the funny man didn't want to.

Mornings, Langley was tasked with things like spraying deodorizing powder inside the funny man's shoes just before the funny man slid them on to his feet. When the phone rang, Langley started bringing it to him. If the funny man could think of nothing to do, he would tell Langley to polish something and he would, the never-used fireplace tools, the convection oven, the mini-cotton candy–maker the funny man had once ordered midair from an in-flight catalog. The funny man told him to stop doing this one day when he saw that Langley had turned to a box of the child's toys, removing the boy's fingerprints from his little toy people and the plastic dragon and the tiny shopping cart that he liked to push around, and the wooden duck that had wheels and leatherette wings that flapped when you rolled it along the ground and the train engine that the child had given a name, "Trainy," and the funny man snapped and told Langley to cut that shit out.

The funny man apologized soon after, but from Langley's demeanor he sensed that he didn't have to, that this was not something that was expected of him. This was sort of fascinating, this casual, unchecked abuse and he began to experiment with it until one day, Langley was bent over, picking up the funny man's clothes discarded carelessly the night before and the funny man decided to boot him in the ass.

LANGLEY STRAIGHTENS, DROPPING the clothes, but otherwise registers nothing and merely stoops again to gather the clothes and places them in a hamper that he then picks up and carries toward the laundry area. The funny man follows and watches as Langley shifts a load from washer to dryer and again as Langley stoops, the funny man boots him in the ass. This time Langley topples halfway into the dryer, clanging his elbow against the metal drum, but still he says nothing.

"This is so terribly wrong," the funny man thinks as he stalks behind Langley toward the kitchen, booting him in the ass every few strides. As Langley pulls eggs from the refrigerator to start the funny man's omelet, the funny man slaps them out of Langley's hands and then retrieves the only one not broken and smashes it on Langley's head. Each escalation is more thrilling than the last, the realization that no one should get away with this, and yet here he is, and as Langley turns to face him, the funny man can feel his own body surge with power.

Langley looks at the funny man, his face unbothered. Strings of yolk stretch between his upper and lower lashes. It is a look of infinite patience, of waiting.

"How do you do that?" the funny man asks.

"Do what, sir?" The yolk runs down Langley's handsome face and collects at his chin and drips to the floor.

"Take it. Stand this. How come you're not beating this shit out of me?"

At last, Langley swipes his hand over his face, collecting the egg remnants and flinging them into the sink. "My last employer concussed me with a phone. This, as they say, is nothing."

The funny man realized he had to get rid of Langley, that he could not stand the shame of having him around, but he already felt too guilty to fire him. He thought about and then dismissed the idea of allowing Langley to boot *him* in the ass and smash eggs over the funny man's head, but the funny man knew that he owed this man something, and the first of his sold-gold ideas sprung into his head.

The funny man calls his manager again. "I've got an idea for a television show, a game show," he says.

"Great," the manager replies, "we'll start filming next week."

"Don't you want to hear what it is?"

"Can we put your name on it as in: *(The Funny Man) Presents* . . .?"

"Sure."

"Then no, it doesn't really matter what it is."

With that, *(The Funny Man) Presents Kick in the A$$ featuring Langley* was born. The concept was simple. Langley would travel about the country and walk up to random people and boot them in the ass. For each kick the person would receive $1000. Once Langley warmed to the task, he was a natural. During his employment with the funny man he had never seen it, but Langley had a gorgeous, disarming smile and when people would turn around, shocked that someone had just kicked them in the ass and saw Langley there, grinning with a fan of hundred-dollar bills in front of his face they too would smile and wave into the camera and on cue say the show's catchphrase, "That's ass-tastic!"

Langley developed a knack for picking the juiciest targets for maximum physical comedy (cruelty), sneaking up behind a mom in the baking aisle at the grocery store and delivering the kick just as she bent to retrieve a bag of flour, sending her tumbling in a white cloud, or pausing at the top of an escalator and waiting for some unsuspecting business-type to bend to tie a shoe so Langley could boot him to the bottom. Once the show gained popularity, they planned sweeps-week stunts, like arranging for Langley to be let onto the field of a Major League Baseball game so he could kick an umpire in the ass.

T-shirts with *Kick Me* and an arrow pointing down on the back and Langley's face on the front sold by the millions. The funny man, simply by lending his name, was entitled to a slice from every ancillary pie, but more pleasing was seeing Langley thrive. He considered it an example of doing well by doing good.

Langley began having to wear disguises to keep people from chasing *him*, offering their backsides up for a boot. He posed for pictures with heads of state, in those cases only pretending he was going to deliver a blow. At the show's peak, Langley had endorsements for shoes and padded "Langley-proof" adult diapers. Whenever a traditional piece of televised entertainment failed, they filled the gap with another half hour of *Kick in the A$$* until Langley had a portion of just about every night of the television week.

And then just as quickly, it ended. The competition came, it upped the ante, and it conquered. *$uckerPunch*, it was called, and this was not about a boot to the ass, but a coldcocking to the jaw. *$uckerPunch* starred a former NFL linebacker (Ronald "the Rage"

Rangini) who had been tossed from the league for chronic steroid abuse. And the prize was not a thousand dollars, but one hundred thousand dollars plus any associated medical or dental costs. Once the contestants woke up from their sudden nap, no one complained. A kick to the ass wasn't so interesting anymore.

There is a special sweeps-week *$uckerPunch* episode, a half-a-million-dollar giveaway involving a very elaborate setup at a wedding. The bride and groom are told that their planned minister has taken ill and there is to be a replacement. The at-home audience is privy to scenes of Ronald "the Rage" Rangini being disguised with makeup and clothed in vestments, but the wedding attendees seem to take no special note of the hulking man up on the altar. This must be because all eyes are on the bride, who is catalog-model pretty in a tasteful, off the shoulder gown that showcases a well-turned back. The groom waiting on the altar a step just below "the Rage" Rangini beams down toward her. Does this remind the funny man of his own wedding day? How could it not? He has not become stone and he misses his wife and the boy deeply. (At this time there are still some glimmers of hopes for reconciliation.)

As the bride joins the groom, they hold hands and the groom bends in for a kiss, but the bride playfully swats his hand and says, "not yet!" and all the attendees have a good, genuine laugh at the groom's expense.

The Rage begins the ceremony, conducting the rituals, a hymn, a lighting of candles, etc. He's not bad, having developed some performing chops during the show's run. When it comes time for the vows, the bride and groom face each other, and the bride does her "I dos" and accepts her ring over a trembling finger.

The groom's turn; he repeats the words: love, honor, cherish, but when it comes time for the part where the minister is supposed to say, "And do you take this woman to be your lawfully wedded wife?" and the groom is to respond with "I do," the Rage says, "Are you ready to go to sleep now?"

The grin disappears from the groom's face just before the Rage snaps off a short right to the head that drops the groom like he's been shot. It reminds the funny man of a toy he had as a child, a toy which was actually his father's toy, found in the attic one day and passed on to him. It was a small wooden horse figure standing on a platform and beneath the platform was a button that when pushed, caused the horse to collapse, its joints suddenly unhinged. When the button was released, the horse snapped back upright, held in tension by the filament that ran through its doweled limbs. The funny man sometimes would lay in his bed, pushing and releasing the button, appreciating how the ruined horse could so quickly be resurrected. As he thinks of this toy, he wonders if he is that toy, unhinged, if there is something that could possibly snap him back to life.

The groom doesn't look like he's bouncing back up anytime soon. He looks kind of dead. The bride's hands shoot to her mouth as she screams, horrified, and she steps on her own train as she kneels to tend to him, her hands fluttering over his body. The groom is moaning, so he's not dead, yet. The attendees stand in the pews, craning to see what has happened. In the meantime, the Rage peels off the fake beard and prosthetics, and strips off the vestments to show the *$uckerPunch* tattoo on his bicep. He taps the bride on her shoulder and she whirls around and starts to jump up and down with excitement. Balloons drop from the church ceiling and confetti cannons fire across the pews. The young people can be seen explaining what's happening to the old people. The bride weeps and shakes as the Rage hands her a briefcase with *$500,000* stamped on the side in gold. By the time the credits roll, the groom has begun to come around. His bride, not quite his wife yet, holds the briefcase in front of him and you can see the effort it takes him to focus on her face.

The funny man can't imagine what kind of barbarian would conceive such a thing as this *$uckerPunch*. He watches it every time it's on.

22

AFTER MAKING THE call to the number on the mysterious glowing card, I awoke in the middle of the night to a gloved hand held over my mouth and a face encased in a neoprene ski mask looming over me. The leather was soft on my skin. I felt more alert than I had in weeks. I thought I must be dreaming.

"Shhh," a man said. "Do not panic. Give me your PIN number." He lifted his hand free so I could speak.

"My what?" My voice was rough, croaking, but the words came with no trouble. I felt my face and the skin was bare and tight. Somehow I'd hacked off my beard, but had no memory of it.

"PIN number, bank authorization number," the man said.

"I don't know what it is," I replied. "I haven't used anything like that for years." It was true. All the money is taken care of for me behind the scenes by others. I am sent account statements that I promptly feed into the shredder without even looking at them. It is one of my favorite things to do. I was not panicking because all emotions had been drained from me. If they wanted to kidnap me and sell me into prostitution, or harvest my organs, what did I care?

"Come on, you know it. It probably hasn't changed. Most people pick one and stick with it."

"Oh-eight-two-six, my wedding anniversary," I said to the masked man. He nodded to someone behind me and I could hear the keystrokes on a palmtop. "Check," the other guy said.

The masked man took off his mask and de-gloved and held out his hand. "My name is Chet and I'm from the White Hot Center." Chet was the best-looking human I'd ever seen. He looked like the love child of Jim Morrison and Marilyn Monroe: high cheekbones, penetrating blue eyes, and even a little beauty mark above his dimple. He had impeccable manners as well, since he wasn't flinching from my smell, or the biosphere that was my palm.

Chet continued. "I will be your center liaison as well as your personal majordomo from this point forward. This is Darrell. He is my assistant. If you ever cannot reach me, which is pretty much inconceivable, Darrell will be available. If neither of us is available, an asteroid has destroyed humanity. We have just made a significant withdrawal from your monetary holdings that we will gladly refund at the end of your stay if you find anything about your experience less than completely satisfactory."

Darrell stepped forward, holding the surface of the palmtop out to me. His mask was pulled up and perched on top of his head like a cap. He looked a little like James Dean. I was being abducted by male models. Was it a dream? It may as well have been. I shook my head and Chet and Darrell bobbled in my vision before settling right in front of me just as before. I reached out and touched the lapel of Chet's jacket, the leather every bit as soft as the glove.

"With your thumbprint you are signaling your agreement as well as pledging to keep your experiences at the White Hot Center in the strictest of confidences under the harshest penalties," Chet said.

I pressed my thumb to the palmtop's surface and after a couple of beats, Darrell nodded again.

"Now, why don't you change into something comfortable? We've got a long journey ahead of us."

I stood unsteadily and peeled the loincloth from my body. It kept its shape as I dropped it on the floor.

"I could use a shower," I said.

"We'll take care of that," Chet replied. "Now get dressed."

I did as I was told, throwing on some sweats and a T-shirt with a windbreaker. I jammed my sockless feet into a pair of tennis shoes.

"Good enough," Chet said. "Let's roll."

Together we walked out, down the elevator and into the lobby, Chet and Darrell flanking me on either side, holding me fully upright. It had been awhile since I'd stood like a man. Under their leather trenches, they wore black suits with crisp white shirts, no ties. Their masks bulged in their pockets. I didn't get the feeling I was captive, necessarily, but neither was I thinking I could get away. I felt more curious than afraid. This was the kind of thing that doesn't happen, but it was happening. As we passed the concierge desk, I could see the doorman slumped over and sleeping, his head cradled in his arms. A black SUV with dark windows idled at the curb with the back door open. I crooked my head over my shoulder at the doorman.

"Don't worry," Chet said, "he'll be fine in a few hours. We gave him the same thing I'm about to give you."

A whoosh of air, a stinging at my neck, followed by dreamless sleep.

23

THE FUNNY MAN realizes too late that he has been operating under a mistaken notion of the nature and purpose of marital counseling. At first, he figured it a kind of straightforward penance. His wife was angry, justifiably so, just not about the right things. If he could prove his remorse for causing this anger, eventually he would be forgiven. As the clock ticked down toward the start of his tour he dedicated himself to his twice-weekly sessions, one individual and one in tandem with his wife.

The marriage counselor had been recommended by his therapist. She was an older woman with gray hair kept in a long braid that looked like a llama's tail, and she seemed nice and friendly enough. Her couch, with its big, overstuffed pillows, was far more comfortable than the angular art-deco model favored by his therapist. The first joint session she laid out her three secrets to successful marriage repair:

1. Always tell the truth, even if it hurts.
2. Anger is the most human of emotions.

3. First thought, best thought. If it comes to mind, blurt
    it out.

Her theory, as she explained it, was that most marriages, particularly after the first several years, suffer from over-calculation,
each partner being *too* conscious of the other. A desire to keep
order overrules and suppresses honest and open communication,
which will naturally sometimes involve conflict. Patterns of
sublimation and subterfuge have been established for seemingly
noble reasons—a desire to prevent hurt, or avoid strife, to keep
harmony—but in reality these are a slow-growing cancer ready
to devour the marriage from within. Everything seems fine, up
until the moment the cancer is exposed and by that time, there's
no healthy tissue left.

"I should know what I'm talking about," the marriage counselor
said with a rueful smile. "It's happened to me three times."

In both the individual and joint sessions the funny man initially
stuck with dictum one and insisted at every turn that he had not
slept with his movie love interest. While admitting to her obvious
beauty and general desirability, he listed dozens of reasons why
he could not imagine sleeping with her. He detailed her stupidity
and vapidity and expressed his indifference, nay, his loathing for
her stupid, vapid self. His story about the night of the proposition
was consistent each and every time and each and every time when
he was finished telling it, the marriage counselor was frowning
at him.

"What's rule one?" she said.

"Always tell the truth, even if it hurts," he replied.

"So why aren't you?"

"Why aren't I what?"

"Why aren't you telling the truth?"

"But I am."

The marriage counselor looked at him, the skepticism etched
in her forehead and at the corners of her mouth. "I know you're
lying for two reasons. Number one, when you list all of those
reasons why you wouldn't have slept with her, not one of them

starts with 'because I'm in love with my wife and would never do that to her.'"

"I thought that was a given," the funny man protested.

"And number two," the therapist continued. "Look at that girl. She's incredibly hot. I'm the furthest thing from gay and *I* would do her. You're not secretly gay, are you? Because if you are, we've got a whole different approach for that."

"No."

"Then don't expect me to believe you didn't sleep with her, and don't expect your wife to believe it either because I'm not going to let her."

It's not that the funny man thought it was a conspiracy, exactly. It was not a setup. Everyone was acting out of good intentions, it's just that he had been cast in a role in which he did not belong. Yes, he was lost and distant, uncommunicative, and above all, flaky, but he was not a cheat.

Still, to move things along, particularly because the start of the tour was pending, at the next joint session he decides to confess.

"Okay," he says, "I admit it, I slept with her."

"I knew it!" his wife shouts.

"Me too!" the marriage counselor chimes in.

He and his wife sit next to each other on the couch. She crosses her arms over each other and begins to cry.

"What are you thinking?" the marriage counselor says to her.

"I don't want to get into it," she replies.

"First thought, best thought."

"I don't want to say something I'll regret later."

"Anger is the most human of emotions."

His wife rubs the tears from her eyes with the back of her hand. "I love him. I want to cut his balls off."

"Good, excellent," the marriage counselor says.

"Good?" this from the funny man.

"Yes, good," she replies with an edge to her voice. "Honesty is the only path to healing."

For the remainder of the session they explore far more of the cutting off the balls feeling than the love feeling, and the funny man spends many of his words on sincere apologies for the myriad ways he has failed in the past. He comes to understand that it is indeed good that his wife wants to cut his balls off, that this is actually an expression of her desire to possess him, to have him always, and he is glad to have made this small metaphoric sacrifice, especially considering he gets to keep the real ones. At the end, there are hugs all around and as the marriage counselor grips him close she whispers in his ear, "I'm proud of you, you filthy pig."

IMMEDIATELY FOLLOWING THE session it seems as though his false confession has stirred some progress. On the way home his wife holds his hand across the center divider of the car and that night they make love. It is better than average lovemaking, like his wife wants to prove that it is something the funny man would miss, but this is totally unnecessary because for the duration of their relationship he has missed it the moment the lovemaking is over. Afterwards his wife snuggles close and things feel so right, the funny man feels that he must tell the truth.

"Actually," he says, stroking his wife's hair. "I never did sleep with her."

She sighs into his bare chest. "Let's put it behind us, okay."

"But it's true. I really didn't sleep with her. I just said so because it seemed like it would help move things along."

"Honestly, don't do this."

The funny man sits up, back against the headboard. "Do what? I'm just trying to set the record straight."

"You can't have it both ways. You don't get to be the good guy here. I'm forgiving you, which I think you know is very hard for me, so let's just drop it."

This is one of those crossroads the funny man does not recognize at the moment, which perhaps explains why he takes the wrong path in deciding now that *he* is the victim. He feels heat rush to his extremities and it feels kind of good, actually. He feels alive. Where for most of the previous months he has felt powerless, battered by forces beyond his control, suddenly he feels powerful. Anger is the most human of emotions and he is feeling it big-time, feeling it toward everyone: his agent, his manager, the love interest, Pilar, his therapist, the marriage counselor, the airline industry, all the people who he would like to unleash his fury on, but because they are not there, he will do what is natural and easy and common. He will turn on his wife.

"Maybe *I* don't want to drop it."

"What does that mean?"

"It means that I never slept with her and I want some credit for it."

"Credit?"

"Yes, credit. I *could* have slept with her. I bet I could've slept with a lot of people, but you know what? I didn't and I don't." He is not even sure where the words are coming from. He retains some part of his brain that recognizes them as ridiculous, but they feel so good, even if they are hitting the wrong target. Shooting a gun up in the air is pretty cool too. "I'm pretty goddamn important in this world, mind you. People know who I am. They love me. I bring them great pleasure. There's a lot of fortunes tied up in me, and for once I'd like just a little recognition that overall, I'm not such a bad guy. *I could be a lot worse.*"

His wife's eyes change from furious to devastatingly sad as her face caves in for a moment, but before she speaks, the fury is back, a low rumble.

"You, get the fuck out of here."

And he does, not because she said so, no way, because *he* wanted to.

HIS ANGER IS so liberating he is not sure why it took him so long to embrace it. He unleashes it on everybody, his agent, his man-ager, even his therapist, and for the first time things start getting done *his* way, and it's effing great. Following a session-long rant the day before the tour started, at the funny man's insistence the therapist added a prescription for cylindrical white ones to the mix to help the funny man sleep because he's so charged up all day it's hard to power down at night.

The tour has been renamed "No Apologies for A-Holes" and the concert T-shirt features a close-up of the funny man's multimillion-dollar hand not in his mouth, but delivering a big middle-finger fuck you.

The shows themselves are amazing. It is theater-in-the-round in places more accustomed to tractor pulls and motocross, fifteen thousand capacity minimum, and the funny man stalks the stage like an animal on a chain. It is crazy to do comedy in such an atmosphere, nonsensical; the connection between performer and audience nonexistent. And yet it works. Because of the lighting he cannot make out a single person, but he knows they're there because of the cheering.

During the show, before doing the thing, which absolutely must close the show each and every night, the funny man has installed an eight-minute bit on why it's dumb to apologize, which, in hindsight, will seem hackish in a Dane Cookian way, but at the time feels like it belongs on the comedy shelf right next to Carlin's "seven dirty words." It is nothing like his earlier material, which is mostly gentle and observational with a light absurdity. He's sure it's the best thing he's ever done now that he's tapped into his true, primal self.

I've got one message for all of you, and it's this: No matter what, DON'T APOLOGIZE! I don't care what you've done, I don't want to see any apologies . . . ever. I don't care if you unleash a deadly plague of monkey herpes that wipes out three-quarters of Earth's population. DO NOT APOLOGIZE! I don't care if you've like kidnapped a third-grader and chopped her up and put in the freezer for snacks later, when the cops come for you and you're tried and convicted and you're about to be fried in the chair, you should not apologize. DO NOT APOLOGIZE! Seriously, no apologies, man. What good does it do to apologize? The second you apologize, you've given them the upper hand. You're the loser, you've LOST, man. It's like here, I'm a bitch, slap me, I apologize . . . shit. What if you were right? Once you've apologized, no one's ever going to apologize back. I'm sorry, I made you say you're sorry? Yeah, right. It's total surrender. It's bend over and grab the ankles and let's play hide-the-kielbasa-in-my-asshole time.

And even if you apologize it's not like you get any credit for it. When's the last time someone just said "thank you," when you apologized. DOES NOT HAPPEN, PEOPLE! Like, you know what I hate, when you say, "I'm sorry," and then they come back with, "I should hope so!" What the fuck is that? "I should hope so?" You should hope I don't jam my foot up your ass I should hope so!

Look at the word, even. Break it down to its roots. First part is "apo," which means "from" or "away," as in "go the fuck away, I'm not apologizing." Middle part, "logo," which means "the study of"—yeah, that's right, "the study of." Last part is "ize," which actually means, get this, "pussy." Put it together, and "apologize" means the study of being a pussy. Well, fuck that!

JUST A WEEK into the tour he realizes that a significant portion of the crowd is delivering some of the no-apologies material with him, shouting out the punch lines. He starts holding the microphone out toward them rather than speaking the lines himself and the noise of fifteen thousand people (forty-five thousand when he's playing a football stadium), yelling, "Well, fuck that!" threatens to lift him off the stage.

The separation papers arrive mid-tour. His wife asks for a truly absurd amount in monthly support for her and the child (and Pilar), and the funny man's first instinct is to say, "well, fuck that," but instead he instructs his manager to instruct his lawyer to instruct his accountant to provide whatever she asks for. She has primary custody, but he will have visitation rights, not that it matters while he's on tour, but when this is done, he's right there with both his money and his love. He will not be the kind of father who denies his child's needs, one of which is a father who is brave enough to tell him the way the world works.

Liberated by his anger, he has sex widely and indiscriminately, *and he loves it.* He effing loves it and he's not going to apologize for it, no way. Most of them aren't remotely in his wife's league looks-wise, but he doesn't care. Fat, thin, hair on their faces, hanging earlobes, unfortunate posture, untreated goiters; he does not care because he is a giving person and they want him so badly.

The tour is a phenomenon. He does press in his off hours, appearing any- and everywhere even though the shows are long sold out. He is impossible to get away from. Flip on the television, he is there. Check Facebook, and it is funny man time. He is a trending hashtag, a comedy virus penetrating everyone everywhere. There are discussions of a South American swing so they can take advantage of the capacity at the giant soccer stadiums. For the first time he begins to understand how mighty he really is.

Think about it: The funny man has his own economy, like he is a nation unto himself. There are not just direct employees like his agent and manager and accountant and brand manager and tour director and the lighting crew, but there are people whom he does not pay directly that are thriving because of him. For example, the zit-faced gomer who rolls his pack of smokes in his sleeve and wears cowboy boots in order to look taller, even though he's never even touched a horse, whose job it is to hawk the concert T-shirts and CDs in the arenas and stadiums for a half-percent commission per item. What could that yokel possibly do if not for the funny man? That guy is unemployable. He'd be gnawing on a block of government cheese and sucking on generic smokes if not for the funny man and his record-breaking comedy tour. But thanks to the funny man he probably has an apartment and is saving for a flat-screen television and could maybe even get laid. And what about the tabloid photographers who follow him everywhere and get paid for the pictures of him spewing pink barf into the gutter just before climbing into a limo following a little postconcert relaxation at a local watering hole? Without him, they'd have nothing to do.

And let's not forget every last sorry shit attached to the movie sequel. Look at what he is providing for them. He has saved all of Hollywood. Dozens of thinly premised movies have been green-lit in the wake of his success. Will all of those writers, directors, actors, and key grips be sending him a thank-you? *Thank you, Mr. Funny Man, for making America believe in laughter again.*

He goes even deeper than this. The funny man is elemental. He is the cause of additional watching of television or Internet surfing, file downloading, consuming of media, things that take electricity and bandwidth, which is provided only by employing miners digging fuel from the Earth and technicians laying cable and flipping switches and Bengali customer-service representatives being unfailingly polite in the face of complaints. The funny man is worldwide.

He should commission a study of the GFMP, the Gross Funny Man Product, all of the tangible worldwide wealth that is directly traceable to him. He strongly suspects that the answer, when it comes right down to it, is *all of it*. He's not saying he's a savior, but it's not an unreasonable word. It's not out of the realm of discussion.

LIKE A SAVIOR, he loves being among the people. Check that, he loves being among *his* people, because that's what happens whenever he goes out, he is soon surrounded by *his* people. People who get him instinctively, unquestioningly. At first, he brought a little extra protection, a little muscle with, but soon he realized it wasn't necessary because everywhere he goes he is welcomed like an old and treasured friend, not because he slaps down his Black Card upon entering the establishment and everyone drinks for free, but because *his people* know that he is just like them. Grounded. Real.

After the initial hubbub of his entrance, he likes to sit at the bar because this is where he finds the realist of the real. He buys drinks and they talk about things that matter: interest rates, sports, engine capacity, gas prices, humidity. While this is going on he's also scoping targets for later, the girls he will bring back to the hotel or tour bus, identifying two or three possibilities in case one or two of them are married or otherwise hooked up. Not that them being married is always an issue. More than once, husbands have offered their wives to him, saying it would be an "honor," but sometimes those guys want to come with and watch and the funny man is not into that level of kink.

This night there's a real honey, young, but not too. She is shooting pool while the funny man throws back boilermakers with his new best friends, Earl and Tony or maybe it's Denny and Bert. This is in Grand Rapids, or maybe Ft. Worth. Maybe the accents on these guys are southern. The bar is called Lucky's or maybe Chance's, he's not sure, but what he is sure of is how the honey's shirt lifts up in the back and her jeans stretch deliciously over her ass when she leans over for a shot. He thinks he might see a tattoo there in the small of her back. They're very common, the funny man has come to find out in his travels.

He sends her one drink, then another, and each time she politely salutes him from the tables before turning back to her game. She tosses her head back and laughs at something someone over there says. This is unusual. Usually the second drink brings them toward him like magnetism. Is it possible that she is not aware of who he is? He always dresses incognito, though not too; but no, when he walked in, a cheer went up and his back was slapped dozens of times on the way to the bar. He still feels their imprints on his flesh. He signed hands and breasts and drink coasters on his way to his stool where he could sit and do some serious drinking with Earl/Denny and Tony/Bert.

Earl/Denny looks back over his shoulder. "That's Woody's girl," he says.

"Who's Woody?" the funny man says.

"Just a guy from around," Tony/Bert replies.

"And where's Woody?"

"Not here, I guess," Earl/Denny says, craning his neck around the room.

"How do you know?"

Tony/Bert chuckles softly into his beer. "Oh, you'd know by now."

"Yeah, well, his loss," the funny man says, tossing back the last of his beer. He follows it with just one of the circular blue pills. He has become very well-versed in what these different pills do in various combinations and he knows that one, just one, of the circular blue numbers is right for this particular occasion because it will make things blurry at the edges, like a movie in flashback, like you've already lived it.

The funny man is terrible at pool, but this is unimportant because by making a hash of it, he is allowed to be funny, his stock-in-trade. He whacks balls all the way off the table, even sending one flying into the middle of someone's back, and when the startled patron wheels around, the funny man shoves his hand in his mouth and everyone in proximity cracks the hell up. When it is the honey's turn to shoot he leans over her and says, "Here, let me show you," and nibbles on her earlobe. She is not receptive, exactly, but neither is he getting the total brush-off. This makes it more fun. It's been awhile since he had a challenge and she seems worth it.

He is racking the balls for a rematch when someone taps his shoulder. He turns and is face-to-face with a young guy, maybe a year or two younger than the funny man. The guy's head is shaped like an anvil and his face is etched with deep lines like a cowboy who's seen more than his share of sun, which probably means this is Ft. Worth and not Grand Rapids after all. The guy wears a denim shirt open a couple of buttons and ropey veins trace up over his clavicles to his neck. The etched face is calm, but the man's jugular pulses. The face is so ugly it is undeniably handsome. The guy has the deepest blue eyes the funny man has ever seen.

"I think it's my turn," the guy says to the funny man.

The funny man makes a face and turns his back and keeps racking the balls. No one laughs, so he makes an even more exaggerated face, but still, no one laughs.

"Winners get to keep the table, and you didn't win." The guy's breath blows the sweet tang of pouch tobacco over the funny man's shoulder.

"Woody," the honey says softly, plaintively.

"Oh, I'm a winner, pal," the funny man says to the crowd, but for Woody's benefit, without turning around. The funny man feels a vice clamp on each shoulder and he is spun so he is now face-to-face with Woody. The funny man holds the wooden pool triangle in his hand. The look on Woody's face is unchanged, but the carotid arteries on each side now undulate under the skin like worms pushing toward the surface.

"I'll admit," Woody says, "that in the general sense of the word, you are a winner. By every conceivable measurement, you got the world by the balls, no doubt about that."

"You know who I am," the funny man says. Woody hasn't appeared to be moving, but it is now clear to the funny man that he has been slowly crowding him against the end of the pool table. His ass hits the table edge and he must lean his torso backwards to keep from contacting Woody, which seems like it would be a bad move. He wonders where Earl/Denny and Tony/Bert are. Surely he's bought some loyalty there.

"Oh sure," Woody says. "I know who you are. Everybody knows who you are. The thing is, though, *I do not care.*"

This is where the combination of the little blue circular pills and the pink, ovoid ones are a problem. The little blue ones take the edge off everything, making it all seem like a dream. The pink, ovoid ones tamp down anxiety and fear, regardless of whether or not anxiety and fear are natural and helpful emotions in a particular moment. With enough of the pink, ovoid ones in your system, a ravenous bear could be charging at you from out of the woods and you would stand stupid, knowing you are in mortal danger, but not really caring. As the bear rears on its hind legs to strike with one of its sledgehammer paws, you may get the urge to open your arms and try to give it a hug. Even as the bear cracks open your skull using all twelve-hundred pounds per square inch of its biting power, your world is hunky-dory. For sure, the funny man should be doing something, but he does nothing.

And then the wooden pool triangle is not in the funny man's hand, but in Woody's and the funny man is flat on his back on top of the pool table and one edge of the triangle is pressed down on his windpipe.

"You got a lot, while I only got one thing," Woody says, leaning into over the funny man's face and glancing once over at the honey. "But in about thirty more seconds, if I keep doing this, you're going to have nothing."

The funny man's vision begins to tunnel, closing down until it feels like he's looking through the end of a paper-towel tube, then a straw, then he doesn't remember, and then suddenly he can breathe again. He rolls on his side as his hands shoot instinctively to his neck.

Woody stands over him, his arm around the honey. She looks at the funny man with loveless pity. "Turns out, I got everything, huh?" he says. The lines on his face break into something like a smile. "No apologies, right, my man?"

They walk off together, Woody and the honey, his arm at her shoulders, hers fixed in his back pocket. Woody is right. He has everything. The funny man has nothing, not even Earl/Denny or Tony/Bert, who are nowhere to be found. The funny man decides that even with its hard slate surface and the balls bruising his kidneys, the pool table is the most comfortable spot ever, so that's where he resolves to stay forever.

24

H ER MESSAGES ARRIVE in almost every batch of signing material. They are harder and harder to dig out because the volume of items sent has actually increased, even as the protests gain steam. Since many items associated with me are being destroyed, I suppose new ones are all the more valuable. Supply and demand. Each missive from her lays out more details of the plan, additional angles and eventualities. She is a clever girl, thinking through everything for me, though I'm starting to anticipate the next phase even before it arrives in the mail. It is a marvel how I never miss them no matter how elaborate the disguises, further proof that she and I are bound by forces out of our control.

Check that. At the Center, what we learn is that no forces are outside of our control, it just appears that way, which is why so many people experience setbacks and unhappiness and the general failures that mark our lives. I was this way before I went there, and again briefly after I shot that man six times, but I have resighted my guns on the target.

As are hers. She had her own slight bobbles following my arrest, she also forgetting what we learned at the Center and what we shared between us, but now, each match seems easier than the last and I know because I watch them all. During changeovers she stares straight ahead, her long lashes blinking evenly, her gaze going far beyond the parameters of the court. She is, as they say, in the zone.

DESPITE BARRY NOW working pro bono, money is still an issue because I need as much of it as possible. Fortunately, I have developed my own part of the plan for that.

My agent is surprised to hear from me. The signature work is the manager's business, so my agent has not had much to do with me for some time. Nominally, he still works for me, but without a body that he can move to different places, I am not much use to him. In the life of my agent, I am a chess piece on the side of the board.

"I'm writing a book," I tell him.

"Really?" he says.

"You sound surprised."

"I just figured you're busy, and everything."

"I've got nothing but time," I say. I feel like I can hear him squirm on the other end of the phone. With me a two-time failure and *this close* to incarceration, there's not much to underpin our relationship. Transaction is our fuel, and there's nothing left to transact.

"So what's it about?" he says.

"It's about how to seduce and fuck your wife."

"Ha!" he says, but as a genuine laugh it is unconvincing. I sort of miss the days when people didn't feel obligated to laugh at what I've said. "Seriously, what is it? I want to know."

"It's the story of my life."

I hear the springs of his chair squeak as he leans back. This is his doing-business position. I've seen it many times. "Well, big man, I think you know there's some hurdles there."

He is referring to the fact that a person convicted of a crime is, by law, not allowed to profit from those crimes.

"It's okay," I reply. "It's thinly veiled fiction and I'm not using any names, like when I write about you, rather than calling you Gord, I just refer to you as 'the agent.' Frazier is just 'the manager,' and Beth is 'the wife' until she's the 'ex-wife.' I call myself 'the funny man.' I'm the villain. I'm finding it considerably less painful to do it that way. It's like it's me, but not and when I can't remember something, or can't bear to remember something, or don't know something, I just make it up. I'm pretty sure that most of it's true, except for the parts that obviously aren't. Some stuff I have to make up just so it's a decent story. I'm calling it 'An American Saga'."

I can hear Gord's wheels turning over the phone. "But isn't a saga supposed to be about heroic deeds done in far off lands?"

"I think I've done my share of pillaging. I possess some spoils."

"But if it's fiction, how are we going to trade on the whole behind-the-scenes true-story angle?"

"Wink and nudge, wink and nudge, say no more," I say. "You say it's all made up, but everyone will know it isn't. Or that it doesn't really matter because no one will ever know the truth."

"It could work, I guess," he replies. "People seem to like that kind of thing. Let me put out some feelers."

"No time for feelers, put it out there and take the first decent offer. I need some dough. I'm willing to sacrifice royalties for a bigger front end. If you can sell it inside of two weeks, I'll give you an extra five percent commission." These are magic words.

"Consider it done," Gord says.

There is a silence on both ends of the line that I fill. "I guess that's it, then," I say. "Drop me a line when you have an offer for me." I go to hang up when Gord interrupts.

"Wait," he says. "In the book, what am I like?"

"You're the same soul-sucking bastard you are in real life," I say with all due affection before hanging up.

Technically, this would be my second published book. You can still find the first with my name on it on the shelves, but I didn't write it. I've never even read it. I can't even entirely remember what it was about. It was one of the many things my name was added to with my permission but without my knowledge. It did well, making its own little pile of money. Now that I am writing a book for real I've found it to be rewarding, though difficult. It's pleasing to do something that is entirely my own, a rarity in the entertainment world. Even my trial is not so much mine, as Barry's and the prosecutor's and the judge's and all the people watching and waiting to hear my fate. My life is the fuel for that machine, an indispensable part, but one of many.

The goal, as far as I can see it, is to make the book as true as possible, as faithful to one's experience as you can get, but I've found this often entails straying from the precise way events may have unfolded since the memory falls short of the truth of the matter.

Perhaps this is one of those truths, that we fall short.

And of course there are the things that happened that no one would believe—*stranger than fiction* is the term—and so I'm going to leave them out of what I will share with the rest of the world, but in leaving them out that does not mean they didn't happen or aren't going to happen in the future.

25

WHAT IS THERE to say about the sequel? Does it help to catalog all of the ill-conceived or even non-conceived moves?

1. The funny man was to be the film's director, but he had no idea how to direct a film.
2. The script that he approved when he thought the whole thing was a hoax was actually a thinly veiled rewrite of a classic episode of a legendary television show involving pies and a conveyor belt that everyone would recognize as being ripped off and would for sure bring a massive lawsuit, so it had to be ditched entirely.
3. With no time (nor idea how) to write a new script, the funny man decides that they will simply improvise the entire movie over a loose structure.
4. When this proves a failure, he then decides to shift gears and make the movie about a guy trying and failing to make a sequel to a successful movie. He does this by

bringing various figures from the movie into his production trailer and then encouraging them to tell him
the "truth" about their feelings regarding the other
participants in the movie. He claims that everything is
confidential, that it is all "just between them," but the
funny man, of course, secretly films everything.

5. Most damagingly, at no point does the funny man put
his entire hand in his mouth. All of the other bad moves
were forgivable if he had simply done this, but he would
not.

The funny man amasses nearly six hundred hours of footage,
which he trims to a svelte 420-minute rough cut before slicing to
the absolute bone for a 232-minute final product. Fully under the
sway of his increasingly complicated cocktail of pills as well as his
belief in his own genius, the funny man is immensely proud of the
movie. He believes it reveals something deeply true about life and
humanity and making movies, namely that it's all total bullshit.
He forbids anyone else from seeing the movie, which he refers to
as "the film." The funny man is done with mere "movies." With
nothing to work from, marketing settles on this tagline as the sales
hook: *You liked it before. See it again, only a little bit different.* This is
terribly false advertising (and will in fact result in lawsuits), but
they did the best they could under the circumstances. Millions are
spent promoting something that no one is even sure exists.

But the funny man is supremely confident. He's forgotten what
it might be like to be wrong. He has broken new ground with
this film. No one before has trod where he is now treading. Other
footprints are neither in front of nor behind him. It is like the
poem about Jesus where supposedly Jesus is always there, but when
the guy looks back in the sand he sees only one set of footprints
and the guy says "what the fuck, Jesus, where were you during
those times?" and Jesus says, "step off, motherfucker, where you
see one set of footprints, that's me carrying your weak ass," only
in this case, it's the funny man carrying the rest of the moribund
entertainment industry.

It will be nearly impossible to outdo the original, box office—wise. The funny man knows this, but that's not what this film is about. Trying to do that is a mug's game, a sucker bet, so he has savvily gone the other way. This film is about how that *can't* be done, so you've got to do something else. The lack of box office will actually strengthen the overall indictment at the core of the film. He imagines it will earn him a whole new level of respect from the people who previously have seen him as that dumb guy with the stupid thing. The off-Broadway play may not be necessary after all.

Rampant speculation about the film flies through the entertainosphere, but all of it is wrong, which hugely pleases the funny man. He refuses to do any publicity, save a single interview with the male cohost of the leading morning show that he likes to watch. The morning show is thrilled with this exclusive arrangement and given the near total lack of confirmable information about the sequel, there is a tremendous amount of anticipation for the appearance. The morning show will receive its highest ratings ever even though no actual news will be broken.

The camera light goes on and the stagehand points at the set where the funny man sits facing the morning-show television host, two pals in easy chairs that just happen to be hanging out in front of a camera. The morning-show television host tells the funny man how good it is to see him and looks at the funny man with moist and friendly eyes that seem to indicate sincerity. This endears the morning-show television host to his audience. It makes him seem human.

The morning-show television host looks at an index card on his lap and says, "This has been a really big year for you. So, tell me, what's the biggest thing that has changed?"

The funny man could give a true answer. He could spill his guts to the morning-show host, tell him things he will not even share with his therapist. How when he was nearly killed in a bar in what he's pretty sure was Ft. Worth, as his vision closed down to a pinpoint, he was visited by a spirit that *he's* not calling God, but others grounded in the Judeo-Christian faith might, and this

God spoke to him in the voice of a woman and what she said was, "Whatever you do is the right thing because you did it." And from this moment the funny man understood himself to be divinely inspired, which is what is behind the film he has come to not talk about.

Or the funny man could talk about the more than occasional surge of power he feels as he walks the streets and sees people noticing him, how he imagines that he may be able to knock a building to the ground using only the powerful fists of this powerful man.

Instead, he looks at the morning television-show host, flicks at the crease in his slacks and says, "Well, if I had to pick just the one thing, it'd have to be . . ." Here the funny man looks around the morning television show studio, as though he's delivering a big secret. (This is known as "timing.")

". . . better hookers," he says. Stagehands laugh, and the host hides his smile behind an index card.

"Oops, can I say that?" the funny man says, looking fake sheepish. "Is this live?" Of course he knows that it is live and that it will get him talked about, which is what he really wants. "They can just edit that out, can't they?" The stagehands and the host laugh harder. The funny man wonders if he should stand on the chair arms and pretend to look around for the people who are laughing.

The host collects himself and asks the funny man what he hopes the audience gets out of the new production, what his desired reaction might be. The funny man considers telling the truth, which would be this: "I hope, that when the credits roll, each member of the audience turns to their neighbor and gives into the urge to tear each other into teeny-tiny little pieces that will scatter the theater floor, pieces that we would sweep up and drop as confetti on the next audience at the next showing and over and over again. People would wonder why every show is sold out, yet no one ever leaves the theater."

Instead, he says, "We just want the kids to have a good time. We're all about the good time."

When the interview ends and the morning-show television host breaks to commercial, he leans over to the funny man and says, "Look, maybe after this last cooking segment you'd like to go grab a beer."

"It's nine o'clock in the morning," the funny man replies.

"Exactly," the morning show host says. "Quitting time."

THE FUNNY MAN'S near-death experience has ended his fascination with *his* people, so the morning-show host suggests they go back to his place for "a few." The morning-show host is an interesting specimen to the funny man. He is quite famous himself, far more famous than most of the people he is tasked with interviewing. (Not more famous than the funny man, though.) For years the morning-show host was just a weekend, substitute morning-show host until all of the sudden people recognized his talent and next thing you know they were nudging the chair of the female morning-show host over to make some extra room.

The morning-show host has also reaped some of the spoils of fame, including a marriage to a Chilean supermodel that was often reported as troubled and recently ended in divorce. The funny man has seen pictures of the morning-show host in the tabloids with two mocha-skinned children with dark eyes and perfect faces. They always seem to be eating ice cream together, the cones melting down the children's knuckles. The funny man suspects these are staged in order to demonstrate that even though he is married to a psychotic ex-model harpy, the morning show host is a generous and tolerant father . . .

. . . with a kick-ass bachelor pad in a high-rise almost directly across the park from the funny man's new place. Unlike the funny man, who decided to outfit his apartment with furniture and appliances and stuff like that, the morning-show host has instead installed a regulation-sized batting cage. But this is not just any batting cage. Unlike other batting cages where the pitching machine is two oppositely rotating wheels that squeeze the ball between them, firing it at the designated MPH, this pitching machine features a video screen on which the greatest pitchers of all time are projected at actual size, and as they wind up and throw, it looks as though they are actually hurling the ball. With a press of a button you can be taking cuts at Clemens's heater, Koufax's curve, or Niekro's knuckler.

"This is the coolest thing I've ever seen," the funny man says.

"I know, right?" the morning-show host replies, tugging his tie down and shrugging off his suit coat. He pulls a beer out of the refrigerator, the only other piece of equipment visible, and tosses it to the funny man. "Go ahead," he says. "Give it a shot."

Though years of Little League established that he is terrible at it, the funny man loves baseball. He puts on a padded batting helmet and stands in the cage. He dials up Clemens and the big man seems to be looming over him from sixty feet, six inches away. Every seven seconds the virtual Clemens rocks into his full windup and throws. The pitches seem fast as bullets and the funny man swings comically late at every one of them. He dials the speed down to Maddux but still can't even manage a foul tip. Each cut with the bat is vicious, all of his strength behind it and soon he is winded and staggers out of the cage, leaning on the bat for support. Maybe it's not as cool as he initially figured.

"Let me show you how it's done," the morning-show host says, grabbing up the helmet and bat. In the cage, while the pitches continue to whistle past, he strips down to a tank-style undershirt, revealing a physique the funny man wouldn't mind for himself. Gripping the bat, he begins lacing line drives back at the screen, the crack of bat against ball like gunshots.

"Whoa," the funny man says.

The morning-show host grins and drops the bat. "That's nothing, watch this." He takes a series of in-and-out deep breaths that remind the funny man of Lamaze class before standing astride home plate and taking 95 mph of hard cheese right in the stomach.

"Haaaahhhhhhhh!" the morning-show host screams. The next pitch drills him in the same spot. "Haaaaahhhhhhhh!" For the next one, he takes off the helmet and squats down and points his face at Clemens. The ball impacts square on the morning-show host's award-winning nose and ricochets off his face as if he was protected by a force field. He flicks the machine off, steps out and drains the rest of his beer in three long pulls.

"Holy shit," the funny man says. "How'd you do that?" He had had some beers and some pills before the interview, of course, so maybe he wasn't fully facultied, but he was not hallucinating. This was not elephants playing jazz through their trumpets, surely not.

"Learned it at a magical place, my friend. If you put mind over matter, then nothing matters."

The funny man had been feeling powerful, but now he feels weak and puny next to this specimen. This is unacceptable. "Let me try," they funny man says.

"I don't know, man, it's not as easy as I make it look," the morning-show host replies.

But the funny man isn't listening. He is tugging on his beer and then getting in the cage and cranking up the machine. He chooses Bob Gibson from the menu. Gibson retired before the advent of radar guns, but it is widely held that he threw the hardest ball in the history of baseball. The pitches whiz by the funny man and smack the tarpaulin backstop with menacing force, thunderclaps. The funny man tries breathing just like the morning-show host and counts to three in his head and straddles the plate.

The pitch from virtual Bob Gibson is a direct hit.

To the funny man's balls.

Clemens was a notoriously high ball pitcher, but Gibson, you see, liked to work low in the zone.

Upon impact, the alcohol and anything else that was with it in the funny man's stomach spews forth, nailing the screen a full sixty feet, six inches away. The funny man crumples to the ground even as Gibson goes into another windup. The pitches continue to zip by, just over his head, pinning him down like mortar fire, not that he could've gotten up anyway because he has no feeling in any of his extremities.

The funny man's organs seem to think that a small nuclear device has been detonated in his abdomen and are busy banging into each other, rearranging themselves in the wrong spots,

pancreas and spleen swapped, duodenum wondering if it's time
to retire. Breathing is out of the question, which in combination
with his instantly accelerated heart rate puts him in a genuinely
dangerous medical situation. For several seconds the adrenaline
keeps the pain away, but once it fully floods this system, all that is
left is the ache. The funny man moans like a ghost.

The morning-show host is laughing uncontrollably because the
funny man has just executed the oldest and most enduring comedy
routine there is. Shakespeare has no fewer than forty-nine direct
or indirect references to characters getting "struck in his majesty's
kingdom." When archeologists first uncovered the storyglyphs in the
ancient pyramids they discovered drawings of one man being kicked
in the balls underneath those little skirts dudes wore back then, while
others stood on laughing. There are cave etchings where a hunter-
gatherer is shown getting a wayward spear to the balls. Chaplin, the
Marx Brothers, the Three Stooges, *America's Funniest Home Videos*.
It's funny because it's true. It's true because it's funny.

Getting it together, the morning-show host enters the cage and
turns the pitching machine off and hands the funny man a fresh,
cold beer. "Here, dude, use this."

The funny man cradles the beer to his testicles and this helps
some. He can now conceive that this is not necessarily death that
has come to visit him. Very close to death for the second time,
recently, but not death. There have been no visits from spirits this
time, though, just the ache, the ache, the ache.

After ten or so minutes he is actually able to stand, albeit
hunched like a dowager, and gimp over and collapse against a
column in the morning-show host's living room. The beer is warm
now and he drinks it.

Every time the morning-show host looks at the funny man,
he cracks up into a fresh round of giggles. He waves his hand in
apology. "Sorry, sorry, dude, honestly, I'm sorry," but he just can't
keep it together. Ultimately he is overcome with hiccups and the
funny man smells the vaporized beer fill the room.

"Holy shit, dude," the morning-show host says. "You are one
funny mofo. I can't wait to see that movie."

26

I AM ENJOYING my new sense of purpose. I sleep very little, but mornings I wake completely alert. I've been concentrating on my core with the exercises, abdominals, obliques, that plus the back and shoulders, lats/delts. Those are going to be key if I'm to make it. In the mirror, I see my shape changing, firming up, a jawline forming. The waistband of my boxers no longer bites into my belly flab. I've felt better only once in my life.

After exercising and before getting ready for court I make my lists and one of the items is to write a letter of apology to Barry. Earlier on in the trial he said how what people are looking for with me is closure, some way to shut the book on me and my sorry story forever. I've been holding them hostage, he said. Now, when I do what I am going to do, I will be denying that experience. There will be no closure. I will leave only mystery behind. (But maybe they will enjoy the mystery, who knows?) He also will not have his chance to take his "not guilty by reason of celebrity" defense to the Supreme Court. I imagine without a client that there is no actual case.

When you cross into the White Hot Center, it is through an entryway that serves as a kind of hall of fame, a nearly endless series of head shots framed and encased under Lucite. They reach floor-to-ceiling and the ceiling is more than twenty feet high. Each is illuminated by its own individual light and collectively, it makes it look like the room is being lit by the celebrities themselves.

Chet and Darrell walked on either side of me, relaxed, nodding greetings to others that we passed. I considered the possibility that I was dead. I tried to recall the final events before the arrival of Chet and Darrell at my apartment, but things were vague.

I remembered nothing from the trip, but as I was awakened, I could tell that we were at sea on a small craft, and as we approached the dock, it was apparent that we had arrived at some sort of island. The weather was warm, dry. The breeze on the boat felt good on my face. It was dusk, suggesting we'd been traveling almost a full day, but for all I knew it could have been multiple days. In the dying light I could see white sand beaches with palm trees behind them.

Chet sat across from me on the boat as we bobbed toward the dock.

"Why do I feel so good?" I said. I really did. For the first time since I could remember my brain felt like it was the right size and situated where it belonged. The purple scrim that fogged the edges of my vision for so long had lifted. Everything was crisp and clear. When I breathed deeply my lungs didn't hurt. I could barely even tell I was breathing. Everything felt effortless. I smelled myself and came away with lilacs. "What did you do?" I said.

"We cured your addiction, to those pills anyway."

"Just like that?" I replied.

Chet nodded. "That's a fairly easy thing, just a matter of readjusting the old brain chemistry, tuning it to the right frequencies. We're very good at that, but then, we're very good at everything." The boat bumped against the dock and Chet leapt easily ashore and secured it to the pier with a pristine white rope. He offered me his hand and hauled me behind him. Darrel was waiting for us.

A SHORT WALK up the dock escorted by Chet and Darrell and a ten-minute ride in a golf cart with a perfectly silent motor and we'd arrived at the main building. It looked like a cross between Jefferson's Monticello and a beach resort country club, all pillars and white paint with a large looming dome, a bronze phoenix sculpture affixed at the peak.

I of course recognized every picture in the hall, but I paused in front of one of them. "That's Mitch Laver," I said.

"Indeed, sir," Chet replied. "Cohost of *Hello U.S.A.*, the number-one morning show in America."

"He was here?"

"Indeed again. One of our greatest successes. When he arrived he was on the weekend shift talking up charity curling matches to cure cleft palate and screwing chicks with cellulite. Now, well, I think you know all about him."

An almost imperceptible pressure at my elbow and Chet had me moving along as he filled me in on the initial details. "There will be a greeting and welcome from Mr. Bob after which I'll show you to your room where dinner will be waiting. After that, you'll want to catch some sleep because the sessions start first thing in the morning. There will be others there, but we recommend not interacting or conversing in any way at this time. It upsets Mr. Bob, and besides, there will be plenty of opportunity for socializing later when you are ready and it is productive."

Clearing the hallway, Chet deposited me in a neoclassical rotunda, every square inch of which seemed to be fashioned from marble. Up close I could see the small fissures mapping the walls. This shit was old. A small platform raised four feet or so off the ground stood in the middle surrounded by people just like me, Q-ratings off the charts, no introductions necessary. Chet took a glass goblet of sparkling golden liquid from a tray offered by a blue tracksuited waiter with the phoenix insignia I'd seen on the card on his breast and handed it to me. "Welcome," Chet said. His face was simultaneously beautiful and handsome. "I'll see you after Mr. Bob's remarks."

None of the assembled spoke to each other, apparently having been similarly admonished by their handlers. We took shy sips from

our goblets and maybe shared the barest of nods. Protocol among
the famous is always a little bizarre anyway, since introductions are
redundant when the mere existence of your face announces your
identity. In general, we cover by acting like old friends—two-
handed handshakes, cheek kissing, backslapping, you old so-and-
so-ing regardless of whether or not we've ever met. But waiting
for Mr. Bob, we acted like seventh-graders at a social.

We did not have long to wait. A man in a tracksuit identical to
the waiters, only in the brightest white imaginable and with the
phoenix insignia in full stitched relief on the back like something
from a motorcycle gang, made his way forward and I must have
blinked or looked away because I could've sworn he floated to
the top of the platform and hovered for a moment before settling
down. He looked to be in his mid-fifties, trim, medium build,
with a long, hawkish nose, balding save for an orbit of hair reaching
around the back of his head extending ear to ear. His voice was
strong, commanding, but also calming.

"Welcome," he said, "to the White Hot Center. I am your host,
Mr. Bob." He took a moment to rotate sixty degrees, making brief
eye contact with everyone in his field of vision.

"It is popular to call this sort of enterprise a 'retreat.'" He made
air quotes around the word and wrinkled his long nose. "But this
is not a helpful word, *retreat*. Under every circumstance to retreat
is to give in. We hear it all the time that it is important to retreat
and recharge, but this is a mistaken notion propagated by losers.
While you are at the White Hot Center you are not at a retreat, you
are at an 'advance.' If you retreat, to get back to where you were,
you must cover previously traversed ground. What is the point of
this? You have worked hard to march over that ground and there
will be no re-marching. We are here to help you march forward
to what is next, not to go backwards to what was and what has
been." He turned another ninety degrees and made eye contact
with a different portion of the attendees.

"We do this," he said, "by teaching you a very simple, very
ancient, very elemental concept that we call 'the Law of Desire.'"
More air quotes. "Human beings want things. It is really just

this simple. We are human and because we are human we want things. A certain musical artist, whose picture you may have seen in our entryway, famously said, 'You can't always get what you want,' but we showed him differently, didn't we? Before visiting us, one would have thought it wasn't possible for a sixty-seven-year-old man to have a physique as lean as a teenager and also continue to rock people's faces off with songs that are more than forty years old, but guess what? It can happen. It happens by focusing on what is important, and what is important is the wanting. Only when the wanting becomes strong enough, shall we get what we want. When people do not succeed, it is a failure of desire, and nothing else. The only limits on the Law of Desire are physics, but even so, physics are not completely understood, which is to say, there are many things you want that people will say are impossible, meaning truly impossible, not merely difficult, and yet, if you put into practice what we teach you, you *will* achieve them."

I thought of Mitch Laver taking a 95-mph fastball to his pretty face and walking away none the worse for wear.

"I am here to help you in this pursuit. To put it most simply, to help you is my desire and I want it very badly, which is why we have a hundred-percent success rate."

A pleased murmur rolled through the crowd.

"Ah ah ah ah," Mr. Bob said, waving his finger. "Do not think that because our success rate is perfect that it will be easy. On the contrary, it is very hard, but because we want it so badly we do not quit, ever, even if it nearly kills you. Our logo is the phoenix because the phoenix is forged in fire. While being a phoenix is very awesome, fire is extremely unpleasant, even for future phoenixes. Until the moment you become a phoenix, fire burns. You should know that you will spend some time in fire here at the White Hot Center.

"Now," Mr. Bob continued, "before we share a toast, let me tell you of just a few of our ground rules. Number one, I have a personal, twenty-four-hour-a-day open-door policy. If you need me, I will be there for you, no questions asked for as long as you need.

"Number two, anyone who tries to avail themselves of my open-door policy without first addressing your needs with your Center liaison is subject to immediate expulsion. You liaison is there for you, make use of them.

"Number three, everyone's program is customized to their specific issues, which means you will be welcome at the White Hot Center for just as long as necessary, but not a moment longer. We will know when it's time for you to go and when it is that time, you will go.

"Lastly, anyone caught within a hundred yards of the southwest compound may be killed without warning. Very serious about this one, folks. Very, very serious. Okay, let's toast! To desire!" Mr. Bob raised a goblet that had magically appeared in his hand and we did the same before clinking glasses with the people in closest proximity. "To desire," I said to a young girl next to me who I instantly recognized from the front of my cereal box. She wore a warm-up suit similar to Mr. Bob's, though hers had a small bunny patch on it.

"To desire," she said.

We drained the liquid. Chet appeared at my elbow just as a female version of him touched the young girl's shoulder.

"This way, sir," Chet said, steering me away, as the girl was led off in the opposite direction.

27

T HE ALMOST UNIVERSAL consensus is that the sequel must be
a joke.

"This is a joke, right?" they say. The nearly four-hour-long
nonsensical rambling heap of garbage is the funny man pulling a
fast one on the entire nation. "Very Kaufmanesque," they say. "If
it's true, that would be like, awesome," they say. The public is ready
to go with it, and that is what the funny man's manager and agent
are encouraging him to do now that they have seen it as well, the
only two people in the theater at their particular showing to stick
it out through the entire run time.

"Let's just put a release out," the manager says.

"Yeah," the agent says, "something like, 'ha ha ha, you fell for
it, suckers.'"

But the funny man is pissed. He is being tragically misunderstood. On the Web site that tabulates all of the reviews and labels
a movie either "tasty" or "putrid," the funny man's film is only 1
percent tasty. He finds the positive review and reads it out loud to
the manager and agent.

"'This film is meant to provoke and challenge, to disturb and upend. It is rare that we are given something that can be safely labeled *genius*, but that's no doubt the case here.'

"See," the funny man says, "this guy gets it. Smithy Carruthers, knows what the fuck is what. What's wrong with the rest of you?"

The agent and manager exchange looks.

"Uhh . . ." the agent says.

"Umm . . ." the manager says.

"Out with it, assholes," the funny man says. He no longer hesitates to call his manager and agent what they self-evidently are.

"Smithy Carruthers is a fake identity owned by the studio. He says every movie they put out is a work of genius." The funny man searches for Smithy Carruthers's reviews on the Web site and sees this is true. "Borderline genius." "Approaches genius." "Gets near genius and brushes up against it and comes away smelling like genius."

The funny man throws the manager and agent out of his apartment and goes to war to defend his film. Because his testicles remain ridiculously swollen he cannot take to the airwaves, so he hits the blogs. He posts messages anywhere and everywhere defending the movie, explaining the movie, explicating the movie for the slack-jawed yokels of America. He expects to be welcomed as a visiting dignitary, to be celebrated for his virtual presence among the anonymous people who usually have to content themselves with shouting into the void, but no, he is beset by savages who can type more quickly than him. Even on the message boards at the Web site dedicated to him and his greatness he seems to be suddenly and universally loathed. It is like they have been laying in wait for him and now have pounced. They are a Venus flytrap and he is their fly, their chunk of ground meat. This is blood sport and he is armed with a peashooter.

The funny man is outnumbered millions to one. No one will jump in on his side. It is the world's largest pile-on. Sites go down, servers crash. The global temperature ticks up one-tenth of one degree because of the extra energy expended delivering the virtual blows. They hit him from every angle, wearing him down pixel by pixel. His fingers blister on the keyboard. His spelling degrades to their level and his balls will not stop throbbing. Finding it impossible to compete on the message boards, he goes to instant messenger in order to take on his foes, one by one, like a martial arts master surrounded by bad guys:

> MovieGuy45: If you have to explain it, it's not a good joke.
> Funnyman: UR right it's not a joke. That's some serious shit up there. If you weren't so stupid you might get it.
> MovieGuy45: That's what she said. Lol!
> Funnyman: That doesn't even make any sense.
> MovieGuy45: Like ur movie. ROTFLMAO!
> Funnyman: eat shit n die!
> MovieGuy45: that's what she said. Lol, ROTFLMAO! LAWSMAHOIYF!
> Funnyman: what the f does LAWSMAHOIYF mean?
> MovieGuy45: LAughing While Sticking My AssHOle In Your Face.
> Funnyman: Seek help, you sick fuck
> MovieGuy45: That's what she said. Lol!

Finally, by the end of the day, the funny man gives permission for his agent and manager to release a statement saying it's all a big gag, but at that point, no one believes him.

He is ruined. He is misunderstood.

To the extent possible, the mess of the sequel is cleaned up. The film had been pulled from theaters by the end of the opening weekend and all of the cast and crew were given bonuses by the studio in order to buy their silence and prevent the slow trickle of tell-alls from showing up in the media. A company run by two fourteen-year-old South Koreans was hired to scrub any evidence of the funny man's typing tear across the Internet.

The only one who wasn't willing to shut up about it was the funny man. The studio had used its leverage to keep him out of any of the mainstream outlets, but when a woman named Dagmar Neuborgen, host of Duluth cable access's *Sewing Time with Dagmar*, managed to get an interview request through, the funny man flew himself to her studio (the Neuborgen homestead basement) and because no one was paying any attention to him, did his best to do something to grab some attention.

But nothing worked.

As he sat down the funny man complimented the Neuborgens on their paneling, saying he'd never seen anything like it, which was the truth, and declined the offer of tea, accepting plain water in a mug with a picture of a cat wearing a sombrero. Looking at himself in the monitor he tried out some different smiles before settling on one he called "pleasantly bemused," which he wore as the red camera light snapped on.

He tried everything. He compared his comedic influence to the holy trinity: Bruce, Pryor, Carlin. He laughed, he raged, he stalked the Neuborgen basement, clawing at the paneling like a cornered animal. He considered, then abandoned, then reconsidered some choice racial slurs. He looked at Dagmar Neuborgen's crucifix nailed to the wall, at the handsome Christ figure's feet, nailed, one over the top of the other, and said how he identified with the man, how he now knew what it was like to die for someone else's sins. The funny man stared into Dagmar Neuborgen's cornflower blue eyes and thought that those eyes must be why Mr. Neuborgen had fallen in love with her, and she shook her head sadly and said, "None of this is very original, is it?"

AFTERWARDS, THE FUNNY man spends his time gazing out the apartment windows, searching for protestors, but the world has taken no special notice. The video pops up on the Web site designed for the purpose of sharing videos like a famous comedian-actor having a meltdown on a cable-access show and sees it only has seventy-eight views. He looks one hour later and sees seventy-nine views. Three days later it is eighty views and he realizes he is the only viewer.

There is now nothing left for the funny man save his once weekly overnights with the boy and a last stab at marital counseling.

At what will turn out to be the final session, the funny man holds a foam ball that the couples therapist has encouraged him to squeeze any time he feels anxious or angry. The therapist has been talking like the funny man and his wife are making great progress, but this is true only if the progress is toward a final dissolution of their marriage.

The ball is stamped all over with the name of an antianxiety drug. The funny man knows that some people would call this ironic, but he knows also that that would be wrong. His wife and the marriage counselor look at him. It is his turn to talk. He doesn't want to admit it, but he is so completely wounded by everything.

"I think, I guess," he says to the ball, but speaking to his wife, "that when it comes right down to it, I feel like you never really believed in me and I hold some resentment over that."

"Ha!" the wife says. "Haaaaaaa! Ha! Ha! Ha!" She fakes wiping a tear from the corner of her eye and grabs the foam ball from the funny man. She shakes the ball at him. "That's the funniest fucking thing you've ever said, you fucking shitball." She fakes throwing the ball at the funny man's face and he flinches.

The marriage counselor, the impartial arbiter of their marital disputes, looks at the funny man and frowns and says with an edge to her voice, "Look, it's important that both parties want to work on the issues, otherwise we're wasting everybody's time."

His wife has launched into a list of supportive things that she has done that even the funny man must admit sound impressive and yet he somehow he still feels empty, a sponge of need that drains as quickly as it is filled.

"Maybe I'm a terrible person," the funny man says.

The funny man's wife deflates, slumps in her chair and speaks down to the ball, "Do you see? Do you see what I'm saying?"

It is his wife who pulls the plug on the marriage and he is sort of grateful for it, though he is also devastated at the act. It is the objectively right thing to do, but he never would've had the courage to do it himself.

She always was more than I deserved.

When the divorce summons comes, the funny man goes to his lawyer's and breezes past the receptionist without pausing and enters the lawyer's office without knocking. He picks up a bronze-cast model train engine off of the lawyer's desk and tosses it from hand to hand as he paces.

"How many zeros?" he asks the lawyer.

The lawyer holds up a lot of fingers.

"Can I afford that?"

The lawyer nods.

"How long?"

The lawyer holds up five fingers.

"Weeks?"

The lawyer shakes his head.

"Days?"

The lawyer nods. The funny man wrenches the train engine in his hands and groans. If he cared about things like money anymore, he would be caring deeply at this moment, but he cares about nothing.

The funny man sighs. "Make it happen," he says.

28

"WITH MIND OVER matter, nothing matters," Mitch Laver said to me after taking virtual Roger Clemens's heat off his face. That's what they preach and teach at the White Hot Center.

Mr. Bob wasn't lying about people not understanding the true boundaries of physics. When it comes to the physical world we have our known knowns and our known unknowns, but we also have our unknown unknowns. The White Hot Center traffics in the unknown unknowns.

You'd understand if you'd been to the White Hot Center.

It started with the sessions. Mornings, Chet would fetch me from my room at first light and escort me to the training center. The grass would still be wet with dew, and as we walked we'd pass foraging peacocks and peahens. Chet wore an all-black track-suit. Mine was canary yellow. Only his had the phoenix insignia. Clearly there was some kind of code behind the colors, but I'd been unable to figure it out. Except for my trainers and Chet, I had been almost totally isolated from others. A slight, Asian-looking woman delivered the meals to my bungalow and someone (Chet, maybe) was cleaning up after me and restocking the canary yellow tracksuits and fresh underwear in my wardrobe, but I never saw them. When I wasn't in training, I would be eating, and then shortly thereafter, sleeping, jostled awake by Chet the next morning.

Blacktopped walkways snaked around the grounds, little white chain fences reminding everyone to stay on them. Buildings of every imaginable architectural style were visible across the hilly grounds. I could see a Le Corbusier, a Gehry, Gropius, Mies van der Rohe, Koolhaas. My own bungalow where I mostly slept off my treatments was clearly a Frank Lloyd Wright. It was like a child playing with models had planted them all over the grounds. Later, I asked Chet about it and he said that in some cases, certain guests would fulfill their remunerative responsibilities with commissions.

But at the start, it was just the walk and then Chet rapping three times on the door to a low, domed hut-like structure. The door would yawn open and Chet would nudge me inside into the darkness. The hut was filled with a gelatinous goo that sucked me in through some kind of peristalsis, pulling me deeper until the only slice of light disappeared as Chet shut the door behind me. For what seemed like hours—but who knows how long it was?—I would sit, suspended in the goo, and then a voice that was more like a vibration that my body just understood asked me questions. It was a lot like therapy, only as conducted by gelatinous goo that spoke to you in vibrations.

The questions might be something like, *What is your first memory?* And I would tell the goo all about when I was two, maybe three, and my mother and father and I were taking a train west to New Mexico for a family reunion and they had left me in the sleeper car, strapped down to the bed by some kind of netting so I wouldn't fall off as the train swayed. I remembered, more than anything, wanting to turn over from stomach to back, but I couldn't because the netting was pressing me down, keeping me safe, but also killing me because I so badly had to turn over.

I said that I told the goo these things, but it was more like I thought them and somehow the goo understood those thoughts.

And why do you remember this? the goo said/vibrated/communicated, after I shared my first memory.

"I don't know," I replied.

Because you were trapped.

I didn't really see it that way, but who was I to argue with the goo?

Another time it asked about my first kiss and I remembered Meredith Babcock, the lead in our fifth-grade musical. She had a solo, an Indian squaw singing about the white man's march over her tribal lands as they laid the track for their iron horse, the railroad. She was simultaneously heartbroken at the loss of her ancestral home and resigned to the march of progress, but you can't stop progress. Not with a song, anyway. At the end she's adopted by a robber baron and goes to Harvard and becomes a lawyer and sues the federal government for reparations.

We all wished her ill. We wanted to hear a crack in her perfect pitch. We wanted her to fuck up big-time. At lunch, we punched her sandwich flat inside the brown bag and told her she sucked. At recess, she'd climb to the top of the jungle gym equipment and read a book while we threw clods of mud at her. In the halls, we kicked her heels and threatened to push her down the stairs. Sometimes we'd chase her halfway home, shouting I don't remember. She'd throw her head back and call us "cretins." We had no idea what that meant.

Deformed idiot, the goo chimed in.

I thanked the goo for the information, and told him how I was going to be part of the tech crew, do the lights, but then one of the square dancers broke his arm at recess and I was all that was left to fill in. They said if I didn't do the dancing they wouldn't let me do the lights, so what the fuck was I supposed to do, that's like blackmail. There wasn't time to mimeograph new programs, but they said they would marker off my name on each and every single one, which even at the time seemed like bullshit, but I couldn't be sure, so I caved. I didn't even have time to learn the steps. I just wore some jackass checked shirt and blue kerchief around my neck and marched around. My partner had psoriasis, so instead of holding hands when we were supposed to hold hands she shoved her balled-up fist into my palm. In class she used to pick at the scabs underneath her desk and flick them to the carpet. At the end of the day you could see a whole collection down there. I don't think she even noticed she was doing it. Once, on a field trip, her mother was one of the chaperones, and the girl was picking away, and I saw her mother slap her hands and grunt at her.

"We must have been the fucking worst," I told the goo.

And is that who you kissed? The girl with the psoriasis?

"No," I told the goo. I told the goo that I had kissed Meredith Babcock, that it was after the play at a party at one of the parents' houses and somehow we were playing spin the bottle. We made sure not to invite her in as part of the circle, but she was watching while pretending not to care, and when it was my turn the bottle stopped in between two people and pointed at Meredith Babcock and she said, "Let's go."

We went to the backyard, behind a bush, the designated kissing spot. I told the goo that as I followed her I watched her long, straight black hair swish in perfect rhythm with her steps. We knelt behind the bushes and looked at each other. I was eleven and had no real interest in kissing anyone. Meredith Babcock looked at me and blinked several times and she said, "Do you think I was good?" and rather than saying anything, that's when I leaned in and kissed her and I hoped that was an appropriate answer.

And why do you remember that?

I didn't know.

Because of the wanting, the goo said.

We progressed like this through most of my life, dredging up things I wouldn't have figured I remembered, along with other things I'd never forget, like the incident with my father when we thought he'd stabbed me with the ski pole, or, what I'd done to my own son. The last question of the day was always, *What do you want?*

I replied with abstractions: "to be happy," "to be loved," and the goo must've been unhappy with these answers because it would quiver and surge and expel me out of the hut at Chet's feet and he would gather me up and take me home.

At the end of another unceremonious dumping, Chet and I started walking together back toward my quarters. It seemed as though my session had ended earlier than usual. Dusk had already fallen, but that day I could see some light still hanging across the horizon. Since the initial greeting ceremony I hadn't seen any of the other "guests."

"Where is everybody?" I asked Chet.

"We do a lot of testing while you're unconscious during the journey here, which allows us to put everyone at the Center on a customized program specifically designed to their particular body chemistry and biorhythms. To paraphrase, you're on your path, they're on theirs, sir."

"How am I doing?"

"Soon you will have a full review and reflection session, but for now, we all agree that you're progressing appropriately."

"Can I ask you a question, Chet?

"Anything, sir."

"Is this place real?"

"What do you mean, sir?"

"Am I dead? Am I dreaming?"

"What do you think, sir?"

"It just doesn't seem possible."

"Who's to say what's possible?" he replied. We'd arrived at my quarters. I could see my dinner waiting for me, steam coming off the plate. It looked like meat loaf.

"I dunno," I replied. "Not me."

"Why not you?" Chet said, clapping me on the back as he opened the door for me.

I went in and tucked into the food immediately. I thought it would be the best food I ever tasted and it was. While I ate, in my head I said, *Why not me? Why not me?*

29

Setbacks at every turn, but what his manager has come to tell him about is a magic word to celebrities, a onetime only get-out-of-jail (metaphorically speaking) free card available to each and every one of them. "It's not all bad," the funny man's manager says to him. He is speaking softly. His movements are slow and precise, like a technician defusing a bomb, which for all practical purposes is what the funny man is. He would like to explode and he knows in doing so, he could do some real damage, could fuck up a few lives, take a lot of people down with him. Free-floating rage, indeed.

"Comeback," the manager says.

"Comeback?"

The manager nods. "People love a good comeback story, something they can root for, something they can get behind, something grounded in real American values."

The funny man likes the sound of the word *comeback*. He was gone, but now he is back; missing, then found. *Come back, funny man! Come back!* He is also crushingly bored in this apartment with nothing to do except wait or not wait for the time to take the next pill. He asks the manager what the plan is.

"Small series of club dates, unannounced, but strategically leaked, handpicked reporter to follow you around and do a profile. We'll give the proceeds to charity, something for orphans or amputees, or orphan amputees. We're thinking a new haircut, something cleaner, low-maintenance. You're both humbled and grateful. If phase one works out, you'll go oversees and entertain the troops."

"Wait," the funny mans says. "Why can't I just do that first? That actually sounds kind of cool."

The manager looks at his shoes, knowing that his snippers are poised to cut the wrong wire.

Recognition dawns on the funny man's face. "Because they don't want me."

The manager half nods and half bows. He could've also said because they don't allow pill-popping addicts to fly on military transports, but he doesn't.

The funny man considers going back to the clubs. He enjoyed the clubs, he really did, the way they would be downright chilly when he'd arrive in the evening, but hot and sweaty with body heat by the time he left. He loved the proximity to the audience, seeing the jokes land and their faces open up with surprise. It begins to sound real good to the funny man, mostly.

"I can't do the thing anymore. I just can't," he says. There are not enough pills in the world to make it tolerable.

The manager's face brightens. "No, exactly, that's fine. That's not for the comeback. We save that for years down the road for the nostalgia tour; no, no, no, no, no, we've got to mothball that for now, make them miss it, exactly right. We're totally on the same wavelength here. No, we need a new thing."

"A new thing?"

"Yeah, something new, that they haven't seen before but still can't stop talking about."

"Fresh lightning," the funny man says.

"Exactly," the manager replies.

AND SO THE funny man sits around the apartment and tries to con-
jure a new thing. Because of the pills, the fully coherent hours of
the day are limited, which is a problem to begin with, and during
those times the funny man's mind usually remains entirely blank.
Later, when the pills have a firmer hold and his body feels like it
is encased in cotton candy, he will experience what he is sure is
an incredible burst of creativity, writing down dozens and dozens
of ideas in his notebook that unfortunately make little sense in the
light of the next day.

For awhile, he thinks that perhaps something involving ears is
promising. He has seen a special on the exotic travel channel where
they visit a tribe of dark, naked people who dangle progressively
heavier weights from their ears until their lobes are stretched practically to the ground. Apparently, in their culture, dangling earlobes
are like large breasts in America.

The funny man spends some time tugging on his ears and finds
them to be agreeably stretchy. Pulling them down while looking
in the mirror, he sees that he looks pretty funny and that people
may laugh at that.

But once out of the drug haze, he thinks through the ear thing
rationally. To pursue it would mean courting a kind of permanent disfigurement, like people who tattoo their faces. There's no
coming back from that kind of thing. Post–face tattoo the first
thing everybody thinks when they see you is, "oh yeah, that guy's
got a tattoo on his face," and it blots out just about everything
else. Everywhere in the world he would be stared at because of his
physical freakishness. Everywhere except the tribe of dark, naked
people, though even there, they would ask him why he is so pale
and his ears hang like a chick's.

So that won't work.

Screaming has been done more than once. Mumbling too.
As has accompanying one's own jokes by playing a guitar that is
smashed at the end of the set. (The same deal has even been pulled
with an accordion.) He is too clumsy for magic and he can't sing.
Singing poorly has been done, anyway. A comedy act involving
constrictor snakes could be fresh, but the damn things are awfully

unpredictable and having a python wrapped around your neck while you tell jokes seems like it might be a distraction.

It becomes increasingly clear to the funny man that everything has already been done. There are no more "things" to be had. On the one hand, this increases his already outsized self-esteem because it reinforces how difficult it was for him to develop the first thing even though it was actually demonstrated to him by an eighteen-month-old baby. On the other, it means there will be no comeback.

Finally, one day, to relieve stress and shake the cobwebs loose, he puts on some music and begins dancing around the apartment. He is not a good dancer, and knowing this, he emphasizes this fact, shaking his limbs arrhythmically, outside of the beat. He concentrates on one limb at a time, shaking it as crazily as he can before adding another limb and another until his whole body jitters in a million different directions. As he catches glimpses of himself in the apartment's reflective surfaces he begins to laugh. "Hey, that's pretty funny," he thinks.

He dances and dances. As evening turns to night, with the apartment lights on, he can see his reflection in the windows and he is now doing a move that involves mostly flopping a single leg around so it looks like the tendons and ligaments of his ankle have become unattached. The foot seems to be able to rotate the full 360 degrees, and even imperfectly captured in the windows, it cracks his shit up. When he tries to put pressure on the foot he realizes that the reason it looks like the ligaments and tendons have become detached is because they have. Rather than pointing straight as it should, his foot points at his other foot. There is pain, for sure. It is hilarious. It is grotesque. The funny man feels a flush of pride. *I am suffering for my art.*

With practice and some manipulation, the funny man finds that he is, more or less, able to put everything back into place before detaching it again and what he has now is a replicable comedy phenomenon. After a week of practice, he makes an appointment to show it to his agent.

He shows it to his agent.

"Whoa," the agent says at the end. The funny man is frowning as he tries to manipulate the foot back into proper alignment.

"What?"

"That's weird."

"Funny weird."

"No, weird weird, gross weird. Cover your face and turn away and don't even look at it through parted fingers weird."

"Really?"

"Hell, yeah. Doesn't it hurt?"

"Not as much as you'd think." The funny man looks down and flops his foot around a little more. He's found that if he does it for too long, the skin starts to turn blue, which *is* a little gross, but the flopping itself, hilarious.

His agent holds his hands in front of his face, not even parting his fingers, trying to block the view. "Don't ever do that in front of an audience."

"But it's good. I know it's good. You're reacting. Reaction is good."

"Laughter is good. Tears can even be good. Shock and horror is not good."

The funny man sits down and tugs his foot back into place so his agent will stop wincing. "What a wuss," the funny man thinks. "This is it," the funny man says. "This is the new thing. This is the comeback."

"I don't think so," the agent says. "I can't let you show that to the world."

Normally, the funny man would simply demand what he wants from his agent and he would get it, but in this case, he doesn't just want what he wants, he wants to be right. It is important that the agent agree, that the funny man be redeemed, not just coddled or handled. "Tell you what," the funny man says, "one show, a test, and then you'll see that I know what I'm talking about."

Relieved that the funny man is not going to take more flesh from his hide, the agent agrees.

30

A FTER ANOTHER TWO weeks at the center, following a relatively light day of treatment and a very gentle expulsion by
the goo, Chet breezed into my bungalow wearing civilian clothes,
a crew-neck sweater, white linen slacks, and loafers. He looked
ready for the post-regatta yacht club reception or a J. Crew cover.
He held a bundle of additional clothes covered in dry-cleaner cel-
lophane over his arm.

"You dress up nice, Chet," I said.

"Thank you, sir, and you will too." He held the clothes out to
me. They looked like carbon copies of what I wore for the press
junket on my first movie, strategically distressed jeans, white
button-up shirt, blue blazer. "Now, no time to waste, we've got
a party to go to."

By this time I'd pretty much figured out the WHC game and I
was wholly on board. If it was stock, I would've made it 100 percent of my portfolio. They did not *take* your memories, there was
no wiping clean of the slate. Rather, they *cleansed* your memories
and they returned sanitized, 99-percent free of psychic harm.

The theory was that over time, the damage accrued, memories piling up like plaque in an artery and at some point the blockage is complete and well . . . we're getting close to hearing about the kind of harm that can cause.

They seemed to be a custom job on each guest, though. Mitch Laver had had his ability to feel physical pain cleared, but when I banged my head on the shower door in my room, I saw stars like I would've any other time. I wasn't sure if all this was a good thing, but I couldn't deny that I was feeling better than I had in a long time, and that things I never should have forgiven myself for no longer seemed so terrible. Everything from the past was at arm's length, like a movie I'd seen once long ago starring someone else.

Just that morning, the goo's final question was, once again, "What do you want?" and I said, "To be with someone," and as I said it, I realized I meant it.

THE FOOD WAS familiar at the party: pureed meats on toast circles, cylinders of Parma ham skewered on toothpicks, cheese puffs. Apparently, even the Center uses the same caterers as everyone else. The faces were familiar as well since all of us were famous, and I'd seen most of them at Mr. Bob's speech. The party was at a kind of mansion-plantation-style house with a grand entryway featuring a double-helix staircase leading upward. We were ushered into several separate drawing rooms with fireplaces and overstuffed furniture frayed at the edges that had been pushed to the walls, exposing large, ornately woven throw rugs. Soft string music came from an indeterminate place, but it sounded live rather than recorded. Everyone was in regular clothes, not a tracksuit in sight, but not everyone was dressed up. Apparently, we had been outfitted to look our best. In some cases that best meant urban-prep casual (me), while in others it meant three-days-from-their-last-shower grunge.

Mingling was at a minimum and if they'd been as isolated as me, I understood why. The only person I'd spoken to on a semi-casual basis since I'd arrived was Chet. The unfamiliar faces were obviously the handlers, the handler/celebrity ratio pretty much being one to one. Without explanation, Chet had left me alone to nibble my canapé and sip from my goblet. (At the Center, the only glasses are goblets.) We all drank the omnipresent Center mead.

As I was about to go in search of a goblet refill, Chet reappeared with one in his hand. With his other hand, he was steering a very recognizable face toward me.

"I believe you two are acquainted," Chet said, exchanging my empty goblet for the full one.

"We got toasted together," I said, and she smiled.

"Wonderful," Chet said. "Perhaps you'd like to spend some time getting to better know each other." He disappeared as quickly as he'd arrived.

I took a good look at her for the first time. Of course I'd seen her face a million times before. She was in my magazines, on my television. Her face looked at me from my box of cereal and I could chew and stare at her like we were having breakfast together. A breakfast for champions. Like the rest of the world I'd followed her path from child athletic prodigy, in a grand slam final at age fourteen, to an early adulthood of as-yet-to-be-fulfilled promise. She was nineteen now, maybe twenty, and she looked it; fresh, healthy, unspoiled. She wore a sheer white top pulled just off her shoulders that emphasized the broadness of her back and straight black pants that emphasized the length of her legs. I remembered she was tall, but being close again, I saw she had a half inch on me. Her hair was down from its usual ponytail, which softened her face from the competitive mask we were all used to. She looked both beautiful and powerful. I felt like a used-up brute next to her, even with all my good work with the goo behind me.

I had no idea what to say. I knew everything about her already, didn't I? She'd arrived fully constructed, fully understood.

"Those are some shoulders you have there."

"Thank you," she replied, half twirling and smiling shyly. "They're what allow me to have such a devastating arsenal from both sides."

"You don't say."

"I did. I did say."

"Yeah, well, my material is killer," I said.

"My serve is a howitzer, the forehand a rifle."

"I've slayed entire audiences before."

"I also have a slice backhand that I sometimes use to drive a dagger into my opponents' hopes for victory."

"When I murder my jokes, I bomb."

"Does that happen often?" she asked.

"It didn't used to."

"When I'm tired, my serve occasionally misfires," she said.

"Does that happen often?" I said.

"Too often, apparently," she replied. She held out her hand. "I'm Bonnie, but everyone calls me Bunny, which I hate with a burning, passionate intensity of a thousand suns."

"Most everyone calls me a washed-up hack."

"Nice to meet you, Hack," she said, smiling.

"You too, Bunny."

We were starting to get to know each other, but I already felt out of words. We weren't allowed to ask, "What brings you here?" And besides, I pretty much already knew. She couldn't manage to win the big one. At a tour stop in Minsk she would be raising the trophy above her head at the end of a fortnight, but in the majors she would devastate her opponents as she moved through the draw until the finals, when she would fold in on herself and lose, often to obviously inferior players. One of the sports weeklies had put her on the cover, a crown askew on her head with the caption MISS RUNNER-UP.

Just as I was about to say, "nice meeting you" and go looking for my Chet life preserver, she placed her cool, dry hand in my sweaty one and said, "I think I saw a pool in the back."

31

I AM DEBATING whether or not to tell my therapist that this will be my final session. On the one hand, it will be a delicious feeling to let him know I am leaving. On the other, our relationship has been changed by his testimony, and even though I am assured that any fresh sessions are re-covered by the privileges of confidentiality, now that I have born witness to how he sees me, it can't help but color our present. The White Hot Center managed to hit my reset button, but I don't seem perfectly immune from fresh wounds.

Sitting in front of him this final time, I realize that I can't not talk about what I want to talk about.

"This is our last session, I'm afraid," I say.

"Are you fearing the outcome of the trial?" We are close to a verdict, close enough that it may come between now and our next scheduled session. It's just that I won't be around to hear it.

"Not at all."

"Then how could you know that this will be our last session?"

"Because I'm leaving."

"And where are you going?"

"I'm going back. She and I are going to be together." I think that I hear a sigh start to leak out of him, but he's too much of a pro to give in to that temptation. He knows that if he sighs there will be a fight over the sigh and that if he's doing his job we shouldn't be fighting over a sigh.

"I know what you're thinking," I say. I believe I do. Having seen him on the stand I now know how he takes what I tell him in therapy and filters it into what he calls the patient's "overall personal gestalt," in short, my modus operandi.

"And what's that?" he replies.

"You're thinking that I'm crazy."

"We've talked about this before," he says. There's an extra wrist flick at the end of the gesture, a dismissal.

When I returned from the White Hot Center, I told him everything. I thought, just maybe, as the therapist to fallen stars that he might have had other clients who had spent time at the WHC. We had one session between my return and the shooting, and I explained how I had been transformed, how I had been washed clean, how I had met someone and that from that moment forward I would be getting what I wanted, that I had been temporarily deflected, detoured by some failures, but that was over, my eyes were firmly fixed back on the prize, which was a lifetime of soul mating with an amazingly sensitive and nubile young woman and that after everything I'd been through, that maybe, just maybe, I deserved it.

I didn't necessarily yet believe that last part at the time, but he pushed my buttons.

"And where is this place?" he says.

"I told you, I don't know."

"And how did you get there?"

"I told you before, two male models kidnapped me."

He responds with the gesture. He is testing me for consistency in my story.

"Two male models kidnapped me, they tranquilized me and when I woke up I was on a boat. For several weeks I spent my days encased in goo sharing all of my memories, many of the same things I've told you over the last several years, the only difference being after I told these things to the goo I felt better, whereas when I tell them to you, I feel like I might be the lowliest shit on the planet, and if you don't wipe that look off your face, I may leap across the room and smack you."

He doesn't flinch. He knows I'm not going to do anything. I hate him for knowing these things. "I wish you could see what I see," he says.

"And what's that?"

"I see somebody who should be working to integrate his life but instead remains rooted in a fantasy."

"How's that?"

"Well, for one, we both know you didn't go anywhere."

"And how do we know that?" I say.

"Because you are the sort of person who is kept track of and no one saw you leave your apartment. Because there is no such place like the one you describe. Because people can't be hit in the face with a baseball and not experience broken bones. Because when people die, they stay dead. I could go on, but why should we bother?"

"If I didn't go anywhere, how did I kick the drugs?"

"Is that what you think happened?"

There is a long silence at the end of which I say, "I'm not going to miss you."

"I have to ask," he says, "are you going to do something foolish?"

"I'm sure you'd think so."

He shakes his head like a pitcher waving off the catcher's signs. "That was my fault. I should've been more clear. You're not going to harm yourself, are you?"

"Of course not."

He stands up from his chair. Our time is up. Somehow he knows, even though he never looks at a watch or a clock. "Then I look forward to seeing you next week."

Maybe it's better this way. He'll be as surprised as anyone, my little bit of revenge for him believing he knows me so well. We shake and on the way out I nod at the receptionist and she tells me to have a wonderful day as she picks up the phone to place the call that will give me exactly twenty-four minutes to be back inside my apartment. I hit the streets and put on my sunglasses and pull a cap out of my pocket and yank it down over my head and even though everybody knows me, as I walk home, nobody recognizes me.

32

THERE WAS A pool in the back, with a patio empty of people and a view that went straight to the ocean. The pool was shaped like a dolphin with blue tiles lining the sides and bottom. The water was perfectly clear. As she approached the ledge she dropped her slacks and stripped off her top, revealing the athletic underwear beneath. With three skips and a double-footed jump she launched herself gracefully into the water at the dorsal fin before swimming underwater to the snout and surfacing, her hair parted perfectly down the middle and slicked to the sides of her head.

As she treaded water her eyes sparkled, beckoning. Her body appeared to be built for movement, the muscles working in efficient conjunction, while I had the body of a nearly middle-aged stand-up comedian. I imagined that I was buoyant, but I was definitely not a strong swimmer. In fact, I wasn't sure I could swim at all unless swimming is defined simply as not drowning. The one time I tried for real, things did not go well. Though there were extenuating circumstances. I had told it to the goo, my answer for its question of *What was a time when you thought you were going to die?*

"Jump in," she called. On her back she frog-kicked to the ledge and rested there in the water, her arms outstretched along the sides.

When I was a freshman in high school, swimming was required as part of the physical education curriculum. The class was coed, the suits school-issued, and it was a kind of hell.

The rationale for the whole enterprise was solid, the swimming a backstop against the flagging fitness of my generation, the first weaned on television and video games. Our thumbs were mighty, but our muscles were flabby. To allow the students to bring their own swimwear would be to risk embarrassment for the disadvantaged, and coeducation would show that we were the same, boys and girls, learning together, even as our morphing bodies most definitely highlighted the differences.

Between classes, the school-issued suits moldered in a soggy cardboard box, a dank pile of failing purple Lycra. They were neither shorts nor Speedos, rather a kind of one-size-sort-of-fits-some hybrid with a tie at the waist and elastic meant to snug up against the legs and seat. The daily laundering had left the fabric pilled and the elastic brittle and fried, making the overall appearance more diaper than swimsuit. Once in the pool, they instantly filled with water, ballooning in the crotch, making what once looked merely ridiculous, absurd.

At least I was in the same boat with the rest of my pale, sunken-chested male classmates yet to experience any of the benefits of puberty: the increased height, mature musculature, doughy faces hardening into chiseled manliness. No, this curse had visited only its worst parts on us, cracking voices, wispy, embarrassing hairs in the pits—soft as down, rather than the coarse curlies of manhood—that nonetheless trapped the smell of cabbaged cooked in iodine after any kind of exertion. My mother had often half-jokingly remarked that she thought teenagers should be locked up, and looking at us furtively changing in the locker room, terrified that someone else might see our pathetic junk, I was inclined to agree.

Somewhat buoyed by the strength of numbers, I exited the locker room to the pool area, towel clutched around my midsection, hiding as much of the suit and my ghostly, hairless legs as possible. The vast majority of the girls sat in street clothes on benches that ran the length of the pool, clutching excuse notes cadged from sympathetic gynecologists that testified to urinary tract infections, the inopportune coincidence of "monthly flow" or other swimming-prohibited ailments. Oh, how I hated them.

I had splashed around at the municipal pool once or twice growing up but had never exactly "swam" before. A pile of kickboards massed at one end of the pool buoyed my spirits. Clinging to the Styrofoam wedge and kicking around for awhile seemed do-able. Certainly the school feared lawsuits. Nobody would be drowned or humiliated. Nobody would be drowned, anyway.

I skirted far enough away from the pool edge to ensure no inopportune slips into the water and everything looked acceptable until I saw Chris Darntoff moving toward me. Unlike the rest of us, puberty had greeted Darntoff both early and quickly, leaving broad, rounded muscles at the shoulders, and a small patch of hair in the cleft between his pectorals. In the locker room, Darntoff would stand naked and make a show flexing his muscles in the mirror, performance as intimidation in front of his as-yet-to-be-endowed classmates. As Darntoff approached, he bunched his hand into a fist, being careful to extend the middle knuckle into a slightly higher peak. Arm cocked back, he drove the fist, pointed knuckle first, into my left shoulder.

"Bam!" Darntoff said, drawing his fist back, and spreading his legs, karate-movie style. "Got ya."

Knowing that a display of weakness meant death, I grinned as I moved all the way past Darntoff. Oh, it hurt, though mostly the arm was numb, neurons shutting down in defense of what they perceived to be a severe injury, but I could not betray this hurt, which would be to beg for a repeat visit from Chris Darntoff's knuckle. This was not abuse, but a rite of passage, a form of bonding, of boys just kidding around.

The sound of a coach's whistle echoed through the pool and Mr. DeFranchschi started yelling. "All right, let's see what we got, here," he said. "Two lines, one boys, the other girls. Swim test time. On each whistle the pair at the front dive in and swim to the other side. I will be judging your swimming proficiency as a benchmark against later progress." He stood in his athletic-department collared shirt, arms crossed, the pit stains creeping out toward his chest. Another whistle blast and we lined up at one end of the twenty-five-yard pool. The other end stretched into the distance and I knew I would never reach it. At least we were starting in the deep end, so if I could make it two-thirds of the way, I could stand and walk my way in.

My arm had shifted from numbness to violent tingling, but still it dangled, wasted and useless. I jockeyed for the final position in the back and hoped for the feeling to return. It didn't.

At the ledge, Coach D. tweeted the whistle, and by reflex I jumped in. (There would be no diving for this guy.) As I surfaced, I heard a laugh go up from some of the swimmers who had already finished. I figured my best and only chance was to start strong, kicking with as much might as I could muster while flailing forward with my one usable arm. Launching into my stroke, I heard Coach D. yell from behind me.

"For the love of god, son, stop screwing around."

But I was not screwing around. I was trying to keep from sinking to the bottom. I quickly become exhausted, swimming in circles thanks to my one-armed stroke. My brain matter swirled around my skull like a tornado and I heard sizzling noises like the water was boiling around me. Coach D. got madder and madder, blasting the whistle and screaming at me at the top of his lungs to cut the crap. I thrashed for everything I was worth and wondered if I stopped and sank if someone would come get me. Everyone else had finished their lap and was poolside, laughing. Even the girls with the excuses looked up from their nails and paperbacks and joined in. Finally, on one of my loops I got close enough to the edge to grab on with my one working hand and Coach D. pounced and hauled me out of the water, hands under my arms, the suit dripping like a soiled diaper. My breath came in heaves. I felt like I'd swallowed half the pool.

"All right, funny guy!" he yelled. "You're done! Hit the showers!" As I shuffled my way to the locker room, Chris Darntoff extended his hand and slapped me five.

"Dude, that was hilarious," he said.

AND SO I recalled it in that moment as she beckoned me from her position at the tip of the dolphin's nose, raising a leg above the surface and wiggling her toes at me, her lovely calf flexing, but unlike my time with the goo when I could feel my heart pound as I reexperienced the memory, this time it's just something not very important that happened a long time ago.

I have to traverse two-thirds of the pool's torso to reach her. It seems very do-able. I hop on one foot as I yank off my shoes and socks and drop my pants, giving thanks for Chet's taste in boxer shorts. I suck in my gut as I strip off my shirt and dive—yes, dive in—the bottom rushing toward me before I arc upwards and dog-paddle with my head above water toward her, undignified, but undoubtedly swimming. With each stroke she grows closer. I swallow a mouthful that burns in my nasal passages and she briefly goes out of focus, but I endure, and there she is, right in front of me, treading water with very little effort.

"You made it," she says. Her legs brush against mine under the water. I have a desire to put my hand on her waist and pull her toward me, so I do. She does not resist.

"Beware, I'm troubled," she says. She smoothes her hand over the stilled surface of the water.

"Aren't we all?" I place my other hand on top of hers. I have never been so bold in my previous life. My ex-wife and I were like two atoms colliding, heedless of what was coming until the moment of impact, or electrons combining. The women on the road were groupie dodgeball. Meredith Babcock propositioned me.

Our fingers twine and she pulls me toward her. Here is a face that is so familiar, but it is like I'm seeing it for the first time.

"I've never been kissed," she says.

"Really?"

I think she might blush. "I've had other priorities."

"I see," I say.

She smothers her face in her palms and then tilts her head up and shouts, "I'm a freak!" and then looks at me and says it so sadly that I swear I feel it in my heart. "I'm a freak." I want to deny it, to bat it away, but we both know she's right and that she's not just describing herself. I have no words, so I lean in very slowly in an effort to remedy the situation. As I approach her eyes close, and I shut mine. Our lips brush . . .

AND THEN CHET showed up. "There you are," he said, his voice filled with false cheer. He held a large towel with the phoenix stitched into it up with arms extended like he wanted to give someone a hug. "I'm afraid the party is over for us. Big day tomorrow."

"Go away, Chet," I said, trying to sound as threatening as possible. I hovered millimeters from Bonnie's face. Her breathing came out in little huffs.

His voice came back hard in a way I hadn't heard before. "So sorry, sir, but it *is* time to go."

Bonnie looked at me and shrugged and ducked underneath my arm and swam a powerful freestyle toward the tail, the water frothing behind her kick. I got out of the pool and Chet encircled me with the towel. He carried my clothes for me as we made our way back to the bungalow.

"I have a question, Chet," I said.

"Yes, sir?"

"Do they teach you about cock-blocking on this island?"

"I don't believe I understand your meaning."

"Never mind, I've got another question."

"What's that, sir?"

"When this is all over, am I supposed to tip you?" We'd arrived at the door to my bungalow. Some nights he stayed and played chess with me, but I was not inviting him inside this time.

"Gratuities are always appreciated, but not expected," he replied. "Sleep well."

In our dreams we are always approaching our goals, only to have our brains snatch us away to some other, unconnected story, and this is what that felt like. After Chet left, I lay in my bed and told myself that while it seemed like a dream, it was not a dream.

Of course, I now recognize the calculation in everything, the integration with everything else I was undergoing as part of the treatment at the Center, but as I slipped into my impossibly soft sheets, eased into sleep by an ambient-noise machine perfectly suited to my aural needs, I cursed that fucker. My only desire was to get my hands on Chet and fuck him up, but good.

33

T HE AUDIENCE IS curious, ready, leaning forward in their seats.
This is back at the club where it all started. The funny man
has not been here in a long time and yet it is unchanged, except that
someone has cleaved the big table that used to sit in the middle of
dressing room and collect beer bottles in two and the two halves
have been crudely fastened back together with two-by-fours nailed
like railroad tracks across the top. He thinks maybe he should be
a dude and spring for a new table. He does not know any of the
performers, but it's clear they are in awe of him. Sure, he's had
his setbacks, but they would kill for the opportunity to rise high
enough to fail so spectacularly as him. No one notices if you fall
out a first-story window.

A woman from the entertainment magazine that dabbles in
politics has been following him around for three straight days and
she stands in the corner of the backstage room and winks at him
when he looks at her. Since she has begun her surveillance, the
funny man has been taking pains to appear grounded, grateful for
the opportunity to perform again, just as his agent and manager

have suggested. He removed the pills from his medicine cabinet because he knew she would snoop there, and indeed, not five minutes after arriving she asked if she could use "the little girl's room." It amazes the funny man how predictable it all is, but this is to his advantage. Knowing what's to happen ahead of time means it's all easy to prepare for. The easiest way to dispose of the pills so they wouldn't be discovered was to take them, so that's what he did and after they kicked in he wondered why this hadn't been his recommended dosage all along.

The woman is young, like right out of journalism school, and she has that green smell about her. She is tiny and dark, with short hair sculpted into a soft fin across the top of her head. She wears black exclusively. Her ears are small and pointed. She looks like an elf as raised and outfitted by eighties new wave musicians. She marvels at the view in his apartment, like she's never seen such a thing before. She uses words like *honor* and *privilege* when she talks about this particular assignment. She has been asking a lot of questions and the funny man can't remember all his answers, but he's sure he's doing fine. He's practically a professional talker at this point. He's lost track of how many questions he's been asked and therefore answered at this point in his career. She's writing lots of things down and the recorder seems to often need fresh cassettes. The funny man imagines it will be a very long article, maybe even the cover. He may or may not have slept with her. There is a feeling there and snippets of images: small, upturned breasts, a trail of fuzz heading down from her belly button that he would not have noticed if he hadn't seen her naked, but while he sleeps hard on the pills, the sleep comes with extremely vivid dreams and it gets hard to tell them apart from reality.

These vivid dreams are still another side benefit of the pills that no one explained to him before.

When it is the funny man's turn to go on stage, he takes his place behind the audience and as the previous performer introduces him he can hear the catch in the guy's throat. It's probably the biggest thing that ever happened to him, introducing the funny man. The funny man has timed the ingestion of the pills perfectly. His head is both soft and clear, his gaze warm and sharp. His performance is sure to be enhanced. There will be piper paying later, usually in the form of sweating and the shits, but the funny man is all about sacrifice, now that he knows what you get for it.

The welcoming applause is eager, aggressive, the claps a little slow, but loud. They have a "you better show us something" quality, and boy, will he. He's shown them a lot in his life and miracle of miracles, he has even more. How is this possible? It is possible because everything is possible . . . for him.

Before the funny man even says thanks for his welcome, he quickly fakes shoving his hand in his mouth and then gives his widest smile and shakes his finger and there's a lot of laughter because everyone is in on that particular joke. It's a good start, just as he planned.

Most of the jokes are oblique references to his recent troubles, self-deprecating and they land with some force and regularity. Often the setups get bigger laughs than the punchlines.

I haven't been up to much lately . . .

The jokes themselves aren't particularly important, though. They are merely the setup for the new thing. It is like a boxing match. No one expects to knock a guy out with body blows, but you need to throw some shots there to get him to drop his hands.

"So, I've been thinking," the funny man says, "that this comedy business just isn't for me." He pauses to allow the audience to boo. "No, seriously, I'm done with it, that's what I've come here tonight to tell you all. For me, the joke's over." More booing, only lighter this time. He seems very serious, like he's deciding to pack it in right in front of them.

"However!" the funny man shouts, lifting a finger into the air to signal attention. "What I am going to do, is dance!" At this cue, the music starts over the public address system and the funny man kicks into his routine where he shakes only one part of his body at a given time. With practice he's gotten really good at it, his whole body entirely still, save his arm from the elbow down, or his head from the neck up. He can even wiggle his ears and move his hair back and forth in such a way that he looks like he's wearing a wig. That took some practice.

At first, the laughter is tentative, but it progressively grows in volume and intensity and some are even clapping along with the music and whooping and the funny man feels fucking great, remembering what it's like to bask in such love. Colors swirl in his vision as he now whips his head back and forth like he might unhinge his skull, which is not planned, but sometime the greatest comedy comes from accidents.

He knows now is the time to strike, now is the time to show them what he has, and he goes still except for his leg, which begins to twitch wildly, and with a practiced flick he is able to disengage the tendons and ligaments that hold his foot at the ankle and he flops that fucker around like nobody's business, really flaps it around better than he ever has before, bouncing it off the stage as it twirls almost 360 degrees, and that's when the cheering turns to horrified screaming.

A woman in the front row yells, "Oh, my god!" and points at the foot and this causes everyone else to look, which is what the funny man was going for, but soon there is the sound of glass breaking as the woman in the front row falls into a dead faint and takes out the cocktail table with her. From somewhere in the back a keening wail like a harpooned seal rises in intensity. Other people appear to be fainting as well, or holding back their hurl with hands over mouths, and still others scramble for the exits. His last image is of a young couple about the age he was when he first met his now ex-wife. They are at a table, a couple of rows deep and all around them is chaos, a panicky stampede, but the young man has wrapped his arm around the young woman's shoulder and with his free hand, he covers her face by pulling it to his chest. "They're going to make it," the funny man thinks.

As the music track ends, the funny man stands on stage under the spotlight, his foot canted almost backwards. In front of him is wreckage. He hurts, but not from the foot.

34

LUCKY FOR HIM, I did not see Chet the next day, because my breakfast tray was brought in by Mr. Bob himself, the first time I'd seen him since the welcoming reception. He wore the same pristine white tracksuit and as he placed my tray on the table next to my bed a couple of splashes of juice hit it but appeared to vaporize on contact.

"Neat, huh?" Mr. Bob said, smiling. He moved to the French doors that led out on to a veranda and threw the curtains open. Like every other day at the WHC, perfect sunlight streamed through. "Want to try something else?" Mr. Bob gestured at the tray. I picked up a small jar of raspberry jam and twisted off the top. Mr. Bob nodded, giving assent. I spooned out some jam and flicked it toward Mr. Bob's chest. It should've been a direct hit, but the fabric was as brilliantly white as ever.

"I bet that saves on dry cleaning," I said.

Mr. Bob laughed way louder than anyone should have. "Ha! Ha! Ha! You *are* a funny man, just like they said."

I was about to say, "To what do I owe the pleasure?" when he made his way over to the side of my bed and sat like he was going to read me a nighttime story. "You owe the pleasure to the fact that it is time for your progress report and diagnosis."

"Diagnosis?" I said. "I didn't know I was sick."

"Of course you did," Mr. Bob said, "but we all agree you're getting better."

"That's good," I replied. I squirmed under the sheets; he'd semi-trapped me with his weight.

"It's very good," he said, "and now that we know what's going on, we'll do even better. Would you like to hear what we're thinking?"

"Sure, of course."

"Wonderful," he said, smiling with his lips, but not his eyes. "You've had some truly remarkable successes in your career, amazing things, but one trend we have noticed is that they have just sort of happened. Now, I'm not saying they would have happened to anybody, but to some degree it seems like they *could* have happened to anybody. This is not unusual in the grand scheme of things, but for someone so famous as you, it's very, very rare. We think this probably also explains your reversal of fortunes. You are simply prone to being buffeted around, if you will. Sometimes the buffeting nudges you skyward, while other times it hurls you to the ground."

He stood up and I took advantage to throw off the covers and sit on the side of the bed. "But you are changing here, that is clear," he continued. "You are coming to understand the power of desire, true desire, focused desire. For instance, I believe last night you had some unpleasant thoughts towards Chester."

"I wanted to kick his teeth in."

"And why didn't you?"

"It didn't seem like the right thing to do."

"Ah!" Mr. Bob said, pointing at the ceiling like he'd made a big discovery. "This all depends on what your definition of 'right' is, does it not?"

"I suppose," I said.

Mr. Bob came over and removed the covering from my plate on the tray, revealing a perfect egg-white omelet, fresh fruit, and synthetic bacon. "And right now, you're thinking that you might like to take a poke at me, even, yes?"

I wasn't thinking that, or at least I didn't know I was thinking that until he said something, at which point an image of me flattening his pointed nose popped into my head. "Yes."

"And why don't you?" He was close enough that I could've.

"I guess I don't really want to, or maybe it's that I don't need to."

He stepped away, hands clasped behind his back. "Yes, you see it now. We make our own right, our own wrong. You are in charge. Wonderful, isn't it? Now, go ahead," he said.

"Go ahead, what?"

"Ask your question?"

"What question?"

"About Ms. Tisdale. If you did not care, you would not want to have strangled Chester."

"Okay," I said. "How's she doing?"

Mr. Bob began pacing, like it was the movement that helped bring forth the answers. "Ms. Tisdale is an interesting case. The opposite of you in some ways. She has no lack of desire or direction in her. It may be that she simply has too much, that it is uncontainable. This is a significant power, but power that cannot be controlled is ultimately harmful."

"Actually," I said, "I was just wondering if she enjoyed herself last night."

Bob seemed pleased at this response, like I had passed some kind of test.

"You will have the chance, I am sure," he said, "to ask her for yourself. Enjoy your breakfast, and the rest of your stay here at the White Hot Center."

He bowed, pivoted, and left the bungalow. I never saw him again. What he left behind was the knowledge that for the first time in a long time I cared about something again, that I was looking forward to what was next.

I wanted something.

35

IT TURNS OUT that the young reporter is beyond ambitious, a real journalistic succubus ready to drain the fame from others to feed her own and she has feasted on the remainder of the funny man's career. It is scraps, but it is something. She recognizes that a march to the top of the mountain requires stepping over some bodies along the way and he is the first of presumably many. Turns out he does make the cover, the photo a shot from the reporter's cell phone when the funny man had fallen asleep mid-question. His jaw hangs, insensate. One hand rests on his little belly like he's waiting for the fetus to kick. His beard is patchy and hair greasy. The headline says WHEN WILL HE STOP FALLING? When the funny man sees it he calls his agent and manager and asks why no one told him that he looks like a destitute wreck.

"We thought it was part of the new look," they say. "It can be hard to tell."

His wife has, upon reading the article, understandably made a motion to return to court in order to modify the custody agreement to prevent any unsupervised visits with the boy. Thanks to the funny man's increasing unreliability, she has slowly whittled down the alone time between father and son, but the wheels of justice do not turn fast enough this time and the funny man is not moved by her pleading and crying. He has some rights left and he is going to exercise them. If rights are not exercised, they get flabby. Besides, he has given her some extra time by arriving two hours behind schedule.

He has added a patch to the pills. There are pills with the same pharmacological properties of this patch, but the patch is a superior delivery system in that it allows for a slow, steady release, and is always doing the work, whether the funny man is conscious or not. Sadly, the new thing has led to a chronic and intractable pain that only the patch can move to a rear burner (though never extinguish). There are some side effects, like how each of his eyes appears to be focused on something different, and the time losses, the inexplicable blanks in his day where he was one place and then suddenly finds himself in another. Unsettling, but manageable.

But he is quite obviously functional. If he were not functional how could he have navigated to the godforsaken suburbs that are the likely cause of his personal rot? The roots of his marriage's dissolution can be traced to the decision to leave the city for these suburbs. Nay, the decline of the entire nation may be lain at the feet of these suburbs. Before the exodus to the suburbs, their omnipresent space, the demands of all that emptiness.

If he were nonfunctioning, could he carry on a civil conversation with Pilar, who holds the boy's shoulders in her unyielding talons as the boy stands with his back to her on the doorway's precipice? Would he shout, "I'll have him back tomorrow by six!" into the living room where he can hear his ex-wife sobbing if he were not of sound mind and body?

And the car seat. Would a man who, in the words of the so-called journalist, "appears willing to chuck every and anything out the window at a moment's notice," take the time and care necessary to transfer the car seat to the rear of his vehicle? That shit is unbearably complicated and it doesn't really make sense to him why the boy still needs a car seat, surely he's far too large, but no, his ex-wife says, until they're blah-blah height, and blah-blah weight, they need a seat and you don't ever let him sit in front, do you?

He has. He has done this, but only because it is easier to talk to the boy this way. In the back he is constantly looking in the rearview for reactions and responses, and in the front, they can actually talk. Besides, the kid gets a real kick out of it. Grown-up stuff. There's air bags if there's an accident, but there won't be. When they're at the apartment, he and the boy have mostly been playing video games where they team up to kill creatures that have been grievously harmed by a release of an uncontrollable virus that makes them drool green viscous liquid out of their grossly meta-morphosed insectoid mandibles and shoot beams from plasma gun hands. What a disease this is! There's not much to talk about in these situations beyond, "kill 'em!" and "watch out!" so being able to talk in the car is a necessity. The boy does most of the killing, but the funny man tries to do his part. At first, the funny man had compunctions. After all, the creatures seemed to be the victims in the scenario, undeserving of such a terrible affliction, but then he noticed their deaths (by Gatling gun or missile launcher) were accompanied by a kind of sighing noise that sounded like relief.

"But the air bags can kill him!" the funny man's wife has shrieked. Who is the unreasonable one with this kind of talk? Air bags are giant pillows. Has anyone ever been killed in a pillow fight? But because Pilar is there watching, always watching, he will install the seat and cinch it down with all its buckles and straps and give two big thumbs-up, which is the signal for Pilar to release the boy from her grip so the boy can walk toward him with his sad little overnight bag clutched in both hands.

Safely, very safely, the funny man drives his boy back to the city. This visit is going to be different than the video game and order-in dinner festivals of recent vintage. The funny man has recently begun worrying about the corrosive effect suburban life may be having on his boy. The boy is still young, but he's begin-ning to get that doughy, fat-kid look. He seems uninterested in sports other than video-game killing. When they visit the judge next time, the funny man does not expect things to go well on the visitation-rules front, but he will instruct his lawyer to go fucking hard at his wife over the whole DVD-player-in-the-headrest-of-the-car issue. He will insist on a soccer league, if not something cooler, hockey or lacrosse.

Today, the funny man is going to show him the city, the real city, put a little grit under the boy's fingernails. The funny man was also raised in a suburb, but it was different back then. Back then kids rode their bikes without helmets and blew up dog shit with firecrackers. Nowadays a suburban kid would find a brick of unexploded ladyfingers and turn it in to the cops. He will not let his kid become one of *them*. He wants his kid to be a ringleader. The kids other kids look at and say, "I can't believe he did that."

The funny man has the whole program mapped out. First, he will show him the city, bit by bit, and then when he is ready he will have his son take the subway by himself and he will see that in spite of what the suburban ninnies of the world think, there isn't a child molester waiting on every corner to snatch you up and take your innocence, as if that's worth anything anyway.

The first stop is going to be a diner, a real diner, not one of the corporate chain places with the shiny and gunkless mini-jukeboxes at the booths stuffed with music that doesn't belong on a jukebox. The funny man and his boy will sit at the counter and the funny man will explain the differences, how the yellowed porcelain of the funny man's coffee cup reflects history and tradition, what the varicose veins on the waitress mean, why those are badges of honor, why it's important that you can see into the kitchen if you look through the pass-through. That the boy's mother used to work in a place like this not long after he was born, if you can believe that.

Because the boy is in the back and hard to see, the conversation as they head toward the city is mediocre to poor, monosyllabic answers to the funny man's closed-ended questions about the status of school, his friends, his history diorama. The funny man apologizes for being late and in the rearview he can see the boy shrug.

The funny man was late because it took a few stops to find a pharmacy that would fill a script. His work on the slip's effective refill date was pretty fucking convincing, so he had to take the first three places at their words that their supplies were out, none of which would have been a problem if the doctor had just accepted the fact that he'd accidentally flushed his whole supply of patches down the toilet. At the fourth place a cop was browsing in the magazine aisle, so that was out. At the fifth place a teenager with a hoop pierced through her nose like a bull's ring, chewing on a fist-sized wad of gum, barely glanced at the thing before shuffling back to the aisles to look for the stuff. The funny man stared back at himself from the magazine cover in a wire rack on the counter. He was counting the days until the next issue when that wouldn't happen anymore. He would've applied the fresh patch immediately upon getting back to the car, but he was already late and he'd found that if he waited some, until the pain began to near its peak, the relief from the patch, the warmth and goodness that spread through his body, was quite wonderful. He wasn't going to slap one on in front of Pilar, that's for sure, and he pretty much figured they could get back to the city before it really became dire.

But the fucking traffic in the tunnel. It must be a parade, always a parade, one ethnicity or another deciding to announce their unique specialness by snarling traffic for hours. The funny man accepts people of all creeds and colors, so why can't they accept themselves and stop marching around demanding things, declaring how proud of themselves they are? *Pride goeth before the fall*, he wants to shout, and maybe he does, because the boy flinches.

The pain is starting to spike with the feeling that the funny man would just as soon saw his foot off with a vegetable peeler as keep it around and this traffic isn't going to loosen any time soon. Fortunately, he's got his little pal who shares half his DNA with him.

"Hey, buddy," the funny man says. "See that bag back there somewhere?"

"Yeah."

"Could you hand it to Daddy?"

"It's on the floor."

"Fantastic, pal. Reach down and grab it and hand it to Daddy."

"I can't."

"Sure you can, pal. Just unbuckle and grab it."

"I'm not allowed."

"I'm saying it's okay, so just go ahead and unbuckle and grab it. Look, we're hardly moving, it'll be fine."

"No, Mom says."

Someday he will remind the boy of this conversation, of the depth of betrayal to all of manhood in general and his father in particular, but right now, he just needs that bag, so spotting a sliver of an opening he jets from the middle lane to the right and then to the shoulder, which is no shoulder at all, but half a lane for the 'tards who walk or bicycle.

The funnyman unbuckles his belt and turns and reaches blindly for the floor on the backseat, but his hand brushes only carpet. The boy looks out the window at the angry faces of the drivers of the cars that must weave around them.

"Am I close?" the funny man asks.

"I don't see it anymore," the boy says.

The funny man sits forward and gropes under the front seat and he feels like he can sense the plastic bag just past his reach but he cannot contort himself enough to reach it and the ankle/foot is really screaming now. It is like in the horror movies where the demon's jaw becomes unhinged and its screams really bellow before it swallows its victim entirely. The ankle/foot is threatening to engulf him. Getting out the driver's side is a no-go because the cars are passing millimeters from the door and he wouldn't actually blame them if they tried to take him out, so he crawls across the front and wedges the door open maybe eight inches since he's so close to the barrier, and after much painful effort manages to wriggle out, face first and to the ground.

He crawls. He crawls past the rear door and opens it and tries to reach inside, draping himself across the boy who is still strapped in his seat in the middle and it's impossible to reach to even the floor, let alone under the seat.

"Out," he says to the boy, flicking the buckles open.

"What?"

"Out. Out. Get out, I need to get in there and I can't, so get out."

The boy looks at the gap in the door doubtfully. As the boy unbuckles fully, the funny man grabs him under the arms and puts him on the car's roof.

"Pull your legs up," he says to the boy. "I need to get in there."

Face pressed deep into the scratchy car carpet is no place the funny man wants to be. He's been negligent in the upkeep and crusty bits of the boy's road snacks leave imprints on his cheek. But he perseveres. The funny man jams his shoulder into the seat back, inching it millimeters forward until there is enough room and his hand closes around one of the bag's loops. Carefully, carefully, so as not to spill the contents, he hauls it back. When the bag is fully freed from under the seat he pauses for a moment and smiles and focuses on the pain. It is at a crescendo, the woodwinds and brass and percussion sections all working at maximum intensity, total cacophony, but one of the best parts, almost better than the moment of salvation, is to know that salvation is at hand, and it is, right under his hand. Above the traffic noise and honking and shouting, and the fog of carbon dioxide exhaust, music fills the funny man's head, a marching band playing just for him.

36

I FEEL SORRY for the sheriff's deputy who must testify about the incident in the tunnel. I think we all do. In many ways he is the headliner, the one we've all been waiting for, and he appears temperamentally unsuited to the task, out of his element and shy. Since my plan has formed and taken shape and I've begun the implementation, I've been viewing my trial differently, half-a-step removed, not divorced from my reality, not like the pills, or how I felt at the Center and prior to the shooting and my arrest, but not a full part of it either. Maybe it's me remembering the teachings from the Center, temporarily abandoned in the postarrest-and-start-of-the-trial panic, but I tend to think it's because I now believe that what I intend to do, what I most desire, is going to come true.

Bonnie is fulfilling her part of the equation. After the coded messages started to arrive, her game soared out of its lovesick trough, as she slid through the clay at Roland Garros for her first major ever. The sports weekly called her a champion, and I flushed with pride. In the pictures she never looked *too* pleased. Wimbledon is next and if all goes well there, we are on target.

The sheriff's deputy holds his wide-brimmed hat in his hands as he takes the stand. His hair is cut so close he looks bald. He looks solid in his formal uniform, reassuring, the kind of law enforcement you'd be glad to see if you were in trouble, yet not too intimidating when he pulls you over for that broken taillight. As he tells us at the outset of his testimony, it was a fluke that he was even there that day, not being part of the city or even county police. He plies his trade where the roads are two lanes and bracketed by wheat and soybeans. He was going to a regional conference, a chance to exchange techniques and strategies with other law enforcers and eat some rubber chicken dinners. They had discount tickets to some midweek theater. The sheriff's deputy drove his cruiser rather than flying because he wasn't keen on planes and it would save a little money. The county he worked for was the kind of place where sheriff's deputies take their cruisers home with them because even when they're not on duty, they're on duty. He wasn't even going to go this time, but changed his mind because he was scheduled to get a citation at the conference for his organizing a youth basketball program in the town where he worked. The chain of choices that led him to that moment is almost endless.

Clearly, he never expected this to happen to him, and on the stand he looks a little shell-shocked. Barry is as impassive as ever, and the prosecutor jitters, but without purpose or focus. From his perspective, there's apparently nothing to object to since the sum total of our defense has been to demonstrate the bottomless depths of my horribleness. If he has worked out Barry's angle, he must be resigned to whatever is going to happen.

First we see the video in its uncut, grainy, black-and-white glory. Out of instinct the deputy flicked his dash camera on, and as he hit his flashers and weaved closer, the horror of the moment became apparent. It's likely that everyone in the jury has seen it before, but in the courtroom it takes on a different gravity. The screen is large, the video enhanced as much as possible. Superimposed circles and pointers direct attention to the relevant figures. After the first showing, the deputy goes through it again, scene by scene, narrating, coached by Barry the whole way, explaining why he did what he did, speeding forward, the sirens and lights, then the gestures, drawing his gun, firing. Jurors hold their hands over their mouths and shake their heads. I may owe them an apology letter as well.

I got a surprise call this morning before I left for court. I was heading out and the phone started ringing and I decided to let the machine pick it up, but as I was about to close the door I heard my ex-wife's voice.

Oh, hey, I guess you left already. I just wanted to say that . . . you know . . . I know this is probably going to be a bad day for you and I've been thinking that . . .

I hesitated for a moment on the threshold of the door, but then I ran to pick it up.

"Hey," I said.

"Oh . . . oh . . . hi. I thought maybe you'd left." She sounded flustered, like maybe she was hoping she'd get to make her speech into the machine.

"Just on my way out."

"How much did you hear?"

"All of it. I was listening."

"Okay, good."

"Yeah." There was a long pause and I listened to her breathe. I remembered this breathing. It is familiar to me as my own, more so, because I've never paid attention to my own breathing, whereas, Beth's, as she slept, I could watch her for hours.

"So how are you doing?" she said.

"Okay, considering . . . not bad."

"That's good," she said. I thought that maybe there was a nagging something about to be appended, how maybe I wasn't looking all that good, but she swallowed it back. "Like I was saying," she said, "I just wanted to tell you that I hope it doesn't go too terribly and everything."

"Nothing I don't have coming to me."

"No, no," she said, like she was forcing the words out. "You don't. They're judging you on your worst moments and it isn't totally fair."

"How else am I to be judged?"

We listened to each other breathe. We held the line, just listening. She said, "Good luck, all right? I'm thinking of you today."

She hung up before I could thank her. I can say it here, for what it's worth. Thank you to the love of my (first) life.

37

NOT LONG AFTER my swim with Bonnie, the treatment regimen lightened up considerably and I was given increasing freedom to roam the grounds and "study independently." For the most part, I wandered unchecked (though never too near the southwest compound), but it seemed all I had to do was think about needing or wanting something and Chet would appear to fulfill that need. One day I was on an early-morning walk that turned into a hike to the top of a small peak at the center of the island. I'd been doing a lot of walking, but had previously balked at trying to make it all the way. However, that day I decided to follow the path upwards. At around halfway I realized I hadn't brought any water. I was about to turn back when Chet materialized in front of me, two canteens slung like bandoliers across his chest.

"Refreshment, sir?"

"It's like you read my mind, Chet," I replied.

"Yes, sir."

I drank heavily from the canteen. It was like liquid ice.

"How is it still so cold?"

"Did you want it to be cold?"

"Sure."

"Then there you are," Chet replied.

"Join me," I said, as I started back up the hill.

"Gladly, sir."

FROM THE TOP, standing in a small dirt clearing, we had a 360-degree view of the island. There wasn't another landmass in sight, though to the north there was a blue-gray haze that might have been a very distant shore. Down one side was an impenetrable canopy of tropical greenery, while down the other I could see the buildings of the White Hot Center, and then a distance removed, with more heavy foliage in between, the southwest compound.

"It's a beautiful place," I said.

"Indeed."

"Where are we, anyway?"

"The precise location of the White Hot Center is not divulged to any nonemployees for obvious reasons, but you can see with your own eyes that we are on an island. Through the simple process of deduction, by measuring climate, the sun's declination in the sky as well as star patterns, it is plain to see that we are in the northern hemisphere, though just barely. I am also authorized to tell you that the White Hot Center is not only for the study of what you're studying, but is itself a sovereign nation whose borders and integrity are recognized by international law. To protect these borders we have a military budget that is, per capita, higher than any industrialized nation save the United States of America."

"But where do you keep all the stuff?" The island was big, but not big enough for what I'd seen of the Center, plus a million-man army.

"Stuff, sir?"

"You know, soldiers and tanks and planes and shit."

Chet shook his head. "Maybe you aren't progressing as much as we thought."

"What do you mean?"

"I mean, with what you have seen and experienced, do you really think we need such obvious brutality to protect ourselves?"

"Right," I said. "Sure, I get it." I didn't, not at the time, anyway.

Sometimes I'd try to draw him out, make an attempt to get to know the real Chet.

"How long have you worked for the Center?"

"My entire existence."

"Seems like forever, huh?"

"It does not seem like forever, it is forever. I am a native of the island. All employees of the Center are."

"No shit?"

"Born and raised, though *raised* isn't quite the right word for what happens here. *Grown* would be more like it."

"Is that what's going on at the southwest compound? Is that why Mr. Bob said we shouldn't go nosing around there?"

"No. Not exactly."

"So what is going on there?"

Chet looked at me seriously. "I could tell you, but then I'd have to kill you, sir."

I laughed, but stopped when his look deepened.

"Don't worry," Chet said, "it would be swift and painless and your corpse would be unmarred. Your remains would be returned to your family with a look of peace and tranquility on your face."

"You're just a big ball of sexy fun, aren't you, Chet?"

"I try my best, sir."

"It must've been something, growing up here."

A hint of wistfulness crossed Chet's face. "I know every inch of these islands."

"Do you ever think about leaving?"

"We leave often. If you recall, I came and brought you here."

"Don't play dumb, Chet, you know what I mean: leaving for good. With a face like yours you could make a fortune as an actor, or model, or probably anything else you wanted to be."

"My understanding," Chet said, "is that those pursuits don't have all that much to recommend themselves. That's what I've heard, anyway. Besides, my parents would kill me."

"You have parents?"

"Of course."

"And do you get to see them often?"

Chet shaded his eyes from the sun and looked down the hill. "Quite often; most every day, actually, if things aren't too busy. My mom says I'm the best thing that ever happened to her and that I better not ruin that by doing anything stupid."

"Like becoming famous?"

Chet smiled.

"I'd like to meet them," I said.

"I'm afraid that isn't possible," he replied. He seemed a little disappointed about this.

"Why not?"

"It is forbidden. You would understand why if you knew what was there."

I drank more from the canteen, just as cold as before. My ankle throbbed lightly from the hike, but the surgery had mostly ended that pain. As the weeks passed at the Center, I felt better and better, dropping some weight, seeing a little bit of muscle tone. No one would've mistaken me for a world-class athlete, but I was ready to take my shirt off in front of Bonnie again. In all my wanderings, though, I hadn't seen her. Our singularly designed paths were not crossing. There was no central reception area where we could ask for a bungalow number or leave a message, so everything was left to chance. (Or so it seemed.)

I don't know how long it was until Chet spoke. "Do you want her?"

"I didn't say anything," I replied.

"Nonetheless," he replied.

I sat on the ground and stretched my hamstrings. "How's my progress coming, anyway?"

Chet loomed, the sun behind him, putting him in shadow. "How do you feel you're doing?"

"Good. Pretty good, anyway. I'm afraid that I'm forgetting things."

"Sir?"

"Not forgetting, exactly. It's not like that. It's more like, I remember them, but before the memories came with feelings."

"It works for us, sir," he said.

"You don't have any feelings?"

Chet cocked his head. "I have many feelings, sir, just none of the bad ones," he said.

"But if you don't have any bad ones, how do you know the good are actually good?"

"That good must come with bad is a myth, sir. Good can be built on good. You'll see."

"You think so?"

"Yes," Chet replied. "We feel you're probably close to completion."

"I feel like I'd like to stay here forever," I said, as much to myself as to Chet.

"I'm afraid that's impossible, sir, for you."

"What does that mean, 'for you'?"

I could see the hesitation on Chet's face. He looked around to make sure we were alone.

"I've said too much already," he said.

"Come on," I replied. "Impossible for me, what does that mean? That it's possible for some people?"

"I shouldn't have spoken."

My brain began to put two and two together. "What's going on in the southwest compound, Chet?"

"As I've said previously, sir, I'm not at liberty to say."

"Which means you do know what's going on?"

"Correct."

"But you won't tell me?"

"Yes. While I am well aware of what is going on in what you refer to as the southwest compound, I will not tell you what is going on. My suggestion is that you go see for yourself if you're so curious."

"Mr. Bob was pretty clear on that front," I said. "Seems like he said we'd be killed without warning."

"I remember it differently," Chet said. "I remember him saying that you *may* be killed without warning, not that you *would* be killed without warning."

"What are you saying, Chet?"

Chet hesitated again. "Probably too much, sir."

We looked at the view awhile longer. The air started to cool as the sun set, but then I wished I was warm and I was.

"Chet?"

"Yes, sir?"

"Sometimes, when I'm asleep here, I dream that I'm back in my apartment. That I'm in real trouble. What do you think that means?"

"I think it means the work here is harder than anyone thinks," he said.

We started the hike to the bottom, Chet leading the way. He was moving impossibly fast, and no matter how much I wished to catch up to him, I couldn't.

Three days later, after a Chet-less hike, I returned to my bungalow to find Bonnie sitting on my front stoop, reading. The book was resting on her pressed-together knees and she looked up as my shadow crossed over the page. Her canary yellow tracksuit looked better on her than on me.

"Hey," she said. "You know what? I really like reading. I never knew it before. They pretty much took me out of school when I was ten, so I never got a chance to find out, but turns out, I dig it."

"That's great," I replied. "The reading part, not the taking you out of school at ten part. That sounds wrong to me."

"Yeah, like child abuse or something, right? It's the kind of thing people get locked up for and here my mom wrote a best-selling book about parenting your champion child."

"Ironic," I said.

"Yeah," she said. "As you can see, I've got some bitterness." She held a hand up to me and I lifted her into a standing position. She closed the book and held it against her side. I couldn't see what it was, but I wanted to.

"Anywho," she said. "I was wondering if you had plans tonight because there's a place that I like to go that I wanted to take you."

"It'll break Chet's heart to not have the chance to kick my ass in chess, but he can get over it."

"Great," she said, starting to bounce away. She walked on her toes, athletic, ready for action. "Wear something dark. I'll be by at sundown."

38

OH, IT IS good. It is *sooooooooo, soooooooo, goooooooooood*. Whatever it is, this stuff in the patch, it drips like honey from the spot on the funny man's back where it is affixed all the way to his bombed-out foot/ankle. It shuts things down, flips switches to off, presses the mute button. Life is fuzzy. Life is good. The exhaust fumes trapped by the tunnel: gone. The honking: silent. And look at this: The shit is magic because the traffic is loosening and the funny man begins to move more than 5 mph for the first time in a long time. Everything is back on track. Maybe a little lying-down time when they get to the apartment, just so he can enjoy the patch a bit more before they head to the diner. The boy can play video games solo, then they'll grab dinner instead of a snack. It's all the same. It's even better, matter of fact. They'll order meat loaf, the one where they cook a whole egg in the middle and you get a portion of it with each slice. The boy is going to say yuck, but the funny man will insist that he try it and he'll fucking love it because there's a lot to love in that meat loaf, as long as you've got enough ketchup poured on top.

The traffic is loosening, but then here's these assholes pulling up next to him and honking and waving their arms like lunatics. God, it sucks to be so recognizable. *All right, fellas,* the funny man gestures with his hand, *I see you, move along now.* But they don't move along and are in fact joined by another car on his opposite side where some woman is doing the exact same thing. *For God's sake, kill the honking.* There's nothing that harshes the buzz more than the honking.

Oh, thank thank you thank you, the funny man thinks. There's a cop with his flashers on, come to protect the funny man from these lunatics. Good luck for him this day, finally. This situation could have turned into a real Lady Di thing, but this cop will save him from the shenanigans, and look, there go the lunatics, peeling off as the cop pulls alongside. The funny man salutes; thank you, Officer, and takes advantage of all the traffic in front of them parting from the cop's siren to go a little faster.

Police escort, sweet, the funny man thinks. Membership does have its privileges. They're going to get home in no time now. Even if the parade is still going, this guy is going to let them cut right through. The funny man thinks about what it might involve to hire someone like this on an as-needed basis to just sort of grease the wheels for him and makes a mental note to check on that.

He said thanks, so why is the cop rolling the window down and what's with the gun? It's a nice gun, pretty big, but why does he need the gun out, and what's the deal with pointing it right at the funny man like that? He's shouting something and pointing with the gun, but no way is anybody going to be able to hear what he's saying. The tunnel just makes all the engine noise echo and swallows up anything under a low roar, and those sirens aren't helping either.

Because of the patch and its muffling properties, it is not immediately apparent that the cop is firing the gun. They appear to be warning shots, but what the fuck is up with that? Carefully, because there's a cop there that's shooting at or at least near him and he doesn't want to antagonize the man further, the funny man signals his move to the curb with his flashers before stopping.

The cop angles his car in front of the funny man's, blocking his way, as if that was even necessary, and slams on the brakes, squealing the tires. He's still carrying the gun and as the funny man exits his own car, he can now hear what the cop is saying, over and over and over. "Jesus, Jesus, Jesus, Jesus." The funny man steps up and says, "What is it, Officer?" but the cop blows past him, his arms reaching for the roof and the funny man turns and he sees his boy there, frozen, his fingers gripped on the window edge. His boy, my boy, on top of the car, his hair crazy wild, dried tear tracks visible through the soot on his face.

My boy, releasing his grip only as the cop—who, come to think of it, doesn't look like a regular cop—takes him into his burly arms, wrapping the boy up so the funny man, so I, can barely see him and stuffing the boy into the back of his cop car, and this is when I fall to my knees and begin to wail.

But this cop who doesn't look like a regular cop is not done with me. No, when the boy is safe in his backseat he turns and he grips my shirt with two powerful hands and hauls me up and throws me on the hood. The cop is screaming in my face as he roughs me up against the car. "What the fuck, dude? What in the fuck!"

I have no answer.

It is the kind of thing that happens, but for which there is no explanation. We read about it all the time, but there are no answers. The funny man should die. Immediately. On this spot. He hopes that the cop splits open his head on the car's hood or that the patch is laced with poison. His life should be flashing before his eyes, but nothing comes because he has no life. It has been taken from him. No, that is wrong, he has thrust it away from himself. Underneath the cop's arm he sees the gun back in the holster, but not snapped down and the thought comes into the funny man's head, "I need that," and so he reaches for it, but the cop is way too fast and strong and snatches the gun first and the funny man is staring down the barrel of the gun, which is what he was after with the grabbing. He smells the gunpowder and feels the heat of the barrel, and he can see that the cop, who doesn't look like a regular cop, is crying and the gun is trembling in his hands. No, his hands are trembling with the gun in them and the cop is screaming, "I should blow your fucking head off!" and the funny man is saying, "Yes, please please do. Please."

PART III
Closure

39

I HAD NOTHING dark, my wardrobe being limited to my canary yellow tracksuit and appropriate undergarments. Chet had whisked away my party duds following our one social gathering, but for some reason, that evening as I went to prepare and dress, I wasn't surprised to see an outfit of dark jeans, black turtleneck and windbreaker in my wardrobe. Everything fit perfectly, of course, and inside the windbreaker was a black stocking cap. I left it in the pocket as I went outside to wait for Bonnie.

As the sun dipped far enough to put the island into dusk, the walkway lights turned on, the halogen humming as it warmed. Before the lamps even reached full strength, Bonnie appeared, dressed in black stretch pants that clung to her lower half in an undeniably alluring way, and a black sweatshirt. She had her hair up in a ponytail that was thrust through the back of a black baseball cap.

"Twins," she said, by way of greeting, then, "We better hurry, or we're going to be late."

I almost had to skip to keep up with her stride as we wove our way down the paths until, with a quick glance both ways, she hopped from the path and started in a light jog.

"I didn't know we could do that," I whispered, but she didn't break stride. The pace was nothing for her, I'm sure, but I had to work hard to keep up. The hikes were coming in handy. We were moving toward a line of unbroken trees, but as we approached I could see a small, single-file path open up that we plunged into. We jogged for another five or so minutes, barely enough light to illuminate the ground. I trusted my footfalls would strike true and I wouldn't roll my bad ankle. Low-hanging branches brushed at my clothing, and I resisted the urge to ask her to slow down because I was worried that she wouldn't. Finally, we reached a clearing and she stopped suddenly and said, "We're here."

The clearing was relatively small and circular. Unlike the WHC grounds the grass was long and wild with weeds and wildflowers shooting up. A little bit of light was thrown into it from our right and looking over I realized that it came from the southwest compound that couldn't have been too far in the distance.

"What?" I said.

"Just wait," she replied. So I waited. My eyes adjusted to the increasing dark. The lights from the southwest compound put a soft, gray cast over the darkness and that's when they appeared, rabbits, everywhere.

"Do you see?" she said.

I did. It was like one moment, bare ground, and then hundreds of rabbits gathered together, sitting back on their haunches, eating grains gripped in their forepaws. Rabbit couples consummated their love left and right and it became apparent why their numbers were so great. Their two great needs, food and sex, were more than abundant. We sat Indian-style on the edge of the clearing. The grass was tamped down here and I imagined she'd been coming alone for some time. We watched together for probably thirty minutes before it ended as quickly as it started, the rabbits disappearing en masse into the grasses so quickly that I began to wonder if it was an illusion.

"You did see that, right?" she said.

"Yeah, it was cool."

"I wanted someone else to see it, to make sure," she said.

"And you chose me?"

"I did."

She laid flat on the ground and looked up at the sky, so I joined her. The nighttime jungle sounds intensified and mingled with what sounded like music from the southwest compound just barely loud enough to reach us.

"We're out past curfew," I said.

"Don't worry," she replied, "nothing happens."

"Good to know." I felt like I should have been frightened, but I wasn't. I was right where I wanted to be.

"There's something I've been wanting to tell someone for awhile," she said, "and I think I want to tell it to you now."

"Okay."

"It's totally fucked-up, I mean totally. Like I can't believe how fucked-up it is, but I can't not talk about it anymore."

"Okay."

"I mean, it's like, you'll-never-look-at-me-the-same fucked-up."

"I hear you," I said.

She took a deep breath and started speaking quickly. "When I was ten, my parents decided for the sake of my tennis that I needed to go to 'the academy.' I was beating the crap out of all the girls my age and even older in the region, but that wasn't good enough, so they took me to see Mr. Popov and I remember him sitting behind a desk with his hands tepeed under his chin as my mom rattled off my accomplishments and then he stood up and walked around and told me to stand. He had on those like old-school tennis shorts, stretchy and super-tight and too short, and he had a big belly, but also an outie for some reason that you could see through his shirt. He pinched and grabbed me, the backs of my arms, my knees, elsewhere, and he said, 'Yes, I think we can work with her.' He smelled like sausage."

The words sounded simultaneously spontaneous and rehearsed, like they'd been rolling around in her head forever without ever getting fully polished.

"Like I said, the school was basically a joke, maybe an hour after morning practice. It was tennis and conditioning, weights, psychological games to make us mentally strong. It was boys and girls and the girls all lived together in a big dorm room with bunk beds and the wall by everyone's bed was decorated with personal stuff. One guess what mine had."

"Bunnies," I replied.

"Duh. Bunnies. I didn't like them even back then, but it was my nickname already, so like everyone gave me bunny shit for my birthday, Christmas, whatever, and I think I was probably a pretty polite kid, so I'd put up the cards or stack the stuffed animals on my bed, but I didn't feel a damn thing toward any of it."

"Uh-huh."

"All the girls were friendly, but we weren't friends, you know? There was always that rivalry thing underneath. They had these poster boards where they ranked us on everything, even like making our beds fastest and shit like that, so you could never let your guard down. I mean, at the time I didn't realize it, this is all afterwards, more recently, if that makes sense."

"Sure," I said. We were lying so close that I could sense her there, and I wanted to reach and touch her somewhere, but I didn't.

"Mr. Popov would come in at night and make a big show of tucking us in, telling us to always get good rest, and to dream of being champions and once a week, after we were all under the covers, he would take one of us from the room. He'd pull the covers back and whoever it was would stand up and he'd hold out his hand and he'd lead her from the room and it didn't take long to figure out what he was doing."

"Shit," I said. "Motherfucker." I felt something inside me start to boil. I could tell that she was crying, but her voice was steady.

"But wait," she said, "that's not the fucked-up part. Here's the fucked-up part. The thing that made me the most mad was that he never chose me. Holy shit, is that twisted? But it's the goddamn truth. When some of the girls got older they would, like, brag about who was the best and they'd look at me like I deserved pity or something. I took it out on the others on the court. I beat their goddamn brains in because he never chose me."

I had nothing to say, so I didn't say anything.

"Pretty fucked-up, eh?"

"Yeah, no doubt about that."

"I'm probably even attracted to you because of the age thing, quasi–father figure and all that."

"Hey," I said, "I'm not that old."

She reached over and patted my leg. "I know that."

She sat up again and brushed nonexistent debris from the front of her sweatshirt. "I thought I'd feel better after saying all of that, but I don't."

"We're damaged goods," I said, joining her in the sitting position. "The sum of our triumphs and tragedies."

"Where'd you hear that?"

"I think I made it up."

"It doesn't sound like that. It sounds like the kind of thing someone might say."

"I guess I'm that someone this time," I said.

For a moment the music from the southwest compound stopped and I could hear light clapping and laughter before it started up again, someone singing a familiar song in what sounded like a familiar voice.

"So," she said, looking at me, one side of her face partially lighted as she turned my way. "What's your story?"

I laughed. "Oh, no," I said. "It's more like a novel, an epic, a saga. I wouldn't know where to begin. Just trust that it's long and sad and stupid."

She patted my leg again. "Tut-tut. I'm sure it's a good one," she said.

"Don't be so sure," I replied, but I told her. You've heard most of it already.

"MINE'S BETTER," SHE said.

"Yeah. I'm not that special."

She stood upright, this time offering me a hand in help. "So," she said. "Our little pity party is over and the night is still young. What shall we do with the rest of it?"

My legs were stiff and I tried to shake them out. The music from the southwest compound swelled and I now felt positive I recognized the voice of the singer, but of course, who I was thinking of was impossible. I thought of what Chet had said to me at the top of the island about the difference between "may" and "will."

"Come on," I said to her. "There's something I have to see."

40

THE DEPUTY SHERIFF'S testimony over, I am all that is left on the schedule and then of course the closing statements. We are bumping up against the Fourth of July holiday so the judge has sent us home for the rest of the week. Barry tells me my time on the stand is to be minimal, his inquiries limited to the night when I allegedly shot an armed robber six times in self-defense. He doesn't want to muddy the waters of the rest of my life with any personal testimony. It's all there, plain as day for people to make of it what they will. I am ready for my testimony, but mostly because it's not going to happen.

Giddy in anticipation of the trial's climax, Barry has called me to his office ostensibly to talk strategy. The conference room is decked out in a mini-replica of the courtroom. I recognize a rehearsal space when I see one. Barry stands behind a lectern. "I just thought I'd run some ideas by you," he says.

I sit down behind what I take to be the judge's desk and run my hands over the smooth surface. "I'm all ears," I say. Barry smiles and looks down at his notes, the only time he'll do so for nearly an hour.

"Ladies and gentleman of the jury," Barry says, "I want to tell you a story, a story of a man who was like any other, until he wasn't. Imagine, if you will, getting everything you could ever want, but somehow everything is never enough."

It's not that the story is bad, just that it's awfully familiar. There are times I have an urge to object, but that isn't the judge's job. My role here is to listen; composed, impartial. I nod occasionally to keep Barry going, but it isn't necessary. He's plenty wound up. My case must be the best thing that ever happened to him, everything he ever wanted, and I feel some pangs of guilt over the fact that he'll never have a chance to deliver this story to its intended audience. We all want to be heard, but only some of us are pushy or needy or damaged enough to insist that someone else listen.

His telling of the story isn't the same as my telling, but from the parts I pay attention to, it's not wrong.

Barry watches me, eyes open and hoping and I realize he's done. I pound my hands together until they hurt. Barry knuckles a tear from the corner of his eye.

"Really?" he says. "It was good?"

"I couldn't imagine anything better," I reply. I go to him and we hug and I thank him for everything, and tell him I'm sorry.

"For what?" he says.

"You'll see," I reply.

I FEEL AS though we take it for granted, but the Internet really is a miracle, and for my personal purposes, it has developed itself on a just-in-time basis. For example, if my stand-up career got underway once the video-sharing Web sites were ubiquitous, I can't imagine anyone paying to see the thing. I would have done it once or twice, someone would have captured it on video, and there it would be, instantaneous worldwide distribution. Rather than an international touring sensation, I would've been a virtual flash in the pan, next to the guy with the bizarrely deep voice singing about "Chocolate Rain," whatever the hell that is, or the baby who loves to tear paper into pieces. I got to control the content and people proved they would pay for it. Now, they say, content just wants to be free.

Well, we all want to be free, don't we?

Conspiracy blogs that posit the existence and location of a special island where the famous and rich go for special treatments, combined with my own experiences and knowledge, and some work with satellite-mapping software allow me to make a better than reasonable guess as to its location. I can also procure a sturdy sailing vessel that is promised to be waiting for me at a certain time and location stocked with all of the necessary supplies. Thanks to the Internet I can learn how to sail without actually doing so. I can even check out a half-dozen sites that promise to offer foolproof steps to disabling a home-confinement monitoring device (though I will not need their advice).

I check Bonnie's Wimbledon tournament results before they are shown tape-delayed on television, where I will savor every moment. She is in the semifinals without dropping a set. The commentators are calling her performance "inspired," which is more on the nose than they know. She strikes the ball with a ferocious purpose. Her serves seem laser-guided. It is as close to perfection as possible.

My agent e-mails me to say that he's successfully sold my book for more than we had figured, which is good news because that money is now spoken for. And now that I'm done with the book I can thank him in a return e-mail and attach the manuscript to the message and wish him Godspeed.

41

EVERY STEP TOWARD the southwest compound, I braced for Bonnie and I to be vaporized like the jelly impacting Mr. Bob's tracksuit. I put on the dark cap and willed myself to be silent and invisible. The music swelled as we approached, growing more distinct before ending with a round of claps followed by the soft murmur of a crowd moving elsewhere. It reminded me of the times backstage, just before the houselights would go down and my audience would be busy whiling away their anticipation and then the lights dim and there is that moment of silence before the first whoops and cheers cut toward the stage. Barry says celebrity is a disease, but it's really just like any other addiction, where you chase that brief high to sustain you through the lows. Every time I went up on stage, it was that moment that pulled me out of the wings, that surge of audience desire, even when I felt like I'd rather jam knitting needles into my eyes than my hand into my mouth.

As we neared the compound I expected guard towers and walls, but there wasn't even a fence and not a patrol to be seen, just the forest line up to the edge of open grounds encircled by tiki torches.

At about thirty yards we went facedown in the overgrown grass and I peered through my cupped hands at a patio with lounges and low tables arranged in little conversation nooks facing a stage area with a couple of guitars sitting on stands, microphones, keyboards, some small amplifiers. The crowd had apparently moved off.

"Maybe the party's over," Bonnie whispered.

But the torches still burned and I could see the red lights on the amplifiers. I told her we should stay.

"I don't have anywhere else to be," she said.

This was true. One of the mantras at the White Hot Center, is to "be the moment," which is the same new-age hokum that any self-help guru is going to peddle, but that doesn't mean it's bad advice. I rested my head on the ground and listened to the grass shift. My breathing slowed until it matched Bonnie's. I pressed her hand to my lips and she rolled to face me and it was too dark to see anything, but I'm pretty sure we were gazing into each other's eyes.

And then the party returned to the patio.

Even Bonnie, young as she is, knew the names of most: Dean, Hendrix, Joplin, Bruce, Belushi, Farley, Ledger, Cobain, the Princess of Wales, Lennon. None of them aged even a moment from the last we saw them. They drank cocktails and conversed. JFK smoked a cigar with John, Jr., the two men seated, side by side, blowing smoke into the lights. Whatever had bothered them before had been washed away. Hendrix's eyes were bright and clear. Belushi was still round, but fit. Cobain had a pretty compelling grin.

They circulated around the grounds, clotting together in different groupings before breaking apart and reforming.

"Awesome," Bonnie said. "No way."

I nodded, afraid that if I spoke I would break the spell. Thanks to our black clothes and the torches between us, we were invisible in the dark. Bonnie crawled forward and I tried to grab her ankle, but she shook free so I had no choice but to follow. As we got closer and closer I thought that she might just stand up and join them and that's when I recognized that she could, that she belonged there and I didn't. Like them, she was a genius in her field, maybe not fully realized yet, but she would be welcomed.

She stayed with me, though, just shy of where the torchlight licked the ground.

Chet appeared and crossed the patio. He hugged and kissed a beautiful blonde with a pleasingly full figure and a beauty mark just above her dimple. I could read his lips in the lamplight: *Hello, Mother.*

Yes, they were talented and I was not, this was abundantly clear, but all of us needed the lightning strike, the luck. Like, for example, the talent agent happening into the malt shop in the case of Chet's mother or being introduced to the second greatest songwriter of his generation, as happened to Lennon. Everyone on that patio had a story and mine wasn't so so different. But just as my "talent" paled next to theirs, I realized so did my scars.

While we watched, Belushi and Farley took the stage together to do a routine that we could only half hear over the laughs, but even just watching them made me bite my forearm to keep from exploding.

At the next break, a young man with high cheekbones and soft, shoulder-length hair entered the grounds barefoot and shirtless, wearing only leather pants. He hugged Chet and leaned down to kiss the blonde. The assembled group began a low chant, "song, song, song, song," and eventually Lennon went behind the keyboards as the young man with the high cheekbones grabbed the microphone. He tossed his hair back and smiled as Lennon started to play. The tempo was slower than usual, sensuous, the melody draping itself over the crowd. The beautiful young man had his share of demons in life, but he'd left them behind on the island. The conversation stopped and everyone sat somewhere. I looked at Bonnie and saw her mouth shaped like an O, just like mine. The lizard king stared at America's sweetheart and sang in a low, rich tenor. When he closed his eyes, he sang of love and fire.

I heard it, with my ears. Yes, sir.

AFTER MUSIC FEATURING every combination of performers possible, the equipment was snapped off and the torches snuffed,
leaving Bonnie and me in the full darkness. We couldn't have been
more than an hour or two from sunrise.

"It's like some kind of retirement village," she whispered.

"For the most famous people ever."

"Who are supposedly dead."

"Yeah," I replied, "that's weird."

"More like impossible."

"Seems like there's a lot of impossible things going on here."

"That's true," she said.

"Like this," I said, pointing to the two of us. "This is impossible, isn't it?"

"Apparently, nothing is impossible."

"I'm glad you said it instead of me," I said.

"Why?"

"Because that means it's real."

ON THE WAY back to the WHC we made our future plans. When
we got out we would be together and that was that, so all we had
to do was talk logistics.

"I could stop playing," she said. "I've pretty much had enough,
anyway."

"Pretty much?"

"It does bug me, to be honest."

"No majors?"

"Yeah, but that's just the fucked-up brainwashing of the academy
and Mr. Popov talking. I'll get over that."

"Or you could just go win one." We had made it back to the lighted
paths of the compound and I reached and squeezed her hand.

"There is that," she replied.

"So, I'll travel with you. I've never been anywhere that I
remember. It'll be fun."

She sighed. "Can you imagine the coverage? The jokes? The
tabloids? It'll be awful."

"We'll ignore it," I said.

"How's that gone in the past?" she said.

"Good point."

"But we'll figure it out," she said.

"Yeah."

We were at the entrance to my bungalow and it got awkward. I had one hand on the doorknob and the other on her elbow as we faced each other. She pulled her cap off and yanked the ponytail holder free and shook her hair and I smelled lilacs.

"Should we say good night?" she said.

"I'd rather not. There isn't much night left, anyway, from what I can tell."

"I'm pretty tired."

"Me too," I said.

"But maybe I can lie down here for awhile and then I'll just go back to my place in a bit."

"I'd like that," I said, opening the door and leading her in. As usual, the sheets were pulled down waiting for my entry. We didn't even get undressed, just laying down in the bed with our clothes on, me on my back, her tucked to my chest, one leg slung over my body. I rubbed my hand in circles on her back.

"That feels good," she said.

It was nothing like the moment Beth and I held each other after we first came together in the library. I was young then and the future stretched infinite, but I also cared only about the moment. It was a gift. She was a gift, a lucky break, a once-in-a-lifetime opportunity where we made the boy who gifted me my thing, the boy who I'll probably never see again.

But with Bonnie, I was making the moment. I had created it. Everyone's got a story and the best ones are those we tell ourselves. I imagined it and then after the imagining it had come true. It is not a perfect substitute for what I had, but it will have to do.

THE NEXT DAY I woke in what felt like my bed, in what looked like my apartment. I knuckled the sleep from my eyes and looked

again and confirmed my initial suspicion. My face was stubbled
and I needed a shower. Chet walked in from the living room.

"Welcome home, sir," he said. He opened the slats on the blinds
and let the sun stream through. It clearly was morning, but judging
from my stubble and my stink, it was not necessarily the morning
after my adventures with Bonnie.

"What's going on?" I said.

"You've completed your treatment, so we've brought you
home."

"I don't remember."

"From past experience, we've found that often people are, let's
say, reluctant to leave, so we find it easier to do it with our guests
unconscious."

"You drugged me."

"Correct, sir."

The room looked like it had from when I left, clothes strewn
everywhere, my curtain loincloth as soiled and stiff as ever. The
air was sickbed sour. I'd been barring the maid service while I was
present, but at least she could have snuck in during my absence. I
saw a firing in someone's future. The only thing that had changed,
apparently, was me.

Chet hovered nearby, nudging some of the debris piles with the
toe of his shoe. "Is there anything else I can do, sir?" he asked.

My tongue was thick in my mouth, my throat dry. "I'm thirsty."

Chet nodded toward the nightstand where there was a half-full
tumbler of water. Lip prints crusted the rim and there was a thin
layer of dust across the top, but I drank it greedily. It was cold and
crisp, just what I was hoping for.

"Will I see her again?"

"Do you want to?"

"Of course."

"Then why should anything stop you?"

I wasn't sure if he was waiting go be dismissed, what our relationship was now that we were no longer at the Center. I'd tried
the servant thing once; it hadn't worked out. "I'm going to take
a shower," I said.

Chet just nodded. My body creaked as I headed to the bathroom, probably a hangover from whatever Chet had given me combined with my southwest compound adventure with Bonnie. The shower was glorious. I utilized every one of my six nozzles, simultaneously pummeling my body from all directions. I believed that the supply of hot water in my building was inexhaustible. I thought about testing the proposition. The towels smelled a little musty, so I went back into the bedroom naked, letting the air dry me.

Chet was gone. I called out his name, first softly, and then loudly enough that it carried throughout the apartment. I slipped into some sweats and stepped into the living room. It looked like a tornado had blown through. Crusted take-out containers and half-empty cans of beans were splattered everywhere. The coffee table rested on its side and three giant slashes had been hacked through two of the couch cushions. Someone was going to have a lot of cleanup work on their hands.

On the street below my window, the whole world went on as before. I missed her already. Fortunately, my cable package included a channel dedicated entirely to tennis. I punched the on button on the remote and flipped to the guide and saw that, just as I wanted, *Bonnie Tisdale: A Life So Far* was showing. It was a soft feature biography, lots of discussion about her youthful genius, talking head interviews with former coaches and competitors. I realized I'd seen it before, but now, it took on a different light. I put the single undamaged couch cushion back in place and settled in. Tomorrow, I would begin putting the pieces of my new life in place.

42

THE NEWS IS everywhere. Hours after winning her first Wimbledon title and her second consecutive major championship, Bonnie Tisdale was found hanging from the beams inside the ladies' locker room at the All England Lawn Tennis and Croquet Club. She left a note, an angry excoriation of her parents and former coach, laying the blame squarely at their feet. I wince at the pictures of her mother, face blanched and distraught. I know something about causing others grief. Even though I knew it was coming, and was necessary for us to be together, I weep softly. I hope it was as peaceful as we thought it would be, that she was transported to the island in whatever way those things happened, quickly and painlessly. I have an urge to call Beth, but I don't. My disappearance will cause her trouble enough, and a call would only add to that.

The coverage is wall-to-wall. There is nothing to say and yet they spend hours and hours saying it. I flip between the predictable mix of experts explaining depression and pressure and the risks of starting children in ultracompetitive activities too young.

I see on-the-street interviews with people clutching pictures of her moistened by their tears and it feels good to know that so many others love her as well, even though they do not know her like I do.

Each of the networks has branded the coverage: "Death of America's Tennis Sweetheart" or "the Passing of a Court Queen." Psychological experts say how inevitable such a thing was given the pressures of our day and age. Everything is inevitable after the fact, though.

Mitch Laver has been dispatched to host *Hello U.S.A.* from London. As I see him see me through the television, I wonder if he suspects anything, if he made his own visit to the southwest compound during his time at the Center. I want to get in touch with him, let him know that I'm in on the secret, part of the club now, but I imagine it's against Center alumni protocol. We know who we are.

The preliminary plans for Bonnie's memorial service are already out of control. Lyrics to popular songs have been reworked in tribute to her. (It's amazing how hard it is to rhyme anything to *tennis*.) There will be a charity match in her honor with black tennis balls and the scoring flipped so each game counts down to love, since we agree that's what we need more of. Some have proposed canceling the U.S. Open in her honor, but most everyone agrees that would be impossible. Tomorrow, she will be relegated back to the sports-dedicated channels and a slice of the hourly loop on the news networks. Next week, there will be bulletins. Next year, there will be a brief mention of the anniversary. So it goes.

Bonnie has a day's head start and an easier route back than me, but her "death" will provide additional cover when my disappearance is discovered, which shouldn't be for a couple of days, long enough for me to make it to the boat and launch, and at that point I will be a needle in the great haystack of the ocean.

Everything is set, including the funding I may need to bribe my way into the promised land.

I have some pictures in a drawer. There is one in front of the first house after the apartment, Beth and the boy on the front stoop, him resting on her out-thrust hip. With the hand not cradling the boy, she points to the ground at the welcome mat. We'd purchased it on our way to take possession of the place, her telling me to pull over at a home improvement store and declaring she'd be right back. The boy and I waited in the car and I asked him what he thought his crazy mother was up to. She hid the mat behind her back as she returned to the car, and once at the house made me close my eyes as she positioned it on the stoop. She whistled with two fingers in the corners of her mouth.

It said:

WELCOME TO OUR RETIREMENT HOME
Twice as Much Husband, Half as Much Pay

I tried to laugh.

"We're going to live and die here," she said. "It's just that the dying part's a long time from now." She kissed me with the boy pressed between us, forgiving me for my faulty sense of humor.

We moved to the bigger house six months later. We brought the welcome mat with us, but it wasn't the same. Some jokes work only once. Some never work at all.

I twist the lid off the Scotch, its vapors reaching up to my nose, calling me closer. I'm taking it easy, though, just a finger and a half in a tumbler, one ice cube, one pill, two pills, fizzing angrily as they dissolve in the glass, like they're upset at being drowned.

I take the photos to the sink and burn them slowly, dousing the embers when the smoke threatens to trigger the alarm. So long, farewell, *auf wiedersehen*, good-bye.

So, closure.

As I turned the corner, I saw the guy dressed in a hooded sweat-shirt and I could see the gun as he said, "Give me your wallet, no funny business."

I was shocked by the gun. I could suddenly taste the fillings in my mouth. I stammered and he grabbed me by the elbow and pulled me down an empty side street and pushed me to the ground and my hood came off and he said, "Hey, I know you."

I stood slowly, my hands held out in front of me. I kept my eyes on the gun the whole time. "I don't carry a wallet," I said. I turned my pockets inside out to show him.

He got angry, agitated. "Fuck you," he said. "Fuck you, you don't have a wallet. You are a rich motherfucker and got tons of money and you're telling me you don't have any on you? If that doesn't beat the band." He massaged his forehead with his free hand. His left leg twitched a little and his eyes were rimmed red.

The thought formed in my mind, a thought I'd had once before: "I want that gun." And the next thing I knew I had it in my hands and the thief was kneeling in front of me, an angry red welt below his eye.

"Aw, fuck," he said, sounding more sad than angry. "You're going to call the cops, aren't you? Are you going to call the cops?"

I hadn't thought that far, but it sounded right to me. "Yeah, I'm calling the cops." I reached for my cell in my jacket pocket and flipped it open.

"Please, please, please don't, man, don't. Just let me go. Keep the gun, let me go."

"I don't think I can do that," I said, still holding the phone open.

"Shit shit shit shit shit shit shit shit," he said, pressing his forehead to the ground like he was praying. "I'm a two-time loser, man. This is going to be three strikes, and on a famous dude, no less. They're going to throw the book at me. I can't go back to jail. Do you know what happens in jail? I . . . can't . . . go . . . back . . . to . . . jail."

We had a standoff, and he looked at me closely. "You don't look so good, man."

"What do you mean?"

"I mean you look like shit."

"I'm in love," I said.

He kept looking at me and then frowned. "Okay, maybe that's it. If you say so." He sank further to his haunches and hunched over, like he might be praying.

"I'm sorry," I said. "I don't know what else to do." I squinted at the numbers on the phone, but the rain pounded down hard.

"I'm just so tired, so so tired," he said, rising slightly. His shoulders shook as he began sobbing and then lifted his head up and looked straight at me.

"Shoot me," he said.

"What?"

"Shoot me. Kill me. When you shoot me, just make sure you kill me. I don't want to be no veggie or cripple. I want it over."

"I can't do that," I said.

"But you have to," he pleaded. "I need you to. This is it for me, I know it. It was it for me a long time ago. You'd be doing me a favor."

"But then I'll get in trouble," I said.

"No you won't. Look, no one's around. You shoot me, you wipe the prints, you take off, it's done. It's my gun. No one will ever know it was you."

"I'll know."

"Honestly, man, it's the kindest thing you could do. I'd do it to myself, but I'm a Catholic and I can't do that shit. It'll be like an act of mercy. I'm telling you, it's what I want."

He looked up at me and I could see it in his eyes. He wasn't lying. There was no White Hot Center for this guy.

He smiled. "Thanks, dude," he said. "Oh, and hey, that thing you used to do, with your hand in your mouth, that shit was hilarious."

I don't know why the earwitnesses say he begged for his life. The man knelt quietly and made no sound as I emptied the gun into him.

Who could've anticipated the cops driving by that very moment? I don't blame the thief, whose name was Daniel O'Dell. Daniel got what he wanted. We all should. It's the American way.

I RECOGNIZE THAT, unlike Bonnie, they will not be welcoming me to the island. I'm not delusional. The southwest compound is for legends who choose to leave on top and I am much closer to a career valley than any peak, but I am sure that running the place is not cheap and among my sailing provisions I have a hefty sum of cash stashed and ready to go. Beth and the boy will have plenty, and anything my legacy earns following my disappearance will go to them. Maybe there will be some sort of D.B. Cooper movie about my flight from the law for them and Gord and Frazier. There may be Elvis-like sightings of me across the country, which could turn into additional profits. I have some guilt about leaving the boy, but the sad, sorry truth is that for a long time he has been better off without me. I will be reported as yet another casualty of fame, and maybe I am, at least from their perspective, but here is the full story, the true story.

Maybe a storm will sink my boat, or my calculations on the island's location are off, or I'll get pulled over for a minor traffic violation on my way to the coast and they'll recognize me and I'll get hauled back. Maybe the White Hot Center's vaunted defense system, if it really exists, will terminate me before my boat gets within a mile of the place, or if and when I arrive Chet will snap my neck and shove my carcass into the ocean, but maybe instead he will be a little glad to see me and I will be an exception to the rules. It is the exceptions that make the rules.

Perhaps if I get there safely, I will write that play I've been thinking about.

I open the curtains to my favorite view and switch on the music and I start to dance. I take just one or two additional pills and a final swig of the Scotch. I feel good. I really really do. I do.

I shake each limb in turn until it is the leg with the monitoring bracelet's turn. I shake and shake until it looks like my ligaments and tendons have become detached at the ankle. It looks like they have become detached because they are. The bracelet slips off rather easily and I leave it behind in the middle of the room, my final legacy.

Curtain down, lights up. I exit stage right, limping.